DEATH AT INVERANNAN

David Clark Keachie

ISBN: 9781073826872

Published by Amazon KDP

For Jacqueline, Neve and Adam

With great thanks to Aileen Sherry, Gordon Heaney and John Young

SYNOPSIS

The last two years, or the best part of that time, I, Adam Darnow have been working for the Allanton crime family, also known as the Portfolio. I've been trying to stay alive and, due to the dangerously surreal situation I find myself in, retain my sanity. Those being my twin purposes, I can only confirm that I am still, definitely alive.

I was, before all this, a student, then a journalist and now I'm playing the part of an enforcer, an organizer, a supply chain specialist for the narcotics industry if you could imagine such a thing. I play my part in the efficient delivery of the expensively poisonous – and lucrative – supply of shite which gives a high but then breaks, ruins and takes lives and for that, for all that, perhaps I deserve all the bad things which come to me.

There are advantages, I won't lie. I'm rolling in money. I have a lifestyle you would envy (other than the actual depravity which I participate in as part of my work, of course). I am respected, probably, and feared, quite definitely. My old self has been placed on suspension and my new persona has been in charge this whole time. I'm not sure if this new character is indeed the permanent me, but more of that later.

I've also been alone, largely, during this time. This may be because I've been busy, or live in a city where friendships are hard to make, or even because it's tricky to find common ground when you're living on the outside of the respectable world. Recently I've been more successful on that front, which has made me contemplate my egregious life. I've come to realise that I have a few aspects of my life to sort out, which can perhaps be encapsulated in one critical question.

Can I get out of this business?

1 ADAM LOSES A FOOT

I am deeply, deeply, troubled by the disappearance of the man's dismembered foot. We have all the other constituent limbs and components accounted for, ready to be disposed of with the surety of never becoming part of the evidence against us. The foot, on the other hand, as it were, is a problem. It could quite possibly have my DNA on it, having helped saw and pack it into a nice, tight black parcel bag; ideal for transportation to the incinerator, but not so ideal when my utterly incompetent Edinburgh operatives don't manage to get it from the floor of the building, into the van which transferred the other 95% or so of our victim onto the industrial incineration facility just outside the capital.

It is a problem which requires my immediate attention, needless to say.

I leave two of the guys to operate the incinerator and make damn sure that there is nothing left to concern me at that end. I drive back into Edinburgh with the two others, to find the missing appendage which we need, very much, to close down the last of this irritating problem. I park the van outside the unit. There is, as usual, no-one else around the decrepit building, once an engineering facility and now used by the local guys to store whatever they need, short-term. It also has an excellent shower room, originally used by the former employees of the engineering firm, Swarfega cutting through the oil after a hard shift. Now the facilities are being used by me to dispose of a talkative operative who had, inadvertently or deliberately disclosed information about us to a competitor's agent, along with some premature information about the imminent termination of arrangements pertaining to his source of narcotics. This indiscretion had, in turn, caused something of an instant turf war locally; expensively ended by our wider organisation and calmed locally by some of my more competent negotiators. My instructions for this intervention had been clear that the arsehole that started the problem was not permitted to live in Edinburgh anymore; I extrapolated this with my own interpretation that my voluble employee would no longer be permitted to live, full stop.

So, with some anger on my part and a desire to resolve my tasks in Scotland within the week to allow my return to higher living on Friday afternoon, I had dealt with him myself while handing out the redundancy payments for the Scottish bases. Now, however, my haste may have been my undoing. His left foot, I think, was not in the unloaded van when we arrived at the incinerator; a puzzler, as it was definitely bagged and accounted for, lying at the side of the van before we left the unit.

On arrival back at the industrial unit, a cursory check confirmed that we had cleaned, disinfected and bleached the area thoroughly before leaving; no sign of a black plastic bag, a foot or anything else.

I stand, looking down on the spot where the bags had sat before loading. 'OK boys, where do you think it went?'

The two men look at me with blank faces. 'Dunno. It was put in the van boss. There wisnae anything sitting there, for sure.'

Danny, the more senior of the two, has a Fife accent and, previously, I had thought him and his crew competent.

Now, I inhale, trying to calm myself and then mentally retrace our steps.

The other guy, Tam, then volunteers his thoughts on the mystery. 'It's just a foot. Mibbe it's just fell out the van or something.' I look at him and he makes a don't-know face. Resisting the urge, I stay silent.

From the corner of my eye, I see something move in the shadows of the far corner of the unit; walking as noiselessly as I can towards it, I peer into the dim corner where it sits. A feral dog, mangy as hell, sits askew, chewing on the mangled remains of the foot and ignoring me while it sustains what looks like its first decent meal in a long time. My eardrums then nearly explode as the Fifer standing behind me raises his pistol, rather unexpectedly and very near my right ear then shoots the beast. Its head explodes onto the cement wall, the blood of the mongrel mixed with the foot in a god-awful ensemble. I turn to him as he lowers his gun. 'Got him' he smiles at me.

I continue to watch motionless as Tam turns the Fifer round by the shoulder and punches him full in the side of his face, a heartfelt blow and one which renders him prostrate.

'Bastard – that was just a wee dug!' Clearly, Tam is fonder of stray dogs than Danny could have imagined.

This is getting too annoying for words, so, when the angry and slightly tearful Tam has finished glowering down at his semi-conscious colleague, I pick up Danny's pistol, put the safety on and end Tam's canine-related reverie by breaking his nose with a sharp crack of its handle.

He reels back, nasal blood cascading onto the concrete floor and looking for a moment that is thinking about fighting back; not an advisable course of action given that I am both holding the gun and capable of kicking the shit out of him with or without it. He backs down, holding the palm of his hand out towards me while the other tries to stem the flow of blood, then mumbles something incoherent and stumbles off to the shower unit while his colleague slowly gets to his feet.

'What the fuck happened there?' Danny asks no-one in particular, the last few moments a shambles of noise and pain for him.

I looked at his pummelled visage and just shake my head. 'It doesn't matter. Your job is to clean up that foot and dog combo, make the wall and floor nice and clean again then take a bag with both of them to the incinerator. If you fuck this up, you two are in the next bags.'

He nods and glances at me uncertainly. 'Are you not coming with us?'

I shake my head and look at him. 'Believe you me, I have had enough of you fucking idiots for a lifetime.' Taking the clip from the gun and throwing them one after another to Danny, I leave them to their duties, all the while wondering how they had managed to ever run their operation here. I close the rusting door of the unit for the last time and walk for a good thirty minutes before reaching a busier part of the city, jumping into a taxi to Waverley Station, where I pick up a car and head north, out of the city and heading for Perth. My plan is to conclude my business over a couple of days in the highlands and then fly back to London, where after a quick pack-up and transit, I'll be on a flight to France and

4

a long weekend with Sasha. She is returning to Melbourne after this weekend, so it will be the last chance I get to see her for a while, unless I can get some time off when all this is done.

During my drive out of Edinburgh, after trying to find something decent to listen to on the oddly-programmed car infotainment system, I mentally review the day's events; I rarely, if ever, feel any emotional regret over my actions. If there ever are misgivings, they generally are about the effectiveness of my actions, whether they were too little or too much. I did, early on and following a discussion on the subject with John, decide that the most serious mistakes were caused by under-reacting to local problems. With that in mind, all our distributors became aware that, rather than causing me to visit to deal with an incident, they would be better just over-reacting themselves. They all knew how our methods worked, how to avoid leaving evidence; how to eradicate risks and most importantly, how to ensure the business operated securely and productively. Only in cases like here in Edinburgh have I been required to intermittently react without planning; when a fairly senior guy fucks up and the others aren't sure how to play the situation, and it's a problem. If this guy gets dealt with by a member of the team, half the others go in a huff or worse; if a boss level guy from London turns up, there's fuck all they can do but play along and get back to being a team afterwards, no-one there to blame and just me to fear or hate or respect or whatever their little heads think. This time though, there's no team to go back to, just the uncertainty of life without our supply of narcotics, and the probability that the vacuum will soon be filled by newcomers.

Even before I was told of our new corporate direction, I had been increasingly wondering what my shelf-life was for this work. It was around my fourteenth month of employment with the Allanton crime family, known to us as The Portfolio, and my third session of psychiatric counselling when it occurred to me that I should perhaps re-evaluate the morality of my participation in the supply of illegal drugs and the whole associated murder/violence thing. I genuinely hadn't been troubled by sleeplessness or remorse; nor had I felt what you'd consider negative emotions towards the work, quite the opposite. My re-evaluation of the whole thing really just started as an exercise in probability analysis. I'd been on my own a few times in these situations and even if I had taken a couple of heavies with me, I was walking each time into a seriously criminally violent operation with dozens of guys who could turn on us, or more importantly, me.

My psychiatrist, Dr Schaffer, an American practising in London, is aware that my work may be at least in part illegal, but not specifically what I do. She listens to my guarded analogies where I try to explain situations, not sure myself if I'm trying to prove if I'm a permanent fucking psycho or whether I can, at some point rejoin the human race as a functioning adult. My analogies are advisedly all business-based. I figured out that there were enough psychopaths, narcissists, weirdoes and high-functioning lunatics in the field of management that I wouldn't stand out unduly in their company. It worked a treat; she quickly categorised me as an emotionally fucked up high-flyer who showed enough signs of needing psychiatric treatment that she'd be able to pay the annual fees for her kid's private schooling from her extortionate charges to me alone. Our sessions gave me the only outlet available to discuss my feelings openly; she provided insight and advice on how to explore my inner self and I ignored this completely, but understood some of what she was trying to highlight for me. While doing this, of course, I immediately realised that it all had to end; so when John Allanton told me that the narcotics business was to be no more, I hid my relief but felt it inside, a prickly excitement for prospective freedom and perhaps even an opportunity to put my misdeeds behind me before my luck ran out.

So, as I leave the city of Edinburgh behind me and drive over the Crossing into Fife, my thoughts turn to the future. The business is closed in London, Manchester, Birmingham, Glasgow and Edinburgh, the last city withdrawn from, our outlets now closed and packets of hard cash given to each of the core operatives as compensation and reward for past contributions and future silence. I am not sorry to leave that life, although I have enjoyed parts of it. Exactly why I enjoyed these parts is still being clarified by psychoanalysis, so I focus my thoughts on the aspects I enjoyed less; meeting with scumbags, travelling at short notice into situations where my good health was at risk and of course, the feeling that my life had been hijacked by this, all this. No, I tell myself, if I've lived and prospered through this, it's a result for me.

I had been dubious, to say the least, about the introduction of new risks to the security of the Portfolio. The business is based on a hierarchical structure, multi-tiered, cellular and with each having minimal knowledge of those above and their peers to maintain the safety of themselves and others. The mafia used it, the resistance in France in WW2 used it and so, even in our global and hence more complex business, we use it too. It protects from insurgents, investigators and those open-mouthed after too much product or booze, or both. I preferred the key soldiers, as we call them, to be cautious by nature and aware of the consequences of disclosing confidential information. John Allanton had given me a number of lectures on how to organise a secrecy-intensive business, which I found highly informative, leading me to tighten and monitor my network on a more concentrated basis, working for some time now with a specific security officer, Zoe, appointed by John a few months back.

Zoe is one of the best qualified and most focused officers in our UK operation. Since leaving The Insider, I had primarily confided in John regarding the deeper movements of the business. However, her appointment to our management team filled a much-needed functional gap in defences. Zoe is also ex-military, well-known to John as a previous employee of Allanton business associates in Germany and trustworthy in the extreme. She had indeed quite rightly doubted my credentials for the post I held, however, I believe she has now amended her thoughts on that front, as she has seen my approach and also worked with me to implement the new security measures. These have covered dozens of actions, such as the monitoring of social media accounts; restructuring our financial controls; setting up a network of contacts who can report concerns and a more developed and incisive continuity plan. In short, Zoe keeps an eye on everyone and I move in when it looks like someone is about to fuck up.

So, both I and Zoe were completely, utterly and without reservations, opposed to the hiring of the Treasurer. Regardless of any personal dislike, we did not feel that the inclusion of a single-point-of-risk like Tim Balliol was helpful to the security of the business. We had no doubt that Balliol was capable of enacting complex financial transactions and therefore useful to the family, but he certainly was not necessary from our perspective. To us, he represented a solution to a problem which doesn't exist and throws a set of serious risks into the core of our organisation.

Three days after the surprise of being introduced to our new colleague, Zoe and I are still trying to make these very points to John.

'I know you think he's a prick, but he has skills we need.' John opens his hands after hearing our concerns.

'He is definitely a prick, but that's not what we are complaining about.' Zoe tells him calmly. 'He has access to financial information which could put every one of us in jail for the rest of our lives.'

'So have you, and Adam, and me' he counters. 'It's the same thing. Any of us could go crazy, go to the authorities and it would be all over. We have current and existing measures which counteract any unwise actions and it's the same for Tim.'

I haven't spoken too much yet, Zoe being the designer and expert in our security formation. Still, I share her concerns and have a few of my own, maybe more given the way I too was parachuted into the business. I glance up at John, who is sipping coffee and looking like he wishes he were elsewhere.

'Take me. You brought me in because of what Sir Mathieson thought I could offer and what I had done, okay, with due diligence, but a risk and a big one at that.' I hope that I'm not going to raise any undeserved suspicions about myself here, but I have to make the point.

'Balliol doesn't have that much to lose, the threats aren't there; I knew what you had on me and what the outcome would be if I went rogue, but this guy's only living relative is some old uncle that he doesn't give a fuck about anyway, so if he turns out to be untrustworthy, what's the threat on him?'

John nods. 'I understand your point. It's not ideal, but his track record means that if he is pressured by the authorities, they couldn't turn a blind eye when we let them know what we've got on his background.'

Both I and Zoe know that this was the key piece of information, as yet unknown to us.

'So what is it?' she asks impatiently.

John looks at us solemnly. 'Just don't leave any kids with him.'

'Fucking prick.' Zoe spits, turning away.

'I know, I know', says John wearily, but he's here for a reason. Please'. He gestures Zoe to sit down again.

John looks serious. 'I have something of an announcement for you which might explain Balliol.' We exchange glances.

'He is, apart from any shortcomings, one of the best when it comes to moving and cleaning money. This time, we have to move a significant amount of our reserves like this. In fact, we need to clean all our financial reserves.'

I am not really sure what John is telling me here and a quick look at Zoe shows me that she's confused too.

John continues. 'In short, we are ceasing our narcotics activities within a very brief period of time and from that point on, the Portfolio will be just that. Property transactions, globally and within the legal frameworks of every country we operate within.' He sits back and looks from me to Zoe.

Zoe exhales. 'Good time to get out boss. The tide's changing and the newcomers aren't going to be easy to hold ground against.' John nods at her and I keep quiet, letting Zoe give her encouragement unaided.

John resumes his briefing. 'Exactly. We know more and more competitors are coming in, already here rather. We could expand and fight back, which would be expensive and not a guarantee of winning; or, we cash out and go legitimate. Balliol is transferring the missing funds from his previous employer and then will start on our various reserves, with the purpose of moving it all into a corporate financial framework. This will not just be untraceable; it will stand up to just about any investigation or due diligence.'

He goes on. 'After this, the business will withdraw from all locations. Adam, you will coordinate the termination payments to all staff. Work with your hub guys to cover the whole thing, including giving advice to the men that they should take the money and fuck off quietly to somewhere sunny. They'll know all about the Albanians and the others who will fill the vacuum and without our backup, they will need to think carefully about hanging around and still supplying.'

This all sounds like a damn fine plan. While making vast sums of money has been great, I have also been acutely aware that it certainly wouldn't be forever. If this exit strategy keeps me alive, I'm all for it. I need to figure out exactly what he wants me to do and then if John intends for me still to have a job here.

'So, we set up a schedule to visit the facilities and the transfer stations. I take them their pay-off cash and say bye-bye?' I look to him for guidance, but he just makes a face which suggests that they just need to do what he says.

'How much are we giving them? I mean, we could just withdraw and let them sink or swim?'

John shakes his head. 'No, and I'll tell you why. These guys have made us a fortune. They have limited knowledge individually. However, if the authorities suddenly find that there are ex-suppliers getting into trouble across the country, they will finally figure out that our hitherto shadowy business actually employed them. Give them enough time to pick up these skint and pissed-off blokes and there is a good chance that they will be able to piece together enough information to identify us. That is not the way to go, but I will tell you what is.' He stands and pours himself another coffee from the pot in the corner of his office.

'We give them all the equivalent of a year's salary – not the skims or the bonuses, but enough to let them get away or to give them time to get on with something else.' I can't believe what I'm hearing.

'How much will this cost? I mean, there are lots of guys out there, a few hundred.'

'We have been preparing for this contingency for some time by building a separate hard cash reserve. This fund is not currently on our books and is physically stored in a number of secure locations, so don't concern yourself about the cost, this is a decision which has already been made. It's not for everyone working for us, just the key staff and the permanent employees. The low-level guys will just be dropped; they wouldn't know anything even if they were picked up. What we need to do is pay out to anyone who has information which could help an investigation.'

I get this now; it's a clever if expensive move. 'OK, so we let all the teams go at the transfer stations and the hubs. That's not so bad. What about the front businesses? Do we just let them all go too?'

John tells us exactly how it's going to work and I'm impressed. The cover businesses are all in the names of the local guys, so if it's a clothing supplier or whatever, they get the business to keep if they want, or they just sell or liquidate it and head off somewhere else. He tells us the rough order he wants it done in and that he ideally wants it done over a week-long period, ten days maximum. It's a tight timeline but I tell him that I'll get the list drawn up and see what we need to do to make it happen. I head to my office to think and Zoe to hers. He didn't mention our head office yet, I guess that might

13

need a one-to-one conversation so I didn't raise it. Hopefully, since I've been included on a few property deals, I'll still be working here and staying in my rather superb apartment in Knightsbridge, to which I have grown rather attached. I have also grown fond of being rich as Croesus, spending time expensively with Sasha and, whatever happens, whatever I have to do, this all has to be continued.

☐

3 TIM JOINS THE PORTFOLIO

Of his three primary colleagues, he disliked Zoe, found Williams aloof and couldn't communicate with Cheryl. However, neither of these interpersonal situations was new to Tim Balliol. As a consistently and inherently misanthropic individual, he had serially failed to engage on a personal level with any of his employers, colleagues or peers in the past ten years, or to be specific, anyone he had met since leaving university. The alcohol-fuelled camaraderie of university and the then-apparent capacity for anyone to fit into some group or other in further education, meant that he was hitherto unaware of the extent his social awkwardness, or at least of how much of a pain in the arse everyone thought he was.

After qualifying as an accountant, Tim had left his first two internships convinced that both organisations were dysfunctional and populated by small-minded, unfriendly types who only socialised in their comfortable groups, shunning outsiders and newcomers. His third and fourth workplaces, where he enjoyed excellent salary and locations, proved to be even more unwelcoming and often argumentative environments, despite, like his internships, starting well at interview before disintegrating over the course of the first few days. So it was that Tim moved from job to job, references gladly given, in part because he was a shit-hot accountant but mainly because he, for some innate reason, was the most dislikeable person that one could imagine. In conversation, he would openly offer opinions which would variously and accurately be described as inconsiderate, ill-informed, fascist, sexist, homophobic, Neanderthal, racist, and on one occasion, drawing serious concerns that he was sexually attracted to reptiles. His colleagues would, as with all new additions to their teams, initially welcome Tim with smiles which would turn sour over their first chat at the lunch break. When joining in, he would spout his perceived wisdom on current affairs, learned from his choice of newspapers and online sites, often at the point where sensitivities were sharpest. In his fourth post, he was given a suspension within a week of his arrival. The rather abrupt investigation and the feeling of unfairness of the disciplinary meeting gave him a sense of dismay at how his logical description of the lead-up to a terrorist atrocity could have been taken so sensitively by his colleagues, when it was merely intended to explain how best any subsequent crimes could be avoided. Tim didn't mince his words, that was his style and he had little sympathy for liberals who didn't want to hear the truth about other religions.

He then moved to a promoted post elsewhere which started well and from a business perspective, enabled him to demonstrate his now considerable expertise. This again turned into a hate-filled and then solitary job for Tim. Despite this hostile environment, he indeed prospered and learned there, his value to the company such that the owners provided him with a precious office of his own and as much home-working as he needed. He continued his studies too, back then, to better move forward in his chosen profession and after some time, Tim moved to another company which actually head-hunted him, through which channels he knew not.

It was in this new organisation that the skills of Tim Balliol were truly recognised. After a discussion with his superior about its various strands of income, both hidden and open, Tim understood that here he could apply his abilities to the full. He developed a more practical application of the processes for international banking, of taxation and its avoidance and, critically, how to keep this income away from prying eyes and turn it into assets which could be used or invested for his employer. Tim Balliol was now working for the wrong sort of company. However, the business gave him the respect he had lacked in those earlier jobs, his colleagues here markedly different as they too guarded their privacy and shunned frivolity.

All had been well there until a management restructuring, which manifested itself as his boss being restructured into a bullet hole-filled corpse after crossing the wrong people. Tim found himself temporarily unemployed and in hiding until further notice; a position that was broken by an offer of employment by John Allanton, the man indirectly responsible for his previous employers' demise.

After one phone call and a hastily-obeyed instruction to get into a taxi from his most anonymous and cost-effective hotel, Tim found himself in an office in an industrial estate near Bromley, sitting across from Allanton and another younger man with an expression Tim could not read at all. He always prided himself on being able to project a detached calmness in interview situations. However, here he found himself spending the first quiet moments of the meeting mentally calculating the probability that he would not survive it. He also realised when they spoke to each other, that the other man was Scottish, that he'd met him briefly once before and that was more than enough. Despite being young and innocent-looking, Tim was fairly sure he was the one who had terminated both his employment and employer the previous week.

'Thanks for coming here Tim, I really appreciate it.' John Allanton smiled at Tim generously.

Tim nodded, uncertain whether the pleasantry was perhaps sarcasm.

John went on. 'I know that the changes in your company have been unsettling, however, I wanted to let you know that we are now managing the organisation on an interim basis and that you still have a vital role to play if you are willing to do so.' He sat forward slightly and looked at the frigidly immobile Tim.

'We have a few tasks which we'd like you to make a start on as soon as possible. There are, as you know, a number of your company assets which are for good reasons difficult to pin down. We need these moved into a structure accessible by our own colleagues. Do you understand?' Tim nodded, this instruction clarifying his presence and hopefully his continuing ability to breathe.

'I have some information on the estimate of the value of assets we expect to transfer. Can you give me your understanding of the total?' Silence now as the two men looked straight at him, causing him to redden as he occasionally did under extreme pressure.

'Yes, although current estimates of some physical assets vary depending on the disposal scenario and market values.' Tim sat for a moment before becoming aware that the silence would continue until he provided the figure.

'I would estimate that we have some £7 to 8 million offshore and an equivalent or slightly larger amount in UK assets, mostly stocks through a number of investments. Although a number are electronically transferable at short notice, there will be some considerable work involved in reattributing others, particularly without the…involvement of my previous employer himself.'

John smiled at him again. 'It is possible though, for a man of your talents to make all these transfers happen?'

'Yes, I do have some delegated powers under my condition of employment and as a signatory for the business.' Tim replied.

The Scottish guy reached under the desk and placed an envelope and an ID card onto the table.

John smiled at Tim reassuringly. 'This is the address of your new office and some basic information. You can consider yourself my employee now Tim and I trust you can carry on the excellent work you did previously as Treasurer for your former employers. We will see you at 9am tomorrow.' John shook his hand, although the other man did not. Tim was ushered back to the waiting taxi and taken back to his hotel, where the driver told him he'd pick him up at 8am the next morning, with no further dialogue or information offered. At least he was unharmed, had a job and John Allanton seemed to like him, although, in Tim's experience, many jobs started like that.

The primary function which Tim served in his first week at his new post was exactly as stated by John Allanton. Every meaningful asset which had he had hidden, moved, placed at the end of a trail and otherwise protected from sight had to be assigned new ownership. More specifically he had to utilise a complex and fascinating sequence of asset holdings and investments under the general title of the Portfolio. He and three accountants sat for five days, until 10 pm each day until the work was completed, during which he became absolutely thrilled by the intricacy of the Portfolio. It wasn't perfect and he noted these imperfections to tell John Allanton about, little gaps where the business could be tracked across companies, countries, shells and signatures. It was nearly there, but Tim was for all his many faults and personal proclivities, a perfectionist who was intrigued by the patterns of numbers and accounts. Tim, a man riven with faults, perversions and quirks, had one outstanding aptitude, besides his encyclopaedic understanding of international finance.

He thought like an Auditor.

Tim was a deeply strange individual, which perhaps even helped him in his profession. Tim carried out his work with the mindset of a person who thinks he is being followed by a cleverer person, a suspicious one at that and one who knows the same rules as Tim. This mindset baffled and amazed the three shadowing accountants he was allocated at The Portfolio. They were impressed by his conventional skills but far more so by his singularly cunning and cutting-edge country-by-country knowledge of people, of loopholes and weaknesses, of places where paperwork could be shredded after changes made by his contacts in offices far and wide. It took bribes, it took pressure and it took nerve, but Tim Balliol transferred almost £14 million in scattered assets to John Allantons Portfolio in just five days. So, it required little else to convince John Allanton to continue the employment of Tim Balliol, despite his many personal flaws. Tim was part of the team, for at least a while, if previous workplaces were any guide.

Due to the busy start to his job, it was later than normal when Tim properly interacted with his colleagues in the new business, pissing them off almost exactly one week later than usual.

He had been introduced to Zoe on the Tuesday of the second week, her role being markedly different but interlinked to his duties. She sat with him and prepared to be patient, having been briefed on his personality and reputation by John and Adam. There had been some disagreement between the two men on the merits of continuing both the employment and life of Tim Balliol after the transfer was complete, however, John knew that until they fully understood his skills, they would be better advised to keep him around. His three accountants would learn from Tim, tolerate him, smile at him and make damn sure they understood what he was doing.

Zoe also had been told to be accommodating for Tim.

'Welcome aboard Tim' she greeted him with her best attempt at a friendly smile.

He looked at her askance, his brown, uncombed and oily hair covering his glasses until he flattened it back with his left hand. Zoe continued, recognising his social awkwardness in all its glory.

'I'm responsible for most aspects of security and we need to discuss the management of risks on the accounting side of the business. I'd welcome your thoughts after last week's look through our books.'

Tim looked now at Zoe with a distinct sneer. 'I could spend all day telling you about the risks you have. It's a shambles and you're just lucky that you haven't all been caught yet. Just being complicated doesn't mean it's untraceable you know.' A rude rebuke, causing Zoe the first flush of embarrassment she'd had in an awfully long time. Tim then smugly lectured Zoe for fifteen minutes on the ease with which an investigator could trace property investment funds back to their source, profits from the businesses which would not hold up to scrutiny.

She reigned in an impulse to press her thumbs into Tim's eyes, forcing herself to break her negative thoughts and listen to through his analysis of the files that he had brought with him.

Zoe calmed herself and focused on the value which he represented rather than the manner in which he offered it. 'This is great work, Tim. I'm really pleased you are going to fix all this and I'm looking forward to your report next week. Next Tuesday at 2pm. OK?' She rose and left him to ponder, enjoying the puzzled look which Tim exhibited as he realised that he had inadvertently been delegated to fix the problems with which he had so successfully humiliated Zoe.

Zoe left Tim and walked upstairs and into Adam Darnows office, where he looked up to see her arriving. Adam was impressed by her apparent calmness after meeting the excruciating Tim.

'Well?' he asked. 'Was I right or what?'

Zoe sat heavily across from him. 'He is the most annoying bastard I've ever met. Ten seconds in I could have cheerily strangled him.' Adam laughed; a rare and brief sound but infectious, making the tension ebb from Zoe, momentarily relaxing her enough to laugh with him.

'He knows his stuff though. I thought we were tight on the international connections but we're not. Definitely a shifty little shit though, not to be trusted unless we are tight on him. Cheryl and her guys won't let him touch anything without an explanation, even though some of his stuff is really hard to follow. We've got a list of his contacts too, we're looking into each of them to make sure they are genuine and get some details on them in case we need to intervene.' She told him one of the examples that Balliol had used to demonstrate their weaknesses. Adam adopted the glazed expression he could not avoid when anyone started talking about accountancy, which only abated once Zoe had finished.

'Are you back?' she asked with more than a hint of annoyance.

'Yeah, if I must.' Adam smiled that smile again, the one where Zoe couldn't stay annoyed for long. She knew that he a flipside, but it was easy to forget when they were just here, in an office like normal people, doing a job, being colleagues.

'So what do we do about him? He has skills but he shouldn't be here, no loyalty and a weird personality. We're throwing open our books to a potential high-risk defector who John wants to be our temporary Treasurer for some reason.' Zoe threw her hands up in frustration.

'John has something else on him, something personal. He wouldn't tell me but I know he wouldn't put an unmitigated risk in place without good reason, not now when we're moving legit.' Adam sat back and yawned, which he did repeatedly on those rare days where he was required to actually attend for eight hours. 'My assumption is that he'll be here until the assets are signed over and moved on again, then he'll be passed over to me to deal with.'

Zoe shivered imperceptibly. 'Well, sooner the better.'

Big Jim Galloglas had spent his childhood enjoying life in apartheid South Africa, the tail end of the good times, but still a most privileged upbringing with a wealthy family and a house replete with servants and swimming pool. As the world changed around him, the young Jim and his family found himself displaced first to Zimbabwe, then in his young adulthood to a reclusive yet intermittently hedonistic life in Hong Kong and thence to his current domicile in Thailand. His business life had taken him all over the world, but the pleasures of Thai life forever drew him back there.

In the winter of his years, the experiences of his peripatetic life over, he had time to reflect on a life spent in the sunshine of other people's money. His apartment, one of several property investments which were funded by his late father's accumulation of wealth, paid him and paid well. He had, to all intents, spent his whole life as a member of the idle rich. His parents had both died relatively young after revelling in the delights of excessive smoking and drinking in a fast set of Johannesburg. They were traditionalists and so left the bulk of their capital and investments to their oldest son, whom they preferred anyway. Their youngest son was a military man, rarely returning home over the years after this financial slight, and so Big Jim Galloglas became the scion of their business, taking advantage of his brother's absence to incrementally cut him from even the fringes of the business. He did pay him annual dividends, which through dint of the younger Galloglas failed investments, were more or less wasted until the last one, the one which could not be cashed in as the younger brother had passed away, unknown to big Jim.

Over the years, the guilt at taking advantage of his brother's absence stayed unassuaged in the back of his mind, until the news of the death reached him, the unattended dividend payment having triggered an investigation. Jim Galloglas' agent was dispatched to Belize, where the brother had apparently spent his last days. There the employee bribed access to a police file, thence to the post-mortem and its photographs which proved at a glance that George Galloglas had died many days before the official date recorded and in a manner most violent. There were no records of him flying to Belize either, although the investigator knew that there were many ways for a man to travel unknown, even now. He reported the grim news to his boss and returned after arranging a memorial plaque on his behalf, a token to give the dead man a marker, somewhere.

Big Jim Galloglas immediately employed an investigative organisation to determine the events which lead to the death of his sibling, a picture of the causes and events which would let him understand how and where his brother, long-lost as he was, came to his end.

The mortal departure of his brother coincided with Big Jim's cancer news, which meant that he too would be going the way of his parents and for the same reasons. He could afford any treatment, but for what he had, money could not make much of a difference. Instead, he found himself no longer caring about his investments, their futures pointless for once, no-one to benefit once he faded away; his last will and testament would send the bulk of his estate to his last remaining, distant cousin, a person so far lost in time and memory that he would not have recognised her if he passed her in the street.

It took his investigators a number of months and considerable expense, however, the file they passed back to him made him feel deep anger again, the malaise of his malign cancer overtaken by the desire for revenge. The report told him that his brother had almost certainly been assassinated by his employers, a mafia-style global mob who stayed in dark shadows and weren't to be approached lightly, or with any intent to survive. George Galloglas had apparently become entwined with them during his army days and thereafter. He'd fronted some business in Scotland for them, went the report, until all of a sudden he died on a random trip to Belize, of all places. His investigators weren't as naive as the authorities, the combination of improbability and lack of forensic evidence making them dig deeper for the answers. They found what had happened back in the UK, by finding out the gossip using bribes and critically, from one anonymous tip-off which was confirmed by their subsequent investigations. It had been a set-up, and after not much longer and one more expensive and very careful leg of the investigation, his men managed to get the names and places of where to gain revenge. Big Jim Galloglas was an old, finished man now and revenge would be his last dividend to the brother he owed; it would be the only reparation he could make for the life he had denied his brother and the inheritance these men had denied him.

Jim Galloglas was dying of cancer, not so young as his parents, but younger than he would have liked and leaving him with this as-yet unrequited sense of anger, a core deep need for revenge and, given that he couldn't take revenge of the cigarette manufacturers who had caused his disease, he would refocus this vengeance on the bastards who had killed his little brother. Three days after the report was presented, Galloglas had arranged a visit from a business colleague and old friend, a man whom few would trust but not Galloglas, who knew that his money would talk with this one.

Mark Roghan approached the house from the wooden patio at the rear, looking for Galloglas through the lounge windows, into the dark teak-lined space, once the epicentre of a party lifestyle but now giving the appearance of a rather decayed time capsule, not helped by the untidiness caused by the lack of recent cleaning. Galloglas libido had largely but not entirely deserted him, as did a series of female housekeeping staff who he unsuccessfully attempted to crudely proposition. Roghan eyed the room with the look of someone who really, really did not want to be there. He was also an expatriate Afrikaner, who had once, long ago, shared the same experiences as his friend Galloglas, although marriage and healthier living had given him a more nuanced appreciation of a decent home life. A life which Galloglas had eschewed, along with any vestiges of hygiene and the capacity to operate a washing machine without professional assistance.

'Bloody hell mate, you've let the old place go a bit!' Mark Roghan held his nose as he entered, seeing Big Jim Galloglas on the sofa in what looked like a pale linen suit, riven with an assortment of stains and odours to which he would have preferred never to have set eyes or nose on. The walls were decorated in an odd combination of African native art and Asian paintings, neither of which appeared to have been selected with a discerning eye.

'Fuck off' growled Galloglas. His voice was never sweet, but the recent years of whisky, cigars and cancer had given him a croak which was appallingly guttural and moist. He turned to see his friend enter the room and struggled up to shake hands. Roghan had intended to give him a hug, but the stench kept him at distance. They smiled at each other, for an instant before they began their business. A whisky poured, they sat across from each other on the low, yellowing leather sofas which stank of years spilt drinks and of canine sleeping.

'I need you to put out some work for a military contractor.' Galloglas handed Roghan what appeared to be a long-lens photo of Sir Mathieson Allanton.

'Who is he? Looks like a professor.' He handed him back the photo.

'He's the fucker who killed my brother. One of his men did anyway but he was the boss, so it's him I need. Name of Allanton, some fucking drug dealer who's just retired, based now in the Med or in Scotland so I'm looking for a European resource and a fucking good one.'

Roghan nodded. 'I don't have anyone that far away but I do know someone who might. A guy in England that I've done business before with, reliable so far. I can give him a call, see if he can help?'

Roghan looked sombrely at Galloglas. 'I didn't know you even had a brother.'

'Yeah, he was sent to school in the UK when we left South Africa, the old dears were too busy having fun to take a young kid along. Was in the British Army for years and we weren't in touch. He was still my brother though.' A coughing fit reminded Roghan that he was dealing with a man for whom time was at a premium. 'How long will it take to arrange?'

'I'll call him soon as I get back to the office. It will not be cheap though, if this guy is big in the drug business, it's a risk mate.' He looked up at Galloglas.

'Like I give a fuck about the risk.' He told him, handing the file over.

At the end of the next day, in his pleasantly plush office in downtown Bangkok, Mark Roghan extracted the file from his wall safe and read through the highly detailed contents. The target, Sir Mathieson Allanton, was likely to be on his yacht on the Mediterranean at the start of the season, although the transcript of a hacked mobile phone messages to his son indicated that he had booked a flight to commence his spring and summer of cruising, and a note of his first ports of call, but was considering delaying it if the weather had not picked up. This left Roghan with something of a quandary as such a man would surely have more than one property, perhaps several. The next few pages of the file showed that Allanton had been photographed in London but had apparently closed down the apartment he used there. He had been traced north, to a remote Manse with an address in the west highlands, which had apparently been in his sole domicile before his retirement. The investigator's pursuit of the fate of the late George Galloglas had pivoted on this information, the brother of their employer being the owner of the Inverannan Estate. From this link, they had pieced together enough information to complete the picture. They couldn't bring George Galloglas back from the dead for his brother, but they could help avenge him and make a damn fine living in the process.

Other than this, the investigators had found no information that Sir Mathieson Allanton frequented any other properties and was generally a creature of habit. Roghan smiled to himself and placed the call to his man in England. After that, Roghan sent him a copy of the redacted file, Galloglas name removed, to let him see what the contract required.

His middle-man, with an accent as thick as Thames mud, called him back two days later to tell him that, in his opinion, that the job would best be completed by sending separate contractors to each location, starting the action at the most likely, the yacht. This would, of course, at least double the cost but Galloglas, after a brief call from Roghan, approved whatever expenses were needed. Roghan knew that Galloglas was wealthy. Their shared investments over the years were seldom lower than in the hundreds of thousands of US dollars. He had by now committed some big numbers to procure the assassination of Sir Mathieson Allanton. Roghan, unlike the terminally afflicted Big Jim Galloglas, was still concerned that reprisals could follow such an act, and he did not want him or his family targeted by anyone angered by the murder of this old criminal. The high cost of the arrangement and the assassins were partly to ensure that the confidentiality of the deal was ensured, and this Roghan emphasised vehemently to the middle-man.

Roghan, in turn, was assured by the middle-man that the work would be completed successfully and without fuss. The asset who had accepted the first contract, the one in the Mediterranean, was apparently an ex-military mercenary who was looking for some high-paying work, already living not far away and knew the area well, which exactly fitted the bill. The contract in Scotland would have to be paid out even if it were not required, as the costs of mobilisation and time would be the same for the men involved. The middle-man told Roghan that the contract in Scotland would be carried out by a small group of highly trained and motivated men, led by someone he could absolutely rely upon.

Roghan knew from experience that, assuming the information was accurate, the success of the Mediterranean mission relied upon the professionalism of the middle-man arranging it and, ultimately, the expertise of the assassin. What wasn't apparent, just yet, was that the former was, as soon as any funds were in his possession, generally to be found drunk and incapable in a local pub east of London and the latter was an overweight incompetent who had barely managed to avoid a dishonourable discharge from the army on two occasions. The contract in Scotland, well Roghan was sure that it wouldn't be needed, but good to have a Plan B. He ended his communication with the middle-man feeling assured that the contracts were in good hands and updated Big Jim Galloglas that their plans were moving along nicely.

The Inverannan Estate had undergone surprisingly little change in the months since the unfortunate demise of its progenitor and benefactor, George Galloglas. Functionally, this had hardly even formed a distraction from its primary function as a transfer station for narcotics. The mystery around the passing of Galloglas had been, for a time, quite the dominant conversation among the estate workers in this remote part of the north of Scotland. Over time, as things do, the gossip around Inverannan returned to quiet normality and a new manager was appointed to take the business forward, albeit with some of the larger projects mothballed and, because of this, a reduction in the number of staff employed. The restaurant, hotel and harbour projects had been permanently cancelled; the game shooting was also closed down other than when necessary to maintain the correct balance. A new port and fisheries business had started about forty miles away, coincidentally, so those who were made redundant from the estate slipped readily and quietly into their new employment.

The new estate head, a local called Magnus Gilfillan, had worked closely with Sir Mathieson Allanton for a number of years and became the focal point of the now less-publicised estate. Concentrating on exporting timber, venison and a number of community-based small products, it still provided the area with a focal point for the distribution of its goods to the rest of the country, but now there were no real facilities for guests, except on those occasions where the owners themselves required them. The owners, the Allanton family, were now hands-off in general, albeit with a renewed commitment to green investment and community participation at Inverannan, or so Gilfillan had informed the estate staff and suppliers during his early discussions. The estate vehicles took their products away twice a week, as always, and the suppliers of cheese, ceramics, cloth products and the like were paid on time and as well as before. Some of the energy had gone from Inverannan with the passing of Galloglas, but the more subdued approach suited those still involved; the transportation of narcotics continued in the background as before. The decision to temporarily continue the movement of product here had not been taken lightly and perhaps, those taking the decision had an element of personal bias which would not have been applied elsewhere. The estate had a certain emotional hold on them and selling it on to the wrong owners would leave a chunk of the community bereft of income - and leave several loose ends which could present a problem if not handled sensitively.

Magnus Gilfillan was a more solid character than the previous manager; his demeanour less of the salesman and more of the ghillie. Unsuited to dealing with more sensitive matters, the team in the office quickly adopted the role of overseeing the remaining estate personnel, while Gilfillan capably ensured the supply of illegal and legal product into the estate and out again with metronomic efficiency and critically, the minimum of publicity. He was, however, a cog in the wheel of a greater narcotics business, required to answer to the hierarchy set in place by his previous employer, Sir Mathieson Allanton. Gilfillan had been absolutely loyal to Sir Mathieson as a soldier, but this loyalty was being challenged by being left in principal charge of a significant narcotics transfer operation here at Inverannan. The delivery boats came into the remote mooring on the west coast, down to the estate and thence off south, but the feeling of relief he had when the last shipment had left the estate and there was no incriminating evidence on sight, was becoming more profound by the week. In short, Gilfillan's nerve had recently gone; replaced by at least a bottle of malt whisky and often a hell of a lot more every day. A situation which his employers were monitoring from afar, to ensure that the best interests of the estate were upheld, abetted by the team in the office.

The situation with Gilfillan's drinking came to something of a head in the early hours of a wintry Saturday morning. After spending much of the day and all of the evening in his office alone and panicking about the departure of the packages, he decided that it would be a grand idea to end his reverie by heading down to the estate fishing loch with a flare gun to shoot some ducks which were returning there for some late winter sheltered solitude. Gilfillan looked at the guns in his office cabinet first, crying a little as he did; his hands caressing his crossbow, a weapon he had been deadly with since his teens. He didn't like shotguns much, the recoil annoyed him now and the noise was offensive compared to his preferred weapons. On active service, however, he'd really enjoyed the night shooting, tracers heading for the enemy lines, spitting fire into the absolute dark; so, he opened the cabinet with supplies for the dinghies, where the signal guns and refills were kept. He still called it a Varey pistol but he supposed that was just his age; these ones were bright orange, plastic and to be honest probably not as fulfilling to shoot as those from decades ago, but he would give them a try anyway. He wrestled with his wax jacket until it was up the correct way and his arms successfully inserted, then blundered out the side door of Inverannan House and onwards into the dark.

Soon after, the highland night was disturbed by the blinding flashes of the flare pistol cartridges, the panic of the ducks and the smell of a few beasts unfortunately incinerated as they tried to escape. Gilfillan reloaded a few times, quite efficiently for someone who had drunk as much strong whisky; in his mind he was back in the regiment, shooting those sneaky bastards who wouldn't fight fairly but hid in the hills and villages and set devices which killed his mates and sent their body parts flying over the roads and he fucking hated them, so much. He thought about those places every day and dreamed about them every night and found increasingly that getting comatose and shitfaced with whisky was the only way to sleep. Gilfillan thought himself too old and maybe too tough to handle it any other way, and after reluctantly agreeing to manage the estate, found himself with new pressure atop all the old army nightmares. He had hidden it well at the outset and knew he did his job well, but the blacking out was becoming more frequent and tonight, he simply wanted to shoot something.

Although only a couple of staff actually witnessed the one-man shooting party from a distance, the detritus remained in the grey, cold morning for all to see, along with a still-recumbent Gilfillan and a few charred duck corpses. The estate lads helped him into his office and gave him another drink to settle his shaking hands and warm him up. In the main office, an efficient and committed employee was calling this update through to her sometime partner and business colleague, Adam Darnow.

☐

Growing through my adolescence in a highland village as I did, my father had occasionally warned me of the consequences of drugs; what he couldn't foresee was that the consequences for me would be to become fairly wealthy, successful and feared and all that without ever having a drop of it enter my own system. Back then I had always wondered, given my dearth of disposable income, what it would be like to have money. Serious money I mean; the kind which meant I could buy anything or go anywhere. I now know this feeling and it's absolutely, totally fucking fantastic. I'm currently looking down onto the harbour at Monaco-Ville and its' all lights and money and laughter and money and yachts and money and I just love the whole thing. Of course, I recognize the nagging hinter-thought that I'm here because of my own dumb luck combined with a degree of moral fluidity; such ambiguity means that I can live with myself as an agent of death and misery to abusers of our product. It also helps that I seem to have a supplementary psychological condition which compartmentalises the nastier aspects of the business, if that covers it - and lets me jolly along with my life regardless. I'm working on processing all of this at present, however only in my spare time and when work allows.

Work in fact which had been keeping me pretty well occupied. A combination of operational management and defensive actions were my typical working week in this narcotic behemoth. This organisation is more than anyone could imagine; if a movie were made of it, you'd walk out calling it far-fetched at best and probably ridiculous in concept. That it may well be - but it is real and I, for my small part, am a lieutenant to one of its great stars, the inheritor of the UK chairmanship of one of the most secretive but unlimited companies in the history of illegal drug supply, John Allanton.

In the past eighteen months, I had become ambitiously engaged in the sectors which John has allocated me. I nodded when he gave me instructions, clarified when required and then implemented them. Same as millions of middle managers, office staff, construction workers and all the others, so it's not so hard to understand how it all happens. You just have to get used to the subtle differences regarding legality and morality, the risks which result in generous rewards, for the moment at least. It's all coming to an end, thanks to John's plan to become safer, richer and free from the worries which beset all honourable gangsters.

My mobile breaks me from my thoughts and I take the call quickly, heading to the side of the balcony, where I can speak without being overheard. I check the number and it's the office at Inverannan.

'Hi, it's me.' I recognise Gillian's soft highland tones instantly, although she sounds like she's worried.

'What's up?'

'It's Magnus. He got really drunk last night and went out with a flare gun. The lads have got him in now, but he's struggling badly, I think his drinking is way out of control now.' She sounds concerned and gives me a couple of more examples of his alcohol-fuelled blunders so I guess I need to add this problem to my list for next week.

'OK. Can you and Eilidh get him into working order for the Monday drop?'

There's a pause, but I know she'll help. 'Yeah, we'll try anyway. He's well gone by the looks of him though. The guys know what to do anyway, so as long as he doesn't do anything daft that brings the Police here we'll be fine. When do you think you will get a chance to come up?'

'Should be Tuesday or Wednesday, but give me a call if anything else happens?' Gillian agrees and we close the call.

I need to go back to Inverannan to finish my work anyway, complete the handing-out of redundancy payments in Scotland and I'll deal with Magnus while I'm there. Before my flight to get here, I had met with Robbie in Glasgow to close down our business there, after travelling around England and Wales all week doing the same. Robbie is an ambitious guy who likes the big money, so he took the packet of cash and smugly told me that he had suspected what was coming and already had some potential new suppliers in mind, as if I could give a fuck what he did next. His parting gift, however, was to let me know that one of his counterparts in Edinburgh appeared to have the same premonition and, contrary to our strict instructions on confidentiality, been somewhat voluble on the matter to people he really shouldn't have. As soon as I left Robbie to his own nefarious future, I had to set some plans in motion to deal with the situation, although my own personal touch will be required to finalise matters in Edinburgh. After that, I'll have to endure the journey back to Inverannan, but at least it's less dangerous than some of the things I have to do recently. I put a cryptic message on my phone app to remind me and walk back to the centre of the balcony to resume my chilling out.

I turn round and look back into the bedroom where Sasha sleeps, my on-off partner of just three months and coincidentally the cousin of my employer. We agreed to keep our relationship secret if at all possible, however, I have from the outset of my involvement with the organisation taken the view that keeping secrets from John would rarely be in my best interest. So, I had a confidential conversation with him and he, with reservations, told me to go ahead but be careful. Sasha appears to have some history of spoiled-brattism, understandable given her extreme familial wealth and the indulgence of her father, Paul Verattis, the Australian businessman and overseer of the antipodean outpost of the Allanton global money machine.

Sasha however, as far as I know, is a sincerely wonderful person under the veil of wealth and beauty; it's a genuine and constant surprise in my life that she is actually with me. Maybe a walk on the rough side for her, maybe to annoy her father or perhaps just going along with relationships as people sometimes do. I had first run into her when I was with John, in London for a family meeting I wasn't allowed to fully participate in and then again at some high-value property stuff in east Asia which required us to travel there and meet some interested parties. We were the backers and the launderers in this scenario, taking on newly-built real estate in emerging locations and all that entailed. I initially thought that John perhaps just wanted some company on these ventures, although I later gleaned an impression that he was preparing me for a more advanced role. John had casually mentioned to me that his daughters would never be involved in the business, apparently known in their family circle as The Portfolio, so maybe there was some motivation there to have a trusted lieutenant available for when needed.

So, with John's permission, I had started seeing Sasha while she was in Europe for the winter skiing and pretending to study at some business school. We met up her apartment here in Monaco-Ville or at my place in London although it was usually me flying towards her at weekends; even the worst of us need a break. She had a cascade of upper-echelon friends who were also spending time here, so we hung out with them in restaurants here at the weekend, mainly, or in the casino and clubs later. I feared that despite my newly generated wealth I was still a gauche highlander, but the Australian psyche does not seem to have the inherent class-awareness of the British. That said, I maintained a fairly quiet and cool demeanour around them, joining in for a laugh when required; enough to be thought well of, but not revealing much else. To them, I was just another mate with money and the loving gaze of their friend who was temporarily and inexplicably smitten by a Scottish ruffian.

It started, as many relationships do, by accident; we were both at a loose end when the discussions ended, sooner than expected, over the construction deal in Singapore. Sasha knew the area and offered to take me for a drink before the collective late meal at the hotel and our respective morning flights home. She took me to a basement bar, just a few hundred metres walk from the business district where we had our meeting. It was decked in neon and soothed with some kind of chill-out suburban jazz so we found a booth at the end of the counter and out of anyone's earshot, music playing enough to cover being overheard but not loud enough to stop us talking.

'So tell me about you'. She looks at me as if I am being interviewed rather than asked.

I have a brief moment to consider my response.

'I'm just working for John'. I shrug.

'Yeah, everybody works for somebody, but what's your thing? You a property guy or a business guy?' She smiles this time, maybe letting me know that she was taking the piss a little.

'I'm a business guy' I tell her without smiling.

'So you say, but John wouldn't bring a heavy here for the property deal, even a baby-faced one. C'mon, what's your gig?'

I look straight at her and give a hint of a smile. 'He's worried that his cousin might get bored between meetings, so he's brought me here to show you how to drink properly and keep you amused.'

'Yeah, I don't think you should plan on showing an Australian how to drink'. We clink glasses and I turn the conversation round to her, where she was brought up and stuff. After a couple of beers, we escalate to tequila and Sasha tells me her growing up stories, crazy college tales and I recount mine, edited where required. All of a sudden its a few hours later and we realise we haven't called in our apologies for missing the business dinner. Sasha finds this funny as hell and we head for a club and then, much later, to the hotel.

She's gone when I wake up and my life pattern continues unabated; I can't remember every part of the night but, other than existential angst, my immediate concerns are that I've slept with John's relative, failed to attend a scheduled business dinner and have no idea if I've missed the morning flight. A panicked check at my watch shows that the latter isn't an issue and I've enough time to shower and maybe meet John for breakfast before we head to Changi for the flight. I jump up and get showered, grab my clothes and stuff the used ones into the bag, call John and join him at breakfast; he's on his own and almost finished but gives me an amused look over when I sit down heavily across from him. I vaguely remember that Sasha told me not tell anyone about last night but it wouldn't have taken great observational skills to notice that my eyes are bloodshot and I hadn't had a decent quota of sleep.

'Rough night?' he asks with a slanted grin.

'Yeah, I'll be OK after I get something to eat.'

'Sasha can be quite persuasive when she fancies a night out. I've had some experience of trying to keep up with her drinking levels so I feel your pain.'

I nod back at him and order the least wobbly items I could see on the menu and an espresso to try and kick start my psyche.

'Yeah. Sorry for missing dinner.'

He grins at me. 'Sasha has a low boredom threshold and we guessed that she wouldn't be there. You missed a great meal though. The chilli crab was superb.' I feel myself paling at the thought.

My breakfast arrives and stifling the urge to be ill, I start to force it down. John tells me he'll meet me in the foyer in half an hour and heads off. I immediately leave the rest of the food and stop the charade; gulping orange juice doesn't help either so I head to reception to get some painkillers and then up to my room to lie down until I have to get going. I message Sasha with vague thoughts of talking to her before leaving; no reply, but at least I tried so fuck it.

I wash again in cold water and put aftershave on to mask my alcohol odours. John meets me downstairs at exactly the time he said, military precision as usual. We don't see anyone else at the hotel or airport and then the flight home is perfect, John good company as ever and me starting to feel better as time passes. I wonder if Sasha will be pissed at me or regretting last night but there is nothing I can do about that just now; I have a slight panic when I remember who her father is but, in the circumstances, he might not find out or if he did, hopefully, wouldn't hold it against me. All grown-ups now I guess.

After we get back to London, a couple of days pass; I'm busy with some supply chain glitches and John is off to spend time with the family. I'd messaged Sasha again and left a voicemail, trying to make sure I trod the right line between cool, keen and stalker. Nothing back so I suppose that is it and not much else I can do. I'm working up in Manchester and busy too, so I have other things to concern me, including trying to avoid being killed by some of the thieving morons I am here to discipline. It goes as well as could be expected and I leave with minimal actual casualties, the main problem identified and resolved. The guys there are generally mental but solid for the moment, which is much-needed at this point in time, there's competition on all sides and temptations of more money with other teams. Disciplinary problems sometimes can be checked before they become a problem and this is one of them; anyone there who heard or seen how we deal with situations like this could be in no doubt that loyalty was preferable to the consequences of disloyalty.

On my way back, I stop at a café near Banbury for something to eat and a break from roadworks and traffic, which bug me far worse than that nonsense in Manchester. My phone buzzes while I'm eating and its Sasha, she tells me she is coming to London next weekend for Christmas shopping and wants to meet. I know I'm smiling after the call; all I can think about, each time my mind goes into neutral, is her.

So, nearly three months on and we're an item, she with her network of friends and apartments and confidence and easy attitude; me with my hidden work, enough money and maybe even charm to see me through. Sasha is so calm and cool in all situations, casinos, parties, it's all normal to her. Me, I'm fucking clueless so getting through situations by asking her in advance what to do and who the people are, planning each outing to make sure I don't embarrass myself or her. It's like Pygmalion but with an undercurrent of serious crime, and for some reason, it amuses Sasha no end.

She leaves the bed and comes out to join me on the balcony, a white silk sheet covering her in the cooling night sky. I still can't look at her without my heart surging, if there is a more beautiful woman on the planet, I've never seen her. She smiles and leads me back into the bedroom and me, I love weekends.

The newly-launched and lustrous yacht, registered for primarily financial of reasons in Malta, was the pride and joy of its owner. His recent retirement, spent between Scotland and the Mediterranean harbours he knew so well from his peripatetic working life, was now a relaxed and mellow circuit of taking the ship to wherever the tourist crowds were not. Sir Mathieson Allanton, the imperious owner of the yacht grandly named "Rex Quiesceret", was usually to be found relaxing on board or at his apartments in prime locations on three of the most investment-savvy and discreet locations. He was a man reaping his just rewards before death or infirmity could take them from him, when they dared.

He dined onshore that night, at the Menorcan restaurant he preferred and shared, at times, with Spanish royalty and captains of industry enjoying the bounty of their elevated position. The seafood was superb and, despite his solitary dining habits, it was as enjoyable a meal as ever he'd had there. He complimented the chef before he left; his handshake to the waiter held Euro notes to almost the same value as his meal; a gesture which ensures not only remembrance but also the best table and service on any future visits. Sir Mathieson had always prized his excellent memory for names and, as part of this, asked and remembered the names of the chefs, managers and salaried waiters at each of his valued restaurants. "Loyalty be my watchword", he thought at these times; a military saying of one of his late uncles, an officer of the 9th Lancers who Sir Mathieson remembered fondly from his childhood.

Sir Mathieson left the restaurant and, although he generally preferred to head directly to the yacht for a gin and tonic to view the lights of the harbour from his vantage point at the end of the jetties, he decided instead to walk off his dinner beforehand. The promenade was not busy, a family resort rather than a tourist hub and one which suited him well. The larger and busier the port, the less he liked the place, in general; he left the yacht at times in Palma, an experience he tolerated rather than enjoyed as it was the most suitable to winter whichever craft he had owned over the years. The "Rex Quiesceret", however, deserved extended use and, in retirement, his winter season would be shorter and merit storing the yacht somewhere more accessible from his apartments. He thought through some of these options as he walked, lost in thought until he found himself at the end of the row of cafes and shops, turning to head back and, from habit when abroad, checking he had his wallet and passport in his inside pocket.

He looked out toward the jetty and the yacht, the dusk and reddish sky bright enough to illuminate his crewed craft as one of the largest currently in the harbour. He had four of a crew, five at times, not including his redoubtable valet, McGowan; valet may not be the definitive description of Benny McGowan, however other job titles, albeit more accurate, were likely to be less complimentary. Suffice; Sir Mathieson retained his services despite the advancing years incrementally reducing his value as a servant and his now near-permanent belligerence towards anyone except his employer. The crew had long since ceased trying to engage McGowan in conversation, or asking him questions, or, god help them for trying, asking if he wanted to join them for a drink on shore. He served his master drinks on the yacht, sometimes, but always dealt with his laundry; a task which, despite the rest of the crews' dislike of him, they had to grudgingly admit he was rather good at. Sir Mathieson was dressed immaculately at all times, giving off an air of retired but still imposing grandeur, a man whose military uniforms were now replaced by linen leisure suits, all cleaned and fresh each morning, cravat added for those breezy days.

Sir Mathieson knew that tonight, Monday, was one of the crews nights off, so only McGowan was likely to still be aboard; some evenings, they sat together in the luxurious sofas at the stern, the only time McGowan spoke in what could be considered a normal conversation; when a few whiskies had been drunk and both men took to remembering days gone past, their days in the military and deeds done. Sir Mathieson, regardless of how relaxed he may be, ensured that the crew were out of earshot of these conversations. Even a retired gentleman must be cautious and security was still a concern to him; his son would have preferred if his staff had been previously known to them, however, they had been vetted thoroughly and, over the period that he'd owned the yacht, he was certain now that their credentials were genuine.

From his vantage point, Sir Mathieson could see his crew walking along the jetty, away from the yacht, their light blue uniforms exchanged for the casual wear more suited to the bars and maybe the nightclub in the capital, some forty minutes away by taxi. Often he gave them a bonus to pay for an overnight, young people needed some space to relax after all, and he couldn't countenance a group of drunken staff members wakening him up at 3 am either. At these times, Sir Mathieson would occasionally also arrange for his own female company for the evening; so the arrangement suited all parties well and retained his privacy completely. Tonight, in this place, that option was unavailable, so a quiet evening beckoned in the luxury of his yacht. He looked at a book- rack in an otherwise unoccupied tourist shop, its wire shelves festooned by inflatable pool toys and poor quality scuba equipment; although not previously a reader due to the busy nature of his career, Sir Mathieson now found himself with enough time to relax and consume fiction, preferring historical literature, as it added an element of learning alongside the underlying wastefulness of fictional works.

He looked up as a half-heard shout broke his attention; leaving the shop frontage, his gaze took in the flames and smoke billowing upwards from the stern of "Rex Quiesceret". In the minutes which followed and from a safe distance, Sir Mathieson guessed that the flames appeared driven by an accelerant, that his yacht would soon be completely destroyed and that it was possible that he was the target. He also decided, quite calmly, that whoever instigated this act, would not spend his last days well.

Walking purposefully down towards the harbour, he was now aware that the flames, fanned by the westerly breeze, were in danger of spreading to nearby smaller craft. By the time he reached the jetty, despite it being evening, a number of what appeared to be port workers were operating a power hose and foam-spraying fire extinguishers which together stemmed the spread and, after some fifteen minutes and admirable effort on their part, all but doused the flames on his yacht. He watched as they greeted the arrival of the Police, followed by ambulances, for who Sir Mathieson did not yet know. He was joined by his crew, returned after hearing of the fire from the bar where they had started their evening and telling Sir Mathieson unequivocally that they had no clue as to how the yacht so suddenly caught fire after they left. They did, however, confirm that Benny McGowan had left before them, to head for a bar they assumed; true enough, half an hour later an inebriated McGowan joined them, compounding his dereliction of duty as a watchman by passing out in a chair behind them.

Sir Mathieson kept as quiet as possible during the entire situation, other than to confirm to the Police that he had no idea what had occurred, which was almost entirely true. After giving statements, which took over three hours of standing and then waiting in a nearby café, the crew chief arranged accommodation for them in a nearby hotel. Sir Mathieson used a landline in the hotel to call his son, who was in London and relaxing after a rather mundane day at the hub of the family business.

Sir Mathieson spoke in his usual calm tones, perhaps tinged with more tiredness than he would have previously, understandable in the circumstances. After brief pleasantries, he broke the news to his son.

'We've had some trouble with the yacht; there has been a fire on board. From first appearances, damage to the whole deck and furniture, smoke damage all over. Thankfully the local chaps got there pronto, so it may not be a write-off.'

'Good grief. Are you OK?' The first thought he had was that it could have been an attempt on his father's life.

'Absolutely; strange thing if it was meant for me though, it happened when no bugger was on board. Me off for

49

dinner ashore, McGowan in a bar getting pissed somewhere and the crew just left for a jolly. Bit surprising, I thought if anyone was to have a go, it would be straight at me, not a botched fire job on the yacht. The deck went up like a firework and the Police clearly think it was down to fuel poured on the deck. Thankfully the doors were locked and the harbour chaps got water onto it before it could spread below decks and into the fuel.

'So...was it a warning?' John couldn't get the pieces together yet.

'I'm retired, so I suppose I'm the wrong person to threaten unless it's to send a message to you.' He pondered.

'Look' sighed John, 'text me the hotel details and I'll fly over first thing tomorrow morning. Adam is up north finishing the redundancy payments, but Zoe and Williams can take my place for a couple of days until we get this sorted.' For one of the very few times in his life, Sir Mathieson felt that he absolutely needed his son to be there, be the officer in charge on this one.

'Thanks, son.' He replied, with some feeling. It had all happened so unexpectedly, from dining alone and deciding to go for a walk into returning to an inferno on his yacht. Sir Mathieson, weary though he was, spent a fair part of that night working on the possibilities and probabilities of the incident. By the time he fell asleep, he did not have the solution, but he did have the method which he and his son would use to get to it.

In the morning, on request and following a significant cash disbursement, he was provided by a laptop by the Hotel Manage. After some difficulty with the hotel Wi-

Fi, Sir Mathieson made the checks that he had planned and made note of. After ten minutes of logging in and flicking between screens, he sat back in disbelief and anger, staring at the screen and flushing with high colour. He checked through the details twice more to confirm the situation before picking up his mobile and selecting a contact, using an encrypted line as always.

'Sir Mathieson.' The line had been picked up in an instant.

'Charlie. Have you heard about my situation?'

'Yes sir, we were told last night. What do you need us to do?'

Sir Mathieson thought for a few seconds, calming the fury inside him and trying to make sure his actions were advisable.

'I'm coming back to Inverannan and I need that new accountant fellow brought up, not to the main house but one of the bothies and made ready for questioning. Tell no-one, and I mean no-one. I'm missing a rather large sum from my account and he's where I'm starting.' He closed the call after his man confirmed his role and the likely timescale. Another hour at the laptop and he was more than certain that someone in the head office had used his access passwords to rob his personal account of a total of 12 million pounds sterling, transferring them, gradually over the past couple of days to accounts in the name of this damnable accountant. To Sir Mathieson, this represented not only the theft of his nest-egg for retirement but a violation of his dignity, his personal wealth stolen by a lesser man, a sneaky little oik that he had clearly told his son not to employ, but demurred as he was retired, and John was in charge now. Almost in full temper, he decided not to tell John, to let him know about this one later, to rebuke him then for hiring the devious little bastard. No, Sir Mathieson would vent his fury personally on this one, until every penny and more were returned to his coffers and the culprit punished, harshly so.

He had made a meticulous plan for his project, not only the tasks themselves but also the potential variations which he might have to deal with. To assassinate someone, to escape and not be traced, well that was something he knew required careful timing and detailed execution, on all fronts. Never trusting anything electronic and fearing that hard copies could conceivably go astray and constitute part of legal prosecution, had he learnt each page of his plan by rote. The paperwork was then destroyed in the shredder and thrown into separate bins near his apartment.

After he left the military, twenty-one years after signing up, he had done some private work, but just training and security. He hadn't fired a shot in anger since Iraq so was perhaps not as game-ready as he would have liked. There was also his weight, which had unaccountably but incrementally burgeoned in the past few years, despite doing his best to walk and exercise when tolerable. Stopping smoking hadn't helped, so he just started again but the weight kept creeping up, his metabolism slowing as the energy of his younger days dissipated.

For this mission, he had started to prepare by looking out his kit and equipment from the plastic security box where it had lain for a few years. None of the clothing fitted, but he didn't want to look like a fucking soldier when he was doing this job anyway, better off wearing the nondescript tourist gear he always wore. The kit was in good order though, handguns and detonators with Semtex which would still be fine for the job ahead, despite being quite old and he hoped, stable enough. He had always been good at that side of things, the rudimentary electronics and primers needed to get a bang going.

This job was all about waiting for the right time, getting in and out unseen and then getting on a tourist flight or two while the local cops scratched their heads and looked for forensic evidence that wouldn't tell them shit if he did his work well. He'd been lucky to get this job; plenty of guys would have jumped at the lucrative contract. He didn't know why it was so high-value, there was minimal security around the target and therefore it was unlikely he'd have to risk anything other than getting aboard and setting the device. This was also preferable as his current physical condition meant that he was both unprepared for combat and similarly for any rapid escape.

He'd done the deal over the phone with an old mate he'd last worked with in Africa a while back, who had no way of knowing that his burly ex-comrade was now more obese than he could have imagined and that his once-square jaw now had two chins beneath it. Their conversations had been brief, the target and his locations all verbally described, with only one image sent to a temporary, anonymous email account. Unfortunately for him, he accessed this image after an afternoon drinking in his local bar in Mallorca so the recollection of the elderly gentleman was both hazy and mainly based on what he was wearing in the photo. His confidence at the time in deleting the email account did not last when he wakened up the next morning to a vague recollection that he had to kill an old guy who favoured beige jumpers and had a cap. At least he had jotted down the name and details of the yacht and all the important information from the calls, such as the port of call and dates, although these were likely to vary if the yacht's owner decided otherwise.

What he did also know was that the job needed doing and doing right. His mate emphasised this, repeatedly. If he fucked up, he'd better keep going with Plan B right through to Plan Z. This old guy had to die, preferably as a result of Plan A.

So, after intensive planning and packing, he travelled by ferry to Menorca, the next island along, a rucksack on his back like any cheap-day tourist and as anonymous a figure as you could imagine. He rented a decent hotel room with a view of the port frontage and waited until the yacht came in, which was, unfortunately for him, three days later than expected; a fact which he established during a call to his contact after the second day of waiting.

'Sorry mate. I told you we're working from old intelligence, we're not live with this one. That's just the way it is.' The voice sounded not one bit apologetic so he had to suppress his annoyance.

'I've got extra costs because of this. I'm going to need another grand, minimum.' There was a pause, which sounded to him like his mate had his hand over the receiver and was discussing this with someone.

'Done. Just make sure you're on the ball here, we don't know if he's coming in for a week or an overnight.'

'Leave that to me.'

There was a click as the call hung up and he smiled at the extra thousand pounds and the thought that all he'd done to earn it was to hand around bars and watch the harbour. He might even have another two or three days to relax if he was lucky. There was a nice bar along the harbour which had an elevated view of the port entrance, so he could sit there and chill out while waiting for the yacht to arrive. He'd noted that the boats mainly come in around late afternoon, so after dark, he was free from his duties to have a few drinks and a pizza without feeling that he was slacking.

It was the Monday when he awakened to a feeling that he'd overslept after a rather beer and whisky-intensive evening in a series of bars along the front. He had no real idea of when or how he'd got back to his room, although he had successfully done so. He still had his wallet and everything so he must have been on auto-pilot. Not much was coming back to him, so he showered and dressed and went down for something to eat and check out the port. He was waiting for his full English breakfast when he caught sight of the expensive and impressive yacht he'd been waiting for. There were a few crackers in that part of the jetty, but this was the best, sleek and beautifully lined, slightly taller than the others too. One of his mates had a boat years ago that he used to visit when they were just out of the army, but even his wasn't a patch on this one, which was class all over, he thought. He managed to wolf down his breakfast but still didn't feel that great as he walked back to prepare for the task ahead. He also sweated a lot now, far more than he would have liked, maybe made worse by the stress of his mission. The day was hot as hell and he felt much better once back in the air-conditioned room and resting on his bed for a while.

He organised his kit exactly as planned; detonators, explosive, devices and the few other items he needed just in case. After double checking everything, he put them carefully into a blue sports bag, leaving his passport, clothes and toiletries inside the large rucksack, ready to be off after his work was done. In the mix of locals and tourists, he wouldn't be noticed but if the police checked later, there wouldn't be anything to be found; his kit was sealed in polythene bags and not a hint was left for a dog or forensics or whatever they wanted to use, he couldn't be connected to the device, not from the room anyway.

He had a chat with the receptionist and told her that he was leaving later today, so checked out and left his rucksack in their office until he was ready. He smiled and thanked her, telling her that he had enjoyed his stay, a typical English tourist here for the beer and the sun. Leaving the hotel with his blue sports bag, he went to the bar to take his vantage point and finalise his approach to the target. The jetty was not particularly secure, unlike some. There was a metal gate, but it was generally left open and the access code not needed. He knew it anyway, having observed a couple of incidences of the 1234 code being punched in when someone had accidentally pulled the gate closed.

There were staff on board, looked like five from his observations. He'd wait until they were all off for a meal at night before planting the device, so he could have a beer now to calm himself and fight off the hangover from last night.

Three hours later, after drinking a few beers to make his stay in the bar appear legitimate, he watched the crew finally leave the yacht. Heading firstly to the toilet, he then walked down the slight incline to the jetty. The crew could be seen walking in the other direction, laughing as they went and no doubt looking forward to a good night out. Pity for them they'd be caught up in this, but he would genuinely do his best to avoid them getting involved. His plan was to make sure the old man was on board, ideally with as few others as possible, place the device, then detonate from a safe distance and make his escape in the ensuing chaos. Failing that, he would shoot the old man, or if the situation demanded silence, draw a knife across his throat and try and get as little blood as possible on him. He had a spare shirt and trousers in the bag, just in case this scenario played out.

His first task was to get to the yacht and confirm that the target was aboard. The metal gate was, as usual open, so he walked confidently along the planked walkway towards the yacht. It was in the third last mooring and he strolled past it to get a look at the occupant. As he hoped, an elderly man sat asleep in the lounge, a whisky in front of him. He didn't look exactly like his vague memory of the deleted image, but neither was there any apparent reason why it wouldn't be him. He even had a beige cardigan on, like the one in the photo.

He stopped at the second last yacht and gazed out to the open sea, happy that he had got this far and was ready to start the action. Despite his excess weight and the impact of advancing years and far too much booze, he felt invigorated now, helped by an afternoon's drinking. He knelt down and set the bag on the walkway to take the ten-inch knife from the end compartment, his decision settled that the elderly target could best be taken down on a one-to-one basis and without noise. He'd picked the wrong end-compartment of the holdall, so impatiently swung it around 180 degrees, which he did too hastily as the weight of the explosives was at one end, causing the bag to fall over the edge of the walkway and into the water below. He grasped for it in vain then watched as it sat for a brief moment on the surface before it descended, releasing a series of dark bubbles as it went.

He knelt on the dimly lit walkway in disbelief, the sounds from the bars and restaurants mixing with the clanking of yachts and the water lapping on their expensive hulls. Having lost all the tools to deliver his various plans, he was now left with the primary option of strangling the old bastard or finding something else to clobber him with. Walking back to where he could see into the lounge of the yacht, he confirmed that the target was still sitting there, unmoved and ready for his demise.

He boarded the yacht at the rear and tugged at the glazed door to the lounge as quietly as he could. The solid-feeling handle was locked and it appeared not to be the sort he could put his shoulder into without waking the target and giving him the opportunity to raise the alarm. He had to find another way in, so he headed around the starboard side and up a flight of stairs. The door there was also locked, so he stole back down to the foredeck to see what he could find.

There were a couple of 20-litre jerry cans there, he assumed for a tender or dinghy somewhere on the yacht. The crew had, perhaps in their haste to get to the resort, left them out by mistake. A quick smell confirmed that it was indeed petrol and this, he thought, might be a lucky break for him. He headed back to the stern and started to pour the fuel at the base of the lounge door, sweating at the effort and now just wishing that the whole sorry mess would be over as soon as possible. Walking back onto the jetty, he reached into his pocket, pulled out his zippo and lit it. He threw the lighter onto the fuel-drenched stern on the yacht and walked determinedly along the jetty and out the metal gate, turning left and walking past a brightly-lit Irish theme bar. He stopped and looked at the elderly man who sat at the bar, who a few minutes ago had been in the lounge of the yacht and, he now realised, had wakened and left the yacht, unnoticed by his intended killer while he found and deployed the petrol. As he walked towards him in a daze, he heard the old man order a drink in an extremely rough and decidedly non-posh voice, which confirmed to him that he had identified the wrong target anyway. His wretched attempts to mentally restructure the situation were interrupted by a god-almighty shout from the direction of the jetty, which prompted a small army of locals to run from bars and restaurants towards the now brightly burning yacht.

He walked back along the resort front as more locals and tourists reacted to the spreading fire in the port area. He needed to get back to his lookout bar and decide what to do next, ideally starting with a stiff drink. He was almost there when he passed a rather distinguished elderly gentleman, who he immediately recognised from his photograph. They passed each other quickly and before he could think of anything to act upon, Sir Mathieson Allanton was striding back to his burning yacht and Plans A, B, C and any other letter were all up in flames too.

☐

9   ADAM GOES TO INVERANNAN

The road straightens out as I leave Edinburgh and head
north, passing the signs for the coast and to the other
side, the inland towns of Fife. The snow falls steadily
now but the traffic is light, far more so than the
insufferable queuing I have to endure in London and the
Midlands. Maybe Scotland does have something going
for it.

I bypass Perth and head for Inverness, through the grim
and snow-shrouded Cairngorms and the Dalwhinnie
distillery, the light malt whisky my father preferred when
his limited budget permitted. I smile to myself as I think
of my parents, out in the sun and their monthly phone
calls their only umbilical to their son. They have no idea
what my life has been like, but are proud of their high-
flying, property-dealing son and his new lifestyle; maybe I
will become the person they think I am, if John Allanton
stays true. One hour later and I'm skirting the traffic at
Inverness, over the Kessock bridge and on towards
Dornoch, the snow on and off the whole journey. The
roads are quiet and easy again, letting me think about my
plans for how to approach Inverannan, the last of our
transport hubs to close. I'd like to have this one done
and quickly, but being Inverannan, it feels like something
else might always happen.

It's getting into Tuesday evening now and I'm thinking
about Magnus Gilfillan. It looks like he'll need to be
moved elsewhere to get dried out and have his problems
addressed with the confidentiality our closing business
requires. Personally, I'd have him strangled and fed to
the pigs but John and Sir Mathieson are fond of him and
probably best not to keep killing Inverannan Managers or

it'll become hard to fill the post. That and the gossip it would generate meant that Zoe gave me quite specific instructions not to terminate anyone in rural Scotland. She's probably right too.

One of the advantages of closing the narcotics business is that we don't need a similar replacement for Gilfillan at Inverannan after his managerial lapse. I just need to pick someone to oversee the legitimate aspects remaining while he's away getting his treatment or whatever he decides. My main job, the one I was scheduled to complete before his duck hunt intervened, is to pay off the team on the supply chain and make sure everyone knows what is expected; to keep quiet and keep their heads down. Inverannan is the most northerly and therefore the last of our supply chain hubs to close, and perhaps the one which I myself wanted to do last too, the one I have history with.

I drive through a few hamlet-sized places and stop at a layby for some fresh air and to eat the crisps I bought in Edinburgh; it's the lightest smirr of snow but cold and feeling like it's going to get worse. Opening the window, it's completely silent here; the breeze and that's it, no birdsong, no animals and not many cars on the road either.

I finish my water and throw the empty bottle into the back of the hire car; about another hour to Inverannan along these loch-edged roads and past the constant mountains. Zoe had messaged me to let me know she'd provisionally booked Gilfillan in for the treatment she had checked out, starting next week if he is willing; if not, he can have some time off to himself, to get well or just to finish himself off with the whisky. I am ambivalent but need this resolved quickly as I've closed the other routes and outlets in the UK and they now represent a vacuum, left for whoever wants to take over and with no more need for our product arriving from Inverannan. Our sources abroad had been the first to be told by John, then onto me and Zoe to pay off all our core teams, well rewarded for their efforts and in Edinburgh, well punished for last minute disloyalty. I was clear with all of them that they should erase all mention and memory of us, the departing suppliers and let the new blood through, no fights and no publicity, if there were smart. Not easy for hard men to take but our ties are severed, their crucial back-up gone and they have to realise that the new mobs aren't gentlemen like us. Better to fly off to sunnier lands and spend their cash on a life of beer and pizzas instead of staying and spending the next year or so getting sewn back together. It was sudden, no notice given, but we planned it that way; best to rip the plaster off in one go, so John Allanton said. Some of them expected change as the new mobs had already moved in around us, but we'd been resident for a long time and had beaten plenty before; the fact was, our money was made and like all good businessmen, we know when it's time to shift investments.

I am deliberately timing my arrival at Inverannan Estate after the last of our product has left; a practice that I'd recently tried to adhere to when visiting any location, in case of a coincidental or planned raid by the authorities. I always ensured that I had a reasonable, recorded reason for my visit to any meeting place; I'm a property portfolio consultant, or at least that's my main legitimate business, which I do indeed carry out alongside my more questionable activities. The official reason for this particular trip is on behalf of the investors who are concerned about Gilfillan's health and the effective running of the estate in his absence. Never mind the demise of the poor sea ducks, which for some reason still annoys the fuck out of me.

There's a snow-coated beach of sorts beside the loch where I've parked, it looks like some kids have been partying there. Black, projecting signs of a wood fire, a few bottles and cans left in a plastic bag lie abandoned and emptied. I walk over to the cold fire and look out across the loch, with not a soul else to see its grey, barren quietness. I uncover a round stone and send it out, not as low a trajectory as I'd hoped; it makes the briefest plink and descends into the chill depth of the Highland loch, unseen for an age to come. Digging around in the snow with my right foot, I uncover a properly flat stone and send it out into the loch, skimming five or six times. I'd love to send a few more out, but the feeling in my fingers is almost gone with the cold and digging out stones from packed snow isn't really viable either.

These few moments after skimming the stone somehow take me back to those crazy few days when I first visited Inverannan as a naïve journalist, trying to write the project up and then investigating the place, god help my stupidity. I probably would never hear from or see my old colleague Emma again, hardly a surprise in the circumstances. Simon Conner could hardly have been considered a great loss to society and thinking back, I would gladly dispose of George Galloglas and his ilk any day without a care. However, it had been the first time I'd killed anyone - there had been a few since and still I haven't lost a moments sleep; it was more that lack of response which bothered me, that was what I was still trying to figure out. Why did I now have no empathy for my – what to call them – fellow beings? I can perhaps be fond of Sasha or I can like John, or Gillian, or Zoe even. It seems to me, as I take a long drink from my water bottle, that compartmentalisation is the key; I can do something pretty grim on a Friday morning, say, then wash up, travel to France and be sitting across from Sasha and enjoying myself with not one fucking hint of regret or remorse over some useless drug-dealing bastard who got in the way. Maybe that was part of it too, I don't see myself as one of them. I might be in the same business, but I'm definitely not them, of that I am sure. So when I need to rain down some punishment on them, it's because they fucking well deserve it and me, I'm just surviving until I get out.

It's bitter cold now, miles colder than back in Edinburgh even and it looks like the snow is indeed getting worse, so I walk back into the car and set back off north-west. The main road is slow going for the most part, despite being well-cleared by snowploughs and gritters, helped also by the paucity of other vehicles. I'm almost run off the road at a tight bend by what looks like a white delivery van, and I check my mirror to see if it's one of the Inverannan transfer vehicles on its final run south. It's gone before I can make out the number plate but I have an urge to check when I get there; if anyone was driving our preferably anonymous vans like that, there would usually be some unpleasant discussions for them when they get back, but I guess now it's not worth my time or effort. In the next thirty or so miles, I drive in almost auto-pilot and think about the steps I need to take. Getting Gilfillan sorted is going to be first, give him his place as the local boss and see what he says. Then, meet with the team at Inverannan and then a representative of the islanders; they are a dependable and stoic bunch and, given that I'm handing them all a year's wages as a pay-off, unlikely to complain.

Snow is falling steadily when I drive along the Inverannan Estate road and the sun flickers once, briefly through a rare gap in the grey-white clouds. The spring buds are reluctantly trying to open out on the trees and I almost enjoy the last part of my journey until I pull up at Inverannan House and get back into character. I'm just getting organised when the side door opens and out walks Magnus Gilfillan, looking like a cadaver with a bad hangover. I get out the car and walk towards him, shaking his hand which is trembling, either through withdrawal from the whisky or nerves at meeting me, or both.

'Magnus, how are you doing?' I see his eyes are red too, the man is struggling badly.

'Been better Adam, I'm sorry you had to come up. Will you come in and we can talk?' I nod and we go inside to his office, I give a quick wave into the office team as I pass their door. Gilfillan's office is old-school, worn leather chairs and a desk covered in inches-deep receipts, letters and wire trays. He sits across from me and struggles to find words, interrupted in his efforts by the phone, which he answers with a terse "not now, I'm busy". He's shaking even worse now and maybe it is my presence giving him this reaction. I stand and put the kettle on.

'Is it white coffee for you, Magnus?' I ask, as kindly as I can.

He nods, still fraught in the situation and trying to stem his increasing shaking by clasping his hands on the desk. I wait to give him a chance to regroup then give him his coffee and realise that, instead of calming down, my silence seems to be winding him up further. I think of the ducks, get annoyed at that again, and then start to tell Magnus directly what is going to happen.

'I'm going to retire you, Magnus.'

He looks up at me in complete terror.

'No, not that - actual retirement. I have arranged to transfer a redundancy payment into your account, conditional on you maintaining silence. Is that acceptable?'

'Aye, of course. I'm not able to do this sir, not anymore.' He blows his nose loudly into his handkerchief and looks relieved to be leaving and still breathing. I wonder what this mess of paperwork on his desk is all about.

'We're closing all the operations down anyway Magnus, the whole thing. I and my colleagues have been visiting them all, paying the outlets off. This is the last place and we'll keep it on as a legitimate business for a period until we decide on the future. Do you understand?'

He suddenly looks even more dazed. 'Aye. It's not because of me is it?'

I give him his coffee and sit across from him. 'No, don't be daft. It's a UK-wide decision. I'm here to close the supply line down. I'd have preferred if you hadn't gone on a pissed-up duck hunt the week before our last consignment leaves, but you're getting redundancy pay like the rest of them, count yourself lucky.' He nods but I'm not sure he's taking it in.

'If I see or hear of you getting pished and talking about the business Magnus, you will be dead the next day. Do you understand me?' I lean forward and he flushes, which is somehow worse looking than the clay colour he had before. He nods and now and has a strained purple complexion like he's trying to function normally while simultaneously controlling heart arrhythmia, delirium tremens and retaining his bowel functions.

I lean back and smile. 'We appreciate the work you have done here Magnus, even though it's taken its toll on you. Will you stay for a bit to help the guys sort through this lot?' I gesture to the chaotic table top.

'Aye, of course, sir. It got away from me a bit, just stuff I should have signed. I've not been well.'

He's not wrong about that. The job has left him debilitated and whisky-ruined, ready to collapse and worn done. I had only briefly met him before he started and he wasn't like this at all. Just a mistake in appointing him and him accepting the job, that's all I guess.

'I'll be here for a day or two, so I'll let you know who will take over tomorrow, OK.'

'Who is to be sir, if you don't mind?' At least he cares enough to ask through the post-alcohol fug.

This is a tricky question as I haven't decided yet. 'You'll find out tomorrow Magnus, but don't worry. A wee clear-up here and then you can relax and get straight.'

'We've got a place for you if you want a couple of weeks break.' I hand him the envelope with documents which Zoe had given me back in London, a letter explaining his redundancy in polite, legal terms just in case, and a nice ending paragraph which refers to a hotel-like facility where Magnus' liver and associated organs can recover in splendid isolation for as long as he needs to start his recovery.

Magnus looks up and smiles for the first time. A sweetly sad smile which tells me that Magnus will be going the other way after he leaves, the way of the whisky.

I leave Magnus to his thoughts and head into the office to have a chat with Eilidh first, but I'm forgetting the time and there's no-one left in the office except Gillian. I sit down at the desk next to her and give her my most normal smile.

'Thanks for coming up. It's been a bit of a shambles with all this carry-on.' She gestures in the direction of Magnus' office. 'I thought I'd better let you know before he got any worse.'

We can hear the side door of the building close and watch Magnus trail across the wide driveway to his Land Rover. He starts it up and rumbles away with what appears to be unnecessary haste.

'Does he always drive like that?' I ask.

'No, but he's tuned to the moon just now. He's either drunk or recovering from being drunk. It's a shame. He is a really nice man without it.' She looks out the window at the receding back of Magnus' battered old four-wheel drive.

She looks at me, perhaps holding back sadness at the thought of the ruined Magnus. 'What are you going to do?'

I know I shouldn't tell Gillian what's happening before I tell Eilidh, but I'm near the end of my termination duties for the business and the niceties of line management are starting to mean less to me now.

'We're going legitimate. The last transfer was today, I'm here to close it down from now on, pay the guys off.' She looks surprised and I can see she's naturally worried about her own job.

'It's OK, the Estate will still run, but without transferring the product. We'll scale back, of course, but you guys will be fine for now.'

'For now?' she doesn't break her gaze from mines for a moment.

'Yes. I need to talk to you all about what to do with the Estate after this; I haven't got any further than that.'

'We do have a few ideas.' She smiles broadly at me and I have a distinct feeling that she has a plan. 'Can we discuss this over a few drinks?'

So, despite me being knackered and having a desperate need to sleep, we end up sitting in the library of Inverannan House, Gillian having procured some snack food from the kitchen and heated it up. Along with a probably-expensive bottle of wine from the well-stocked cellar, we have ended up with the whole place to ourselves and a decent meal to enjoy. Gillian tells me the gossip since I'd last been here, a few months ago in early winter to meet with Sir Mathieson and John to discuss a number of tactical issues. Sir Mathieson hadn't, as far I as know, been involved in the portfolio since then and was now to be found somewhere in the Med.

I want to know if anyone in the community is aware of what has gone on at Inverannan, and if so, how aware. Gillian, for her part, seems to be building towards telling me her business plan for the old place, unless I'm mistaken.

'So' I enquire, 'What will the gossip in the area be like when we stop moving all these vans in and out of Inverannan?'

She sips her wine and looks faux surprised. 'Gossip? Here? Never!'

'Yeah, yeah, this is the north of Scotland and we never, ever blether about anything. Remember I was brought up in a place like this, and if you did anything wrong, it was round the village before you'd finished doing it.'

Gillian sets her glass down for a brief moment. 'If some of the drivers get let go, that will start the chatter off. If they get another job somewhere, the chat will be less. Either way, no-one will actually talk to anyone outside the community. You should know; you tried when you first arrived.'

I nod to her. 'That's true, I found out very little when I had first arrived, however that may have been at least partly because I was a shite journalist.'

'You did your best.' She smiles to herself and picks up her glass again. I'm not sure if I'm being toyed with or insulted, or maybe even praised.

'So what's your suggestion for Inverannan? There's no urgency, it's not going to close just after we stop the run from here.'

Gillian pulls a folder from somewhere behind the sofa where we are sitting and I realise that she has indeed been working on something. She opens the file and shows me a list of projects, each of which has a commentary beside it.

'We have had some meetings on this – Eilidh and the rest of us in the office have come up with a sort of business plan. These are just options, but we think it could be good.'

I'm intrigued now and since I drink wine at almost the same rate I used to drink beer, I'm feeling significantly more relaxed than I was a short while ago. Gillian runs through each of them, which unlike the bullshit that Galloglas once peddled as the future of the estate, look more than viable and capable of keeping the place going. It doesn't take too long and after the list has been completed, she looks at me with her head inclined.

'Well, what do you think?'

'Yeah, really good, I mean I'd have to refer it all to John, but if it's viable I'm sure he'd be up for looking at some financial projections.' She smiles and I can hear a car pull up outside.

Gillian goes to the window and waves down.

'Who is it?' I ask.

'It's my dad. When he heard you were coming up today, he insisted that I get a lift home. You've got a bad reputation.' I laugh, properly, for the first time in a long while.

She grabs her jacket and heads for the door, then turns and comes back. She gives me a long, deep kiss before breaking away and leaving. I'm left, somewhat bewildered, on my own to finish a few snacks and crash on the library sofa for the night.

It's light and bloody cold when I wake. I can hear voices from somewhere near, so I shove my jacket on for some heat and go out to find out what's going on. It's Eilidh and Magnus, having what they might consider a frank exchange of views over something, which stops when I join them in the hallway.

'Adam, I didn't know you were down here.' Eilidh looks calm but Magnus is flustered, the poor man.

'Yeah, I fell asleep in the library. It's quite comfortable if not warm.'

She shook her head. 'We had a room all ready for you, upstairs on the first floor.' Gillian wouldn't have forgotten to tell me, but probably just hadn't for a laugh. I'm not used to getting the piss taken out of me these days but I feel brilliant inside at the thought of such a normal Scottish thing, just happening again as if I was still me.

'I guess I'll head up and get cleaned up. I need to meet the guys this morning Magnus, are they all back from their deliveries?'

'Aye sir, they don't stay overnights any more. The London run gets back up here last, about 7 am, so they will be in the garage now, at least till about 9 am. There's one or two finished early, you'd need to get them here or meet them down at the village'.

'Nip out and tell the guys I'll be over in half an hour, will you?' Magnus nods and sets off, still looking like crap but better than yesterday. I tell Eilidh that I'll have a chat with her once I've finished with the guys and then I grab my bags from the library and head up to get showered, clean clothes on and take the payments out to the guys.

I walk across the now deeply snow-covered driveway and meet them in the freezing garage. I give each of them their named packets, stacked with high denomination used bank notes and let them know that some of them might get re-employed once we know what the future of the Estate will be. They are okay about the whole thing, as you would be if you were given a small fortune in cash and the spring and summer off. I then head inside for a heat and sit with Eilidh for half an hour, letting her know that their jobs are secure and that I will go through the business plan with them before I leave.

Once I finish, I borrow Magnus' Land Rover and, after winding my way along the single-track main road which I can barely see, drive carefully along the indistinct single-track to Loch Baxford to meet the representative of the Islanders, who is waiting on the jetty at the appointed time, a dog sitting by his side. We shake hands firmly and I tell him that there's no more product coming in, the business is closed. He nods and I hand him a plastic folio with more thick envelopes of cash inside for him and his guys.

'Good while it lasted' is all that he says, before he turns and climbs down onto his cabin cruiser, followed nimbly by the black collie dog. I watch as the man of few words releases the moorings and sets off into the gloom back towards the island.

'Not the chatty type.' I say to no-one, pulling my coat around me against the coastal chill.

I drive back along to the main road, then off to the east and Inverannan again. For some odd reason, I feel more inclined to stay here longer. Maybe I'm tired of all the travelling. I have enough time for another overnight before I head back to either Inverness or Edinburgh and then home to London, so I guess I'll clear up the work and just chill out tonight.

I know that I feel a little different here, in the highlands, than I do in London. I'm not sure exactly the reason, but my psychiatrist mentioned the issue of my lack of morality might be linked to the toxic environment of my fictitious city high-flying career. Perhaps the further I am from it all, the less I feel like the guy who works for the Allantons. I'll come back to this, I think to myself.

It doesn't take as long to get back despite the conditions, so I drive into the village first, past the B&B and the pub and down to the loch. I sit in the Land Rover for a while, my thoughts on the past, since I came here and my life changed. Perhaps I haven't yet fully processed the impending migration of the business from criminal to legitimate. After today there will be no more need for me to threaten, or hurt, or kill, or to spend my weekdays with the detritus of sub-humanity. I guess this is a watershed for me, to leave the narcotics business, if it turns out that way. Part of me did not expect to live for long, if I am being true to myself, from the day it all went out of control, up here. Maybe the rest of it was just a reaction to being out of my depth, in danger and perhaps not giving a fuck if I did live. Now though, I think of what I could do. I could live like Sasha, or I could run away back here and pretend it didn't happen. Whatever way I look at it, if I get through the next couple of weeks without being disposed of, I may have choices to make again. Maybe it's just like an interruption to my ordinary life, an extended gap year of murder and narcotic supply.

There's a boat out on the loch, god knows why as it's as cold as I have ever felt and getting snowier by the hour. The boat changes direction and I realise that its destination is a jetty in the distance, a couple of houses remote from the village, no road to reach them on the banks of the loch, surrounded by hills and heather alone. A quiet life, not for many people and no wonder; freezing in winter and packed with midges in summer, only tolerable in spring and a slice of autumn and even then, only for those of a solitary nature.

The snow is starting to cover the car, so I gun the noisy engine and drive back to Inverannan House, the roads still passable but maybe not for long. I skid when I turn into the long driveway, just missing the stone pillars and the sign which welcomes visitors to the Estate. I reverse and then take the corner more slowly, tyres sliding a little but getting around it and along the straight-ish narrow-track to the house. Its lunch time and I'm getting hungry, so I hope the kitchen has something for me to raid. I park at the side again and run in, stopping at Magnus' office, where he is sitting with Eilidh, Gillian and the youngest of the team, Niamh, who I am reliably informed is the smartest person on our books despite being just seventeen.

'Thanks for the loan of the Landy'. Magnus looks at me with the face of a man who could jump from a high building. 'How's it going?'

'We're getting there.' Eilidh tells me, but the eye-rolling of Niamh says otherwise. I smile at them and tell them I'll be back soon. I take the corridor back to the main hall and along to where I reckon the kitchens are. I realise I'm wrong when I get to a dead end with some storage rooms. Retracing my steps, I find a set of small stairs leading down from a niche behind the main stairs. Well hidden that, I think to myself.

The kitchen is below ground level, only the small, high-set windows letting some light into the chilly, old-fashioned chamber. I open the fridge and find a full stock, although there is the issue of me not knowing how to cook any of it, a skill I still lack. On a lower shelf, I find some sausages which I have a rudimentary knowledge of heating up.

The ancient Aga cooker is, however, a challenge too far for me. There are no visible means of starting it and, after releasing gas fumes without any spark of flame, I end up throwing the sausages back into the fridge and finding some fresh bread. I cut and spread butter on it and get some water from the tap, slightly pissed off at not having something hot to eat and bemoaning my long-term inability to operate kitchen equipment. I hear footsteps and it's Gillian, smiling at me and looking like she's torn between saying something at my expense and being professional. She sits down across from me and for some reason, we both start laughing, uncontrollably, me almost choking on my badly-sliced bread, until tears run down both our faces and I put my hopeless lunch in the bin. I wash my face with cold water to get rid of the tears of laughter and Gillian tries to wipe her eyes, the makeup not standing up to the effect of cracking up. Eventually, we're both calm enough to communicate.

'Shall I make something for us?' she inclines her head.

'Please. That would be magnificent.' In an instant, the sodding Aga is alight and the sausages are in the grill, which makes me feel even more of a twat. Ten minutes later we're having tea and hot food and everything is all right with the world.

'Thanks. How did it go with Magnus' office? Looked like a bit of a mess.' I take the opportunity to take a bite of the fresh roll, how I have missed square sausage, Scotland's finest cuisine.

Gillian stops eating for a moment and her shoulders drop a little. 'He's not been keeping on top of anything. Eilidh is phoning round to apologise to all the small businesses we ship for and Niamh is busy paying the bills to keep the electricity on and the tax people off of our back. I think he'd be better off finishing up today unless we find something else he's ignored.'

I nod agreement and tell her I'll speak to him after we've eaten.

'You want to go to the pub tonight?' she asks, rather unexpectedly.

I remember that I still have to pay off two of the guys who weren't at the garage this morning, they were away on some other work they do. 'I need to meet two guys, McVey and Campbell – could you show me where they live?' She nods, still waiting to see if I will go with her to the pub.

'OK. Will we get there though?' I crane my head to see how the weather looks from our subterranean kitchen, but all I can see is a layer of snow at the bottom of the window.

'Yeah, we've got the four-wheel drives. You hire car might not though, and it's to get worse. We might end up snowed in for the winter.'

I give her a genuine smile. 'Might not be that bad.' She smiles back and I definitely, absolutely, feel better when I'm back in the highlands. I head upstairs and it takes about two minutes between telling Magnus that he can go and hearing his Land Rover leave the car park. I had wished him well for the future and he shook my hand, muttered something about coming back to clear his desk but I don't know if he will. Once he had roared off in his appallingly noisy vehicle I have a look around. There's a gun cabinet beside the coat rack, maybe some of his weapons are in there, although after his duck incident I'm not sure he's the right man to be keeping firearms. I have a look at the cabinet, but it's solidly locked and doesn't look like there's a key lying about, so I sit in his antiquated chair and have a think about the situation in hand while I watch the snowfall thicken. Since we're a legitimate business now, I won't need a gun any more either, I suppose. At the start of my employment, John organised some weapons training for me, then some practising in a facility down near Slough to get me comfortable with using revolvers and then rifles, even with night sights, at which I had demonstrated some competence within a short time. After the training, John's guys had given me a couple of revolvers, just in case. I'd used each of them a couple of times, so they gave me replacements, which are still stored safely in my apartment in London, in a professionally constructed false drawer in the hall at the door. With the building security and a series of CCTV cameras leading to my flat, I had a pretty solid and secure home, although I always preferred my relative anonymity as my main defence.

It was this anonymity which I hoped would see me safely through the dissolution of the business. Only my first name, if even that, was known to the teams at the cities; I made plenty people scared shitless and killed a few, but left no trail of evidence other than witnesses who were just as guilty as me, almost anyway. These have all been paid off, presumably dropping off the radar themselves or getting involved with the new suppliers. Either way, the only possible group of people who might still want to find me are friends or relatives of those I've dealt with harshly during the past twenty months or so. The first, other than Galloglas, was Masby, who was such a monumental arsehole that I'd be surprised if anyone would be willing to go out of their way to remember him. The others, well, they were all shits too, or they wouldn't be dead. I had no real idea if any of their relatives would be in a position to look for revenge, or had the wherewithal to do so. Maybe they would be more likely to go for John than me though, although he had delegated all the local stuff to me since just after I started, so he's ancient history in the world of narcotics reprisals. The guy in Edinburgh yesterday, he was a low-life from a crew which was about to be muscled out by incomers, so whatever dealer relatives he had would be busy for a while, surviving and making a living.

There is also the potential for the new teams coming in to make their mark with violence towards us, but John Allanton had sent out enough signals that they could walk in without a fight, straight into the vacuum we left and with not a shot fired. This meant that there was no profit in them hunting around to find their predecessors and, we figured, as someday they might want out too, they would respect our tactical withdrawal as the peaceful business liquidation it absolutely was.

I have my own plans to think through, either as an employee of the now legitimate portfolio or as an unattached citizen of the world. I have enough money, especially if John hands me a year's wages, to move somewhere quiet and let time take care of any angry thoughts of those I've crossed. On the other hand, I would prefer to stay as a highly-paid associate property investor and working with John in a world of clean success, five-star hotels, business class travel and Sasha, a world away from all the things I had done, done well and enjoyed, for the most part. It was a surreal feeling; that I might have come through the whole thing and got away with it. Maybe I could even live with good people again, like I was one of them, without being in character and controlling everything as I've needed to do. Perhaps I need some more visits to Dr Schaffer to see what she thinks, after this sudden opportunity for me to be released back into the wild, as it were.

For now, my official business here at Inverannan is all but concluded, and successfully so. The teams have been paid off, Magnus Gilfillan has slipped away to decide how liquid his future is going to be and I have only to decide whether to head through the snow to the village and get drunk with my friend or to wait here, delegate the conversations and payments to Eilidh for the last two guys and leave in the morning, weather permitting. I stand and look out at the impenetrably heavy snowfall and there's no decision to make. I turn as I hear the door open and its Gillian, smiling and telling me that her dad will pick us up in his four-wheel drive after work, thence to the pub for dinner after a wee visit to the two men, my last redundancy payment and the closure of my tasks.

Just after five, I look out of the library window and see Gillian's dad's huge four-wheel drive crunching its way along the back of the house, its wheels following the tracks of the other vehicles which left earlier. I put on my jacket and walk downstairs, meeting Gillian in the hallway.

'You ready to roll?' she asks, her voice sounds slightly nervous.

'Yeah, no problem at all. You OK?' She nods and after she sets the alarm and locks the main door, we head out into the cold. I sit in the back and Gillian is left to take the front seat. Her father leans over, shakes my hand and introduces himself as Hector MacSuibhne, a proper highland name which jars me slightly as I didn't know Gillian's surname, to my discredit. He's a fair size of a man, a highlander all day long, a mass of bunnet, tweed and Gore-tex. There's a slight but tangible air of disapproval, but I guess that's normal for any father when meeting their daughter's lover, or whatever I was. If he knows my reputation and connection to the narcotics side of Inverannan, it would also be highly understandable if he remains wary. Either way, I join in the little small-talk from Gillian and thank him for the lift.

The road is getting worse now; my car wouldn't have made it to the village. Hector takes me to a house at the outskirts of the village, where McVey and Campbell are apparently waiting for me. How Hector knows this evades me, however, I suppose if it's like my home village, there's a sometimes deeply odd connection between the inhabitants, all living and working together, their secrets kept safe in their little world. I'm wondering if this is all genuine when Hector volunteers that he works with the two men part-time in the forestry and they got a call from Magnus to meet me.

Gillian asks if they should wait, but I tell her that I'll meet her in the pub, and thank Hector again for the lift. The four-wheel drive roars off towards their house and I turn to complete my pay-offs, a job I will be glad to be finished with.

The door opens before I get to it and McVey introduces himself and ushers me inside. His pal stands and shakes my hand too. I recognise both of them from my previous visits, Campbell principally due to his rather retro sideburns and ageing-Elvis-impersonator hair.

'I've got some news for you lads.' I tell them, handing them each a package. They open them simultaneously and look at each other, unable to restrain their smiles.

'Business is closing, as of now. This is your redundancy, the terms being that you keep quiet about anything that ever went on at Inverannan. I don't need to stress the importance that the business places on this and the agreement is therefore that your loyalty continues. This generous payment is a symbol of our good faith and I trust that you accept this simple proposition.' They nod.

We shake hands and McVey seems to want to tell me something.

'What's up – is everything OK?

He looks nervous, something I have grown accustomed to when I am meeting subordinates in a business discussion.

'There's someone in the grounds of Inverannan sir.' He blurted. 'I saw tracks when we went up with Hector to take logs to the Tuath bothy. One man, tracks heading from up the hill, I don't know where he was going but could have been in the direction of the big house sir. There shouldn't be anyone up there now and we are well told not to mess about after hours. I didnae mention it to Hector, he was just giving me a lift and isn't, well, he's not one of us from Inverannan sir, likes to keep out of it, does Hector.'

I thank him for letting me know and shake their hands, leaving them to a financially healthy next few months and me to walk to the pub, wondering who would be crazy enough to brave the extreme cold and snow to get a look at Inverannan, empty and now devoid of interest. If it were the authorities, they wouldn't send one operative; more likely it was just one of the guys out stalking deer on the fly, looking to bring in some meat to keep provisions up and costs down. I decide that, regardless of my desire to be with Gillian, that I had better stay at Inverannan House tonight. I can get the key and alarm code from her, as long as I remember that there is potentially an intruder and don't get forget about it after a few drinks.

After ten minutes or so, I'm at the pub and it's half full of the guys I gave redundancy money to earlier today. They stop talking when I get in, then a cheer goes up and I'm in company with a group of hard-drinking ex-delivery men with more money than they have ever had and a strong impetus to celebrate, as only highlanders can. About an hour later, Gillian comes in and rescues me from a quick-flowing river of whisky and pints. I get us some drinks, leaving enough money at the bar for a few rounds for the guys and, my popularity doubly secured, head to a quieter seat well away from them. There have been some modest improvements to the bar since I was last here, and we get a table beside a new log-burner which lends the room an air of rustic appeal, or as close to it as the place will ever get.

I tell Gillian that she looks great and I mean it, my heart flips when I look at her and I wonder how the hell that could happen, the same feeling I have when I see Sasha. I thought Sasha had triggered some humanity in me, something I'd lost for the best part of two years but maybe it wasn't just her. Maybe I was finding my way back, because I felt hardly any different now than when I first sat with her back then, drunk and still a journalist, before I went south.

Gillian is, as she was then, the best of company. She had been to uni in Edinburgh, so tells me her story and how her parents struggled to pay for it all, the great times and the disasters. I tell her the story of my younger life and she cracks up laughing, then we both do, at the story of my parent's miserly existence to attain their current lifestyle in the sun. Soon, its three hours later and Gillian asks me to come back with her. I nod but tell her that I need to stay in Inverannan tonight as there was someone prowling.

'That wasn't an invite to my bed Adam.' She looks at me with mock injustice and I guess I blush because she starts laughing at me again. Fuck me, I'm still gauche, after all this, I think to myself.

We head out, the cheerios and hollers from the bar seeing us off into the snow again. The guys are now deep into their malt whisky and the barman with them. It's a riotous assembly of guffaws and jokes and, for them, a celebration of not only extra money but a release from the pressure of involvement in the narcotics business. They made it out, I think, and I hope I do too.

So we trail through the snow, arm in arm and soon we're at her home; the lights are on and Gillian takes me into the kitchen where Hector stands to meet us and introduces his wife, Katrina. I'm really quite drunk but thankfully they have been sitting having some red wine, so I hope I'm not standing out too much. I've not been drinking much recently, certainly since joining the Portfolio and it tells, the whisky and beer have gone to my head more than expected and it's with some dread

85

that I see Hector bringing out an almost-full bottle of malt to extend his welcome.

We sit together, laughing and getting to know one another, the whisky going down well and Hector going after it like it was his last day on earth. I can't keep up with him and Gillian realises this, making him miss me out when he refills every second time. Katrina is jolly and has an infectious laugh, telling us about their two sons who both work away as contractors, but come back every few weeks to cause chaos and lighten up their house.

Hector has offered to give me a lift back to the house, but I gradually wonder if he has forgotten he's steaming drunk or is just willing to drive in a highly dangerous state. After the second bottle of whisky has been opened and he becomes even more talkative, we get onto the subject of nationalism, which he and I agree upon, prompting a loud collective rendition of Flower of Scotland, at the end of which Gillian is laughing hysterically at her dad's tone-deaf loudness and my partial-at-best recollection of the words and their correct sequence. Ten minutes later, Hector is comatose on the sofa in the living room and Katrina offers me a lift or to stay in a spare room. Gillian seems to want me to stay, but I really should be at Inverannan, on possibly pointless guard duty, but I am aware enough, just, to know where I should be.

Katrina heads upstairs to get her outdoor clothes on as soon as she leaves, Gillian comes over and kisses me, passionately and warmly, my decision to return to Inverannan now feeling like it is absolutely not the right thing to do. She returns to her chair as her mother comes back in, leaving me rather disconcerted and having to stand up at a slightly awkward angle to get my jacket on.

We're ready to go and Gillian gives me another kiss goodbye, softer this time but no less wonderful.

The snow has abated when we set off, the road in the village not too bad, but the track to Inverannan barely passable. Katrina seems set to ask me something, so I try to let the cold air sober me up a little and with it my vocal abilities.

'So is it all over for you too, Adam?' she enquires, straighter now like she's taking a break from friendliness.

I look at her, the dashboard lights illuminating her face enough to see that she's not smiling.

My well-rehearsed reticence about the business kicks in.

'The business is now property asset-based, nothing else.' I assure her.

There's a pause and I can sense her formulating the next question carefully.

'You have a reputation, Adam. I don't want Gillian to get involved with you, if you're like that, like what they say you are.' There it is. Direct and hard to answer honestly, even if I was sober. I feel like downloading it all to her, the accidental involvement, the murders that weren't this Adam, they were the other guy, the guy with the flat in London who feels great when he puts a bullet in someone, in one of them, the drug dealers, the scum. Instead, I look at her for a moment and know that we are here, at Inverannan and I can't talk, not like that.

'I'm not one of the bad guys Katrina, but I got drawn into some dodgy stuff. It's all over now and I'm clear of it, I promise'

It's more than I should have said and I'm not sure why I did, not to someone I don't know.

She is looking at me, maybe right through the outer protection of my persona, that's what it seems like.

'Good' is all she says, and smiles at me.

Much like his father, John Allanton did not sleep much on the night of the fire on the yacht. After chartering a jet from London City Airport for the next morning, he contacted a number of Allanton family members, as was the protocol for any such incidents. He then updated Zoe, leaving her to coordinate some actions and let the key staff know an outline of the situation.

John packed for his flight and after much thought on the matter ahead, managed to fall asleep for an hour or so before a solitary drive from his semi-rural home to the airport where the jet waited to take him to meet his father.

It was lunchtime when he arrived at his father's hotel, the day dull and greyer than was normal for that place at that time, reflecting his mood at this violent intrusion on Sir Mathieson's life. On request, the taxi let him out at the jetty, which gave him the opportunity to look over the sixty or so metres to where the blackened yacht still sat at mooring. It was structurally complete, although it appeared to John to be unlikely to be easily repaired; he knew that the yacht was well and expensively insured, having spent some time with his father selecting the correct option from a family contact and arranging the requirements of the crew, mooring and running costs. In their line of business, these costs were not significant even for a retired man like his father; quite the opposite, it was another opportunity for their accountancy team to offset income against tax on the more visible aspects of the Portfolio. Nothing better than a free yacht, his father had joked at the time.

John walked along to the small seafront hotel and found his father at lunch inside in an otherwise quiet and rather oddly wood-lined dining area. Ordering an omelette, he sat across from Sir Mathieson and after a glance to ensure they were not overheard, looked straight at the older man.

'Are you OK?'

'Yes, of course I am' sighed Sir Mathieson. 'Except my yacht is rather badly damaged and I'm not sure yet if I was meant to be in it.' He filled his son in on the sequence of events from the previous evening, also explaining his divergence from the norm by going for a walk instead of returning directly to the yacht.

'That said - I am absolutely sure I was the target. There was an accelerant used, but not a device; manually distributed, probably petrol from a jerry-can, from what the Police are suggesting. That means the perpetrator went aboard as soon as the crew left and may have had the impression that the yacht was occupied solely by me at that point.' He sipped his coffee and looked at his son over the cup. 'So who, in your opinion, would try this action, in this way?'

John shook his head slightly. 'That's the thing. We, or you, don't have any shortage of enemies, given our line of work. You're retired though, so why go for you and, if you excuse the crudity, why not just do the job properly?'

'Those are exactly my thoughts. It's possible any number of aggrieved groups or individuals would decide to do harm to me, but this is perhaps more of a warning; not one I appreciate or as yet understand, but a warning nonetheless. I don't have a definitive approach, however, if we continue this conversation in my room, perhaps we can agree on the best course of action. Is the plane still at the airport?'

John nodded. 'Yes, I wasn't sure if you would be coming back with me or staying to deal with the yacht.'

Sir Mathieson smiled. 'No son, I'm returning to active duty, until whoever instigated this assault is in front of me and prepared to answer a number of painful questions. In the meantime, I will take to the Highlands where my security can be guaranteed, so instruct the pilot to make arrangements for the flight to Inverness.' John's shoulders slumped, ever so slightly, at the thought of a return to the Estate; his life had significantly improved since leaving there and spending more time at home. The thought of going back there even briefly was not ideal. That said, it was, from a security viewpoint, perhaps the correct choice.

Sir Mathieson gave his son a beaming smile. 'Come on then John, let us commence the operation.'

Ten minutes later, they both stood by the jetty, watching a team from the local Police and the Insurance Assessors go through the limited forensic evidence in situ; a brief discussion with the senior man on site told them that a jerry-can had been found, no witnesses as yet had come forward and, coupled with the lack of CCTV, it appeared that the investigation was going nowhere fast at this end. However, since the statements and alibis for Sir Mathieson and the crew were solidly confirmed, there would hopefully be, despite delays, a payment from the insurers at some point down the line.

After an hour or so, and with no further involvement required from them, the two Allantons and Benny McGowan left for the airport, after a discussion with the crew, no longer required and being temporarily let go until needed again. Conversely, Sir Mathieson's sojourn in the Mediterranean was over, at least for now.

Benny McGowan had remained, as was his habit, silent during the morning. The other two men felt that he was slightly more red-faced than was normal; however, this generally meant that McGowan had merely misjudged the already industrial quantities of whisky he consumed. He followed them through customs at the airport, onto the small jet and stayed floridly quiet until the flight was in the air.

'Sir!' McGowan blurted, giving John the sensation that he had to talk before his ruddy head exploded.

'Yes, Benny, what is it?' Sir Mathieson looked up from the table where he was jotting down some of his thoughts on the situation.

'I seen someone, sir. He was sitting near the boat when I was heading for the pub – middle-aged, fat, dark hair.'

John looked at him askance. 'That describes almost every man walking around there Benny. Was this individual acting suspiciously?'

'No, he was kneeling down at the back of one of those wee cruisers. Up to no good though, I bet.'

Benny, despite his stress over the matter, appeared to have limited information on the culprit. Sir Mathieson looked like he was about to question Benny further, but paused and reflected that Benny had just identified a generic Spaniard who was unlikely to be of any help in their investigation even if ever found.

'We'll add this character to the investigation, Benny, thanks for letting me know.' Sir Mathieson smiled indulgently at Benny, who nodded, the information now off his chest and able to relax once again. He accepted a whisky, larger than large, and settled into the seat comfortably.

Sir Mathieson shook his head and diverted the conversation to his son on more practical matters.

'Let us assume that this was both an attempt on my life and a warning to the business. The Portfolio is now on solid ground, legitimate barring mild tax avoidance and unlikely to generate this kind of action. Our former business, however, is where we are most likely to find aggrieved parties, agreed?' John nodded, confirming this fundamental assessment of the situation.

'I have taken some time overnight to prepare a list of our potential suspects, which fall into two basic categories; firstly, those who I would count as unfriendly towards us, however, I deem unlikely to have taken this action; secondly those who could conceivably derive some benefit from the action, or would conceivably seek reparation for actions I, or we, may have taken in the past. I suggest we spend the remainder of the flight completing an assessment of the list.'

With that, he handed some handwritten documents to John, outlining a fairly comprehensive catalogue of the organisations and individuals who he considered to be in the latter category. John added two to the list, at which Sir Mathieson shrugged but continued. They spent the next two hours discussing, rating and compiling an analysis of the list, punctuated by minor disagreements over the likelihood of some of their probabilities. Some were deleted after consideration, however, the final suspects, those added earlier by John, generated the most discussion.

'He's dead, or so I heard. In any case, he was never really involved in our line of business, quite happy to lead his own life, of that I have no doubt.' Sir Mathieson appeared highly dubious of these credentials as a potential attacker. His son, less sure, left the name on the list. The last name was unknown to Sir Mathieson.

'Those were locals, Midlands and no further. Not on a scale which would suggest they would in any way carry out this infringement and not when we are departing the narcotics business.' Sir Mathieson sat back and took a drink of his coffee.

'It's not about their current position. We need to consider anyone connected to individuals we have terminated over the past two or three years. Just because they didn't kick back at us at the time doesn't mean anything, they could have been waiting for an opportunity, and our leaving the trade is exactly that. We're not a player any more, from their narrow point of view.' John's voice had risen as he spoke, the frustration at the situation gathering as his father dismissed the potential of individuals to take revenge for murders gone by.

John continued, not even sure if Sir Mathieson was listening closely to his words.

'That's why we monitor them. Zoe has access to their online activity; we pick up what they are doing on Social Media, just to see if anyone is thinking about misbehaving. Some on this list have all just been paid off by us and might have used that money to place a contract on your life, or just took the chance to try it themselves.

Jesus Christ, anyone can fly out here and get a can of petrol, it's the simplest thing.' He sat back, lifting the list as he did and looking at the last few names.

'This Manchester mob, even though they are a target themselves after that Amsterdam thing, they have been trying to move up from being a distributor to being a wholesaler and hate us with a vengeance, along with everyone else on this list that is. In Amsterdam, they misjudged the loyalties of who they were trying to deal with and got chased out. Those guys could be trying to make a name for themselves by killing you, that's motive enough for thugs like that.'

'Have you met them personally?'

John sighed. 'Yes, once. You will remember that I told you that Adam slapped one of their guys down a few months ago and then met with them to clarify boundaries. I thought that was it finished but Adam says they are all crazy, hard to judge. Plus, it's a family business they run – cousins, brothers, uncles – who knows what those idiots could decide to do, they aren't as predictable as the usual outlets, more independent but good earners so we tolerated them. We would have stopped supplying them if we hadn't planned to close down anyway. It's possible that they have taken our withdrawal badly, given the short notice and loss of income, even after the pay-off. They were some of the first to be told, about a week ago if I remember correctly.'

The older man still seemed dubious, distracted and giving little indication of what he was pondering.

John sat forward, his expression hardened. 'There's something else. We have intelligence that they have been heard to threaten revenge for the killing of their man.'

His father looked at him in disbelief. 'I thought Adam had just slapped him down?'

John looked at his father with an expression of guilt. 'Well, things seem to have escalated on-site, it went further than we expected. The rumours are that they appear to be unable to move on from this, so it would seem.'

Sir Mathieson sat back, momentarily weary. 'You should have told me.' John nodded an apology.

'They are top of the list then?'

John looked straight at him. 'No, but I think they are worth spending time looking at. They may have been planning this even before we closed it all down.' His father still looked entrenched in thought. 'We need to allocate our staff to review elements of this list. We can't turn up at their doors and ask if they tried to assassinate you, but we certainly can prioritise our effort, that's for sure. And don't worry, we will get this resolved. After it's done, the yacht will get fixed or replaced and then it will be back to normal for you.'

'Yes, yes.' Sir Mathieson agreed, enlivening as their plan was agreed. 'Let's start with some additional firepower. I always feel better when on the front foot in a show.'

John nodded agreement and set to organising their reserve officer's call-up. One call to the reliable Zoe instigated this aspect of their Continuity Plan, the summoning of former military comrades, who, for generous rewards, were delighted to meet up again for a period of private soldiery on behalf of their former Commanding Officers. They fell into two categories – the older men, Sir Mathieson's, who were effectively retired; and the younger men of John's time in the army.

John knew his men to be solid, well-trained and still fit as a fiddle; Sir Mathieson and John both knew, however, that the older group were gristly tough, nasty, experienced and despite a few of them no longer able to participate fully, those that were would still be able to act without any compunction whatsoever. In short, the Allanton men knew that, regardless of which competitor on the list had to be dealt with, the outcome would the same. John arranged for the right men from his own group to be activated first to help Zoe and Williams gather further intelligence on the list of suspects, the former branches of the Allanton narcotics supply chain and those who had crossed them in the recent past.

Their chartered jet landed at Inverness just before scheduled, a bumpy landing which jogged McGowan back into life. Fifteen minutes later and they were being driven in a Range Rover, accompanied by one other estate vehicle with their operatives on board, to Sir Mathieson's property near Inverannan. Security had been arranged and, after a couple of calls, their key officers summoned to meet them that evening.

'Is Adam there?' asked Sir Mathieson.

'Yes, at the Estate. He'll be there for our arrival, but I've hardly spoken to him, he's been finishing the payments and you know what the phone reception is like up there.'

'Absolutely.' Sir Mathieson replied. 'We might well need his input. If this was the London connection, Adam may well be able to see something we are missing, maybe some more suggestions on why they feel so aggrieved.'

The vehicle followed the east to north-west route they both had travelled many times; spectacular mountain ranges and barren snow-covered moorland, hardly any houses to break up the feeling of heading into one of Scotland's truly wild places. Sir Mathieson loved this journey, not just for the scenery but the feeling of coming home, its safety and the knowledge that outsiders could be identified easily, standing out from the hikers and bikers who travelled around this northerly hinterland. Adam Darnow had temporarily taken over the running of the operation at Inverannan House and, with his two closest employees now with him and a few estate men to help, he felt assured that they were safest there.

In addition, Sir Mathieson had taken one particular, off-plan action, to clarify the situation with the theft from his account; he had one particularly trusted officer back in their London office that could be relied upon to make checks on his behalf. This officer had permissions to contact the bank and determine exactly when and by which method the monies were transferred, each time part of the £12 million was moved. It had been an incremental theft to avoid even low-value flags, his account of the type where large sums were routinely moved in and out, until of course his retirement. This information would hopefully be with him in time to coincide with the interrogation of Tim Balliol and the eventual return of the funds to Sir Mathieson.

The scarcity of mobile signals on their journey to Inverannan meant that John Allantons phone only sprung into life every thirty minutes or so. He slowed the cars at a village where reception at least flickered into life; a few encrypted messages received on his secure app reassured him and Sir Mathieson that their plans were well underway and that their arrival at Inverannan would be the end of this phase, where the risk might not be high, but still present. The road conditions worsened as they drove north, especially the higher ground which, despite snowploughs passing them a couple of times, the snowfall countering and winning the battle to keep the main road open. Their arrival at Inverannan Village was later than expected and it took a struggle to overcome the drifts and get along to the house itself, shrouded in cold, snow and graceful seclusion. A perfect place to stay in safety, thought Sir Mathieson. The access road would soon be impassable by vehicles and he didn't imagine that the village roads would stay open after another hour or so of this deluge. Leaving the car and stepping into the deep snow, he breathed deeply of the fierce Highland air and looked through the driving snow to where his erstwhile protégé, Adam Darnow, emerged to meet him.

Mark Roghan took the call from his man in Ilford, fully expecting that the contract had been completed without fuss, and with success. Instead, he was told that, rather than the job having been straightforward, the target had now fled the Mediterranean and his would-be assassin had left a trail of fire and blunders in his wake. He did, however, have confirmation from the assassin that Allanton had made arrangements to go to Scotland for safety, a place in Scotland called Inverannan. The middle-man had checked the file to confirm the address, The Manse, Inverannan, was indeed the property identified in the report as the previous base for Sir Mathieson Allanton. After some heated discussions, Roghan approved the middle-man to send both sets of assassins to the property in the highlands of Scotland without delay. He was to give them clear instruction to make sure, absolutely and without any doubt, that Sir Mathieson Allanton would die there. The middle-man reassured him that this time, even if they knew they were coming, that all would be resolved.

Roghan closed the call and placed his face in his hands, lowering it to the desk until his forehead rested gently on its polished mahogany surface. He cursed his involvement in this bloody awful situation and the day he ever met Big Jim Galloglas, with his disgusting house, his embarrassing Thai peccadilloes and this god-awful contract. He also knew that people at the top of the narcotics food chain are less than forgiving when crossed and that, if something has to be done, it must be done right this time. Leaving his office without further ado, he drove out the two hours from the city to Galloglas' house to give him this update, taking with him some strong menthol rub, which he spread on his chest and under his nose before entering the foul environment where his friend wallowed. Opening the always-unlocked door to the lounge, Roghan recoiled again at the sweet stench of decay and dogs, which he wondered if they were alive or dead somewhere, such was the odour. Galloglas was waiting for him, already a few whiskies into his evening by the look of him.

'What the fuck happened?' The throaty rasp had a distinct slur to it, making Roghan regret his visit already.

'Our man missed the target. Set fire to the bloody boat and now Allanton is back in the UK.' Roghan sat down while Galloglas set off on an expletive-filled rant about the failure, the ripe and guttural South African accent of his youth becoming more prominent through anger and drunkenness.

He finished after a while and moved to sit across from Roghan. 'So what the fuck do we do now?'

The younger man looked straight at Galloglas. 'I've already set the other contract in motion, this time more men, better armed and better paid. We'll find out later today what's happening, but my guy knows these UK boys, tough lads who he can trust.'

'He fucking said that about the other one!' Galloglas almost choked, a coughing fit hitting him at the same time as the surge of ire.

Roghan nodded. 'I know, I know. We just need to get this done. I'll keep in touch with him this time - make sure they know what is needed.'

'What about this fucking idiot in the Med? He's getting fuck all money from me after that.'

He looked over at Galloglas, realising that despite the bluster and the vitriol, that he was a fading figure of a man, neck skin scrawny from the treatment and the disease. Maybe this thing was all that was keeping him going, so Roghan would need to hang in there too.

'He's still getting paid and he's still active. I've OK'd the funds for him to follow the target and try again, not ideal I know, but he's willing to make amends.' Galloglas shook his head, swearing at nobody in particular. Both sets of contractors were now in the field, for better or worst.

He rose, lurched over to a side table and brought a cheque over to his friend. Roghan looked at it, the numbers far higher than needed by a factor of six. He looked up at Galloglas.

'Just take it. Say it's for an investment we're doing together and that will hide the money if anyone comes looking. Just cash it quickly. I'm a bloody walking tumour now.'

They talked then, small stuff mostly about what Roghan is doing, then onto a few stories from the old days before it's time for him to go. They shake hands and Roghan leaves Galloglas to finish his bottle of blended whisky and fall asleep, blissfully uncaring of the imminent hangover and the torment of his next waking hour.

The next day, Roghan spoke on an encrypted line to his man in England. He in turn told Roghan that the men were indeed well-armed, fully prepared and already on their way north. He expected them to lose contact when they reach the limits of the communications network, into the wild and snowy highlands of the west of Scotland, so they will only speak again when information comes back from either of their two units.

Roghan spent an uncomfortable couple of days without any information or updates and, frustrated by the limbo, tried to contact his man again. The calls terminated after ringing out at the other end. He was lost then, no other way of finding out what had happened and cursed by the ill-feeling of having started something he couldn't control. The cheque from Galloglas had at least gone into his account and cleared and, since he hadn't paid anything out except a couple of down-payments, he was at least financially well positioned.

The down-payments had been transferred to a shell company his middle-man used, with assurances that all was confidential and untraceable, which allayed some of his anxieties. Roghan called Big Jim Galloglas, but that rang out too. Roghan wondered if he might be in hospital now, out of his way permanently, with any luck. With no information and nobody to speak to, Roghan went back to normal then, his work and his family, with just some extra security on the drive home to make him feel better. Even if someone came looking, he'd just give up Galloglas without a thought, the bloody man is almost dead already anyway. Still, Roghan didn't sleep so well, not for a while.

12   TIM GOES ON A TRIP

Tim became increasingly engrossed in his work for the Portfolio, his time at the office passing quickly as he completed the transitional work, only going back to his hotel to sleep and have the weekend off. His work gathered pace, the transition from his previous employer, then the fixing of the Allanton finances, Tim lost in the work and at his happiest doing so. The accountants had to work in shifts to maintain a presence with him, which stretched their concentration and patience with the repellent Treasurer as with all those that had gone before. Cheryl was an exceptional accountant and, despite the mind of Tim working differently from anyone she had ever worked with, she had begun to comprehend his underlying principles. He broke the tracks, that was the critical element, he made these trails go cold like no-one she'd ever heard of; a hundred tricks, to make information go missing after it was processed, to use temporary or paid shell companies with no connections, a myriad other deceptions and loopholes to make the money come out cleaner than clean. Especially now, when it was all changing for the Portfolio and they knew it. Soon the money wouldn't have to be cleaned, that was what it was all about, all this closing down, this Tim Balliol thing. Cheryl didn't know if Tim knew the state of play here, he seemed lost in the work, in the fixing and closing and opening and all that, maybe clever but maybe also naive at the same time. Zoe had told her not to engage him in conversation, and Cheryl didn't know whether that was to avoid giving information away or just to protect her from the insane and bizarre shit that Tim occasionally offered when a subject came up in the passing.

Day after day passed and the winter was almost over when Tim had completed all of his "phase two" work, to self-investigate the Portfolio and make sure that, even if the best that the authorities came in, there was nothing illegal to find. That is, except the live narcotics points of income, the last closures to be enacted before the Portfolio transitioned to complete legitimacy. Contrary to what everyone here thought, Tim had indeed realised from his first interview that he was carrying out a medium-term role at best; he would be finished soon and had conceived his options more clearly than they could imagine, Tim's lateral mind ideally suited to playing out the possibilities and risks of any situation. Tim was acutely aware that Cheryl and her team had been placed beside him to dissect his methods and contacts, his patterns and nuances, to learn from him and render him unnecessary. He also knew enough of this business to understand that the Scottish guy, Adam Darnow, was to be feared, that it was him who would likely be the last person you ever see if you cross this mob. In the weeks he'd been there Tim had hardly seen him in the building and when he did, he made sure that he moved away from him, unseen preferably. In the scenario where a guy like that had a choice whether to kill you quickly or slowly, he didn't want any of his unintentional social blunders to make him opt for the long-drawn-out option, metaphorically and literally.

Tim recognised that he was nearing the point where either he would need to make a break for it, or risk staying and hoping that John Allanton would value him enough to retain his life and service. To that end, he prepared a Business Plan for him, the like of which would have been the pride of any hedge fund analyst across London, Tokyo or New York. Tim had spent his hours away from work and at each weekend carrying out a series of algorithmic, quasi-prediction-based and event-driven calculations which, if accepted by John Allanton, would take the Portfolio from a deal-based profit machine to another level, a level which only Tim could take it to.

His meeting with John was therefore arranged, four hours in the diary and no-one else to be in attendance except Cheryl, who Tim knew was an effective accountant but in no way qualified to take forward this new plan. Tim had seen the current Portfolio returns, knew they were stale in some areas and knew that, if offered, even someone about to kill him wouldn't turn down a tax-free, 17.3% projected per annum return on their already massive fortune. Tim knew John Allanton was smart, a risk taker and someone who he could work with on a long-term basis, if he could convince him to accept the plan and not to let that Scottish lunatic anywhere near him.

Tim had hardly slept that night, his final preparations and the PowerPoint completed at 5 am, his life about to be bet on the Business Plan. He showered, put on clean clothes and his best suit, his brogues for once polished and looking as impressive as Tim Balliol ever had. Of his skills, he knew that selling himself at the interview was definitely up there with his best; he knew that he had the capacity to appear enthusiastic for half a day, or whatever it would take.

He packed his laptop and put the lights out in his hotel room, readying himself for the short commute into the office. It was just getting light now, a hint of the spring morning's return and a light frost even here, in the city. He breathed in the icy air and felt good, positive even, and looked right to check the traffic before crossing and heading for the early, quieter underground train to

Edgware Road and the short walk to the offices of the Portfolio.

It all went dark for Tim as a hood was thrust over his head and a punch landed in his stomach, making any attempt at shouting pointless as his airways were otherwise occupied. His arms were pulled forward and someone pushed from behind as he was thrust into a waiting van. Possibly accidentally, or maybe not, his head crashed sickeningly into the frame of the vans side panel as he was forced forward. A jag in his upper arm, straight through his clothes, completed the efficient kidnapping and for Tim, this was not going to be a good day at the office.

The vehicle took the unconscious Tim out of London, through the accumulating traffic and northwards, past Leeds, then Glasgow, bypassing Perth and thence out into the central highlands. The men took turns driving to avoid tiredness, pulling into small villages to make the rotation happen and get some food. They didn't give Tim too much of the sedative as they had been warned, that this guy had to talk, to answer their questions when they needed him to. They didn't know why they were taking him north; their questions could have been asked anywhere. Still, it was always best to do as they were told, the man above them knew what was going on and that was the way of it.

Tim wakened up, groggy and ill, earlier than they knew. He had stayed still, lying there on the carpeted floor, hooded and bound tightly, which was not actually an unknown or unpleasant experience to him, if only they knew. His captors said little on the journey; just some brief complaints about the closing-in weather and where to get sandwiches were their only comments. Tim did not know who they were, English accents and no names used. They had taken his wallet, keys and mobile and had the audacity at one stopping point to try and get him to tell them his code, no doubt wanting to get all the information they could on him. Tim acted as if the sedative was still working and went floppy when the man tried to lift him by the lapels. Tim was smart.

After he was left at peace for a while, he mentally recalculated his risks and their mitigations and decided it unlikely that John Allanton was responsible for this; a meeting had been arranged where Tim was to tell him how he could make millions, legally and cleverly. Not something a businessman would pass up, even if he intended to do away with Tim afterwards if he didn't fancy the plan. No, this was something and someone else and that did not bode well for poor Tim. His previous employer was last seen with multiple bullet holes in him; it was conceivable that his remaining associates were taking revenge for Tim's willing disloyalty in transferring assets to John Allanton. It was also conceivable that another party were seeking to take over the business in turn from John Allanton and wanted to take Tim away to facilitate a second transition. Either way, they weren't going to kill him immediately, which was somewhat cold comfort to him.

Eventually, the van came to a halt and he was raised to a shakily standing position outside, the air absolutely freezing after the relative warmth of the carpeted floor, the snow deep as he crunched out of the van. His ankle cable ties were cut and he was half-led, half pushed into a building, where he stood alone with his hood still in place. The door clicked shut and the lock turned audibly; little noise and less welcome. Tim reached up and pulled his hood off, the room clearly visible after the blackout of the journey thanks to the van lights beaming through the gaps in the door itself. He was standing in a stone-built area, only a few rustic chairs, a table and an unlit fireplace to break the monotony. One door and two tiny boarded windows gave the appearance of some kind of shepherds bothy or whatever they were called. As the lights departed, Tim walked to the table and tried to use its edge to rub through the wrist cable ties, unsuccessfully. After trying the same approach with the stone of the fireplace and the door handle, all Tim had to show was bleeding wrists and a frustrated demeanour. He wriggled his trousers down and urinated into the fireplace, there being no other options available and having reached a state of extreme desperation on that front.

As his eyes became accustomed to the dark and in the gloom, he spent another five minutes rubbing his wrist cable ties along the rudimentary fireplace lintel until finally they gave way and he was free. He threw the tie across the room and waved his wrists to try and get feeling back into them, flicking droplets of blood onto the floor as he did so. After pulling his trousers back up, his next task was to try and get the door open, which he thought might be considerably harder than the cable ties. So it proved, as the door was absolutely solid. He kicked at it, shouldered it rather weakly then tried to search the room for anything to help pick the lock. Eventually, he had extracted some wire from the underside of a chair and one piece of metal nail from a corner beside the fireplace. He had seen locks picked on television and in movies, but the specifics had evaded him and continued to do so. Almost weeping and having lacerated his fingertips from the effort, he threw the metal pieces into the cold fireplace in frustration.

It was almost completely dark now and, given that he had no blanket or method to heat himself, he had a panicked thought that he would die of cold that night, here in the bothy. Maybe they would come and get him, but perhaps he could find an escape before that, if he applied himself. Tim knew that the days were longer the farther north one was, and if the drive had taken all day, he would be quite some considerable distance from London by now. He closed his eyes and thought of how many miles per hour a van would travel, added the estimate of the stops and taking the weather into account, came to the considered and depressing opinion that he was most probably in the far north of Scotland.

He sat on the closest chair and looked upwards to the rafters and crude joists of the roof. There may be a chance to break through it if he could get onto a joist and kick upwards to the wood and the slates, Tim thought. There were patches where dim moonlight occasionally shone through, so worth a try, no doubt. Placing a chair on top of the table, he climbed onto one of the more solid-looking horizontal timbers, thick with dust and unpleasantly porous. He manoeuvred until his back was resting on the timber and pushed his feet upwards to the roof. There was some give there, so he moved along to a more worn and weak-looking section of the roof. Pushing with all his strength and suppressing the pain in his back, he forced the timbers upwards until his right foot shot through the roof, scraping the skin from his ankle, calf and shin at the same time. As he tried to withdraw his foot, his back slipped from the joist and he swung, suspended by one foot lodged in the roof, blood dripping from his ankle, down his trouser leg, his body and eventually, into his upside-down nose.

'Fuck.' Tim snorted, with some feeling.

The feeling of dangling did not last long, as the roof slates gave way and Tim fell the last two metres or so to the hard floor of the bothy, turning enough in the drop to fall on his upper back rather than his head. He rested there, dazed, winded and bleeding, new agonies taking their time to subside while tears fell down his normally emotionless visage. He gazed up through his tears to the hole in the roof, the source of his pain and perhaps, his method of escape. Tim forced himself to get to his feet, wiped the tears away and, taking his ruined suit jacket off, used it to mop his blood and tears as best he could. Resuming his efforts, he hoisted himself back up onto his joist and, this time crouching on it, pulled the slates and half-rotted timber away until he could get his head through and look at his surroundings. He needed to see if there was any way to get away, to hide even. If he was somewhere remote, that was a problem for Tim, although not as big a problem of just waiting to be questioned and murdered here in the bothy. Either way, Tim felt that he must take action; risks and probabilities must be taken into account and they were telling him that he'd be far better absconding.

All that Tim could see were snow-covered trees. Trees all around, with a hill on one side, covered in trees and snow. It was also cold as hell outside, even worse than in the bothy. He'd need his jacket now that he'd calmed down, even if it was revolting and bloody, it was better than just the thin white shirt he wore. He tore at the slates, pulling them down and dropping them into the bothy as quietly as he could. Once a proper hole was made, he climbed back down and put on his jacket. He ascended for the last time and wriggled through the gap in the roof, which he soon wished he had made larger, his narrow shoulders needing some pressure to get through, causing more scrapes on his already tender frame.

He sat on the snowy roof and slid feet first down to the side and looked at the drop, which although not far, was directly into some snow-covered shrubs and undergrowth of unknown depth. He manoeuvred himself around onto his stomach and lowered his legs over the edge, the slates jagging into his pulled-bare midriff as he went. The last part of his planned descent did not go well as he lost grip and slid agonisingly down the last few feet and fell down onto what he now knew to be predominantly thorny plants and broken pieces of wood. In a haze of points and pain, Tim scrambled through the obstacles and out to a bare patch of ground at the rear of the bothy, where he sat pulling various jaggy items from his sleeves, neck, trouser band and most unpleasantly and painfully, his underpants. There was seemingly no way to make the pain from the vast number of lacerations and punctures to abate, so after trying to numb them with snow, he stood upright with some difficulty and started off uphill, into the forest and using the occasional light of the almost-full moon to try and take as direct a route as possible away from the bothy.

It took Tim most of the night but, with the exception of intermittent stops to assuage the excruciating pain and itching of his cuts, he managed to remain focused on the need to keep walking. He was a remarkably odd individual, capable of stoically enduring the harsher aspects of his life and experiences and analysing them in their constituent parts. This experience, Tim figured, was like transitioning himself from one position, as captor, to another position where he could escape and not be followed. In accounting, Tim was peerless at covering a trail, not being caught and here, well Tim knew that the principles were the same. He didn't break a branch or leave a thread on a bramble. He knew that the falling snow would cover his footprints and even walked along a stream for a minute until his feet got so cold that he almost yelled out loud. Tim had never spent any time in the wilds of the highlands, but he had watched a lot of television and from that, he knew that it would take a decent effort to catch him on foot, if he had luck on his side.

It took Tim a couple of hard hours walking uphill, but he eventually reached the apex of a rocky and snow-blown rise, windy, freezing, and dark, with more nocturnal noises than one would have expected. He had been rather focused on escaping, on not leaving a trail to be followed but was now faced with the reality of being on top of a Scottish hillside while dressed for a business meeting. His feet were an odd combination of throbbing pain and numb coldness, which needed some attention at the first opportunity. His clothing was drenched in sweat and blood which was now quickly drying in the icy north-easterly breeze which had got up since he reached the high ground. Tim realised that he needed to find shelter and help, quickly and while keeping his position hidden from his kidnappers. To that end, he found a clear part of the hillside and tried to see if there were any lights visible from the position he thought he had come from. This in itself wasn't easy as he had started some hours ago, using the position of the moon to guide him; which he now realised was not particularly reliable as a fixed point.

Still, his instinct told him that he had walked far enough from the bothy, hopefully to a point where he would not be discovered by searchers. If he was now safe from that immediate threat, he must now find somewhere to get dry, shelter and hide until he could escape from the area. From his high vantage point, Tim could see lights away to his left, down another part of the hillside but still far, far away. Too cold to sit down and rest for long, he knew that the only option was to dig deeper into his reserves of energy and head for the lights, this time downward, which was bound to be easier.

The downhill stage of Tim's journey to the lights was not however as straightforward as he had foreseen. A sequence of clouds and another downfall of snow darkened the night at one point and he fell down an unseen hillside, only a few metres but his landing on a fallen tree left him bruised and sore. It took him into the lower part of the forest, where he lost sight of his destination. A light came back into view after that, enough to help him pick his way forward and eventually, exhausted and nearing the point of collapse, to a property.

It looked like a holiday home, incongruous here in the wild hillside, white-painted stonework and cobalt blue windows, fenced garden and thankfully no sign of inhabitants. Tim looked through the lace-curtained windows to check that premise and, finding no-one home and the key helpfully left underneath the front-door mat and entered the little cottage seeking respite. He thanked his good fortune that people were not worried about crime in the north of Scotland. The room was lit by a single lamp, on a timer to provide some light for arriving owners, whom Tim did not care about, not one jot.

He found the bathroom and divested himself of his ruined clothes in an instant, showering in gradually increasing temperatures until feeling returned to his extremities. After drying himself on a rough-feeling towel, Tim generously applied some horrible smelling pink-coloured antiseptic cream he found in the bathroom cupboard. Naked and dappled all over with pink cream blobs, he wandered into a bedroom and, finding a thick duvet, collapsed onto the bed and despite the waves of nipping from the antiseptic fighting the various stings, cuts and scrapes, fell sound asleep.

13   THE RETURN OF SIR MATHIESON

I have no idea what time it is, but I hear knocking at the door of my room in Inverannan House. The source of the noise is one office team, Niamh, who tells me that I have a call, which she will transfer to the phone in Gilfillan's office. I shove my clothes on and head downstairs, missing a couple of stairs and jarring myself. I get to the office and shout 'OK' through to no-one in particular. After a few clicks which I'm not sure means that the call has connected, I hear the distinctive voice of my boss, John Allanton. He sounds stressed, which is absolutely not like him.

'I'm in Menorca with dad. There's been a deliberate fire set on his yacht. He's OK but we're leaving shortly. Zoe has made arrangements for the guys to meet us at Inverness airport.' He was rattled; we usually don't speak in detail over the phone unless it was an encrypted call, which this sure isn't.

'No problem. What about here?' My voice is husky and my throat feels like sandpaper.

'We'll be there by the evening, hopefully. Secure Inverannan and get a couple of local guys to keep an eye out for anything unusual.'

'Can I do anything else?'

There was a familiar pause while he was working out his options. 'The Treasurer is missing. Zoe informed me of this problem a short time ago. She thinks this may be linked to the fire.'

The call terminates and I'm left wondering what the fuck is going on. Sir Mathieson is retired, withdrawn from active duty and at least theoretically safe abroad. If this was an attempt on his life, why would the Treasurer go missing at the same time?' Maybe Zoe is reading too much into a coincidence here, but that little shit Balliol has to be found anyway, what he knows could give us a serious problem. I need to call her. I go upstairs and get the number from my mobile then call it from the office phone. My post-alcohol fog is lifted by the adrenalin, but only just.

'Hi.' she says uncertainly. Zoe wouldn't recognise the Inverannan number.

'It's me, Adam. What the fuck is going on? I just got a call from John and he told me about the fire.' Her voice is muted slightly and I can tell she's talking from her car.

'Christ knows. Are you still at Inverannan?'

'Yeah, I was planning on leaving today but they're on their way here. Where are you?'

'I'm just approaching Inverness. Been driving all night, I tried to get you there and on your mobile.' She sounds annoyed at me, but the plight of the rural highlands telecoms situation is hardly my fault. I do however feel slightly guilty that my alcohol-induced sleep may have contributed to me not hearing the phone downstairs. No need to let Zoe know that though. 'Yeah, no signal here and I can't hear the office phone from my room.'

'Bloody hell. Anyway, there's no point going through this now. See you whenever I get past this fucking blizzard.' A click tells me that our conversation is over.

I head back upstairs and into the shower, which along with a couple of painkillers helps to edge the hangover out a little. I put on some clean clothes and go back down to make some calls. A few of the recently-released drivers might be sober enough and willing to help, after their big night in the pub. I get the numbers from Gillian, who seems OK with me, and then get through to three of them who agree to come in, be with me by the early afternoon.

After I close the third call, I remember the gun cabinet. There's a toolkit sitting with Gilfillan's yellow jacket and hard hat on the corner, so it takes no time to prise the door open and let me see what we've got to work with. There are four decent shotguns, boxes of cartridges, a crossbow and bolts and two hunting knives. It's enough for what we need and a well-done to Gilfillan for having them handy. Actually, I think, he needs to be here too, so I get his number too and call him. He answers the phone but I can tell he's rough, although I am in no position to criticise.

'Magnus, is that you?' I hear what sounds like the phone handset being dropped.

'Aye'

He must be trying to figure out what day it is and where he should be.

'It's Adam Darnow; can you come up to the House? Sir Mathieson is coming and we need all hands on deck. Get yourself ready quick; a few of the guys are coming in too. It's a security thing so get yourself sorted, OK?'

'Aye.' He grunts and the phone goes dead. Fuck sake, never work with addicts, I think to myself, not for the first time.

I have a quick chat with Eilidh and Gillian and they set to organising for the arrival of the owners. There's plenty of food and drink in, but the house staff are not, so we all pitch in and get rooms ready. Gillian comes with me to check the rooms for the Allantons and get the fires going to take the chill from the unused space.

'How are you feeling?' She smiles with slight concern in her voice.

'Rough, but getting there thanks. How about you?' I can tell she's feeling fragile too.

'I was spaced out when I got up. Much better now after coffee and fresh air.' We look out the window and the snow looks about 2 feet deep now, worse where it's drifted.

'At least my dad likes you now.' She smiles.

'Why?' I have some gaps in my memory from the latter part of the previous evening.

'If anyone can drink that amount of whisky with him and give him a good argument about what to do with the country, he'll be your friend forever.' I nod, but not having a fully clear memory of that part of the evening, I find myself at something of a disadvantage. It sounds like I have been capable of speaking coherently, so it might not all be bad. I decide to confess my alco-amnesia.

'I can't remember all of that conversation, thanks to the whisky I guess. Not used to it.'

She has a laugh at my expense then turns and holds my hands.

'After you and dad kept the neighbours awake with singing "Flower of Scotland", you both decided that independence was the only viable choice for Scotland and he celebrated by passing out on the sofa.'

'I didn't think that I knew all the words to "Flower of Scotland."'

'You don't, dad kept you right. How is your memory after that?'

'It's fine, thanks. I mean especially the bit where we actually spent a few moments together.'

She goes over and locks the door, walks back to me and despite her parent's admirable efforts, we are finally alone.

We fix up the bed again and put the fire on, ready for Sir Mathieson, laughing together at our post-adolescent behaviour and me feeling again that I've partly returned to humanity but am still tethered to the Portfolio. If this last incident with Sir Mathieson is serious enough I might have to get back into character again, although I'm not sure if I can, not here and not with Gillian. We touch hands and kiss and then we're off our separate ways again, for now.

I get downstairs and remember that Zoe will be here shortly, so get the cold-weather gear that's left in Gilfillan's office on and head out to check if there's any sign of intruders in the grounds. It's a job made easy by the snow, virgin and pristine around the perimeter of the House and gardens, its rate of fall abating helpfully to let me look round. The shotgun is fairly light and I've got it loaded but not locked, the better not to blow my own head off if I fall in the snow. Five minutes later and I've finished my reconnoitre, all is well apart from maybe a couple of areas, maybe the snow would have covered tracks since yesterday, and I start back up to the House as the four-wheel drives crunch their way from the driveway. It's the guys from the village and Magnus, in two vehicles and looking like it was a struggle to make it through. They get out and head for me.

'Thanks for coming lads. Get inside and get a gun, then one of you get back to the entrance and wait. One of you can walk over to the garage and get the heater on, keep an eye on the back road over there. Magnus, you stay here with me.' They nod silently as is their manner and head off to follow my instructions. The respite in the snow is over and it is on again with a vengeance, much heavier than before and cutting visibility down to ten or so metres. I stand silently with Magnus until the men get back out. I give them a quick rundown of the situation, at least as much as I know.

'What's the main road like?' I ask them.

'It's near ready to shut sir. The main parts are passable, but the drifts are getting really bad. If Sir Mathieson is coming later, he'll maybe not even get past Lairg unless the snowploughs are out.'

I wonder if we need a Plan B here, maybe I should re-route them if I can contact John. It's OK making this place as secure as possible, but it's no damn good if we're stuck in here and he's on the open road with his two main men and a couple of reluctant ex-soldiers. Maybe it's nothing but we've got to assume it's a genuine threat and might happen again, so I am pleased to see Zoe arrive in her rather battered Skoda Yeti, skidding her way along the tracks that the four-wheel drives made. She can't quite force her car the full way to a parking area, but gets far enough so that it's not blocking the other cars. She gets out, lifts a rather hefty shoulder bag and walks towards me. I take it from her and we head inside, leaving

Magnus to watch the door and the other men to take up their posts.

'How was your trip?' I look at her and she seems frazzled.

'Fucking worst ever, thanks. I even hit a low wall when I was outside the village, I couldn't tell where the road was and where the pavement started.'

'That's easy, there's hardly any pavement in the village. Come in, we'll get a coffee and you can fill me in.'

We head down to the kitchen and I manage to put the kettle on and make us both a hot drink.

'It's fucking freezing in here.' She looks round at the white-tiled Victorian-era space, her breath visible in the beneath-ground level chill.

'Yeah, I think the heating isn't quite up to the task. Better to keep your jacket on unless there's a fire in the room.'

She pulls her phone out and tries in vain to check her messages. Two seconds later it's back in her pocket after she realises I wasn't kidding about the signal here.

'Tell me about Balliol. What happened?' I ask.

'No idea what happened to him in London. Disappeared, presumably of his own volition, or so I thought. We didn't have eyes on him all the time; we had his phone tracked though. It was switched off until a single brief point, and that's the problem.'

I know Zoe is worried, or she wouldn't be here in person.

'I've left Williams in temporary charge in London because the last signal we had for Tim was up here. Just a few seconds, but his phone activated in GPS coordinates in the area just south of here, either the signal was lost then or the phone deactivated. Either way, for some reason, Tim Balliol is up here and I have no fucking clue why.'

'Would John have him brought here and not told us?'

She shakes her head. 'I've asked him straight out, there's no way he made this happen. I've worked through all the possibilities. Balliol could possibly have been able to see Inverannan as an asset on our property database, although that wasn't the area of business he was working on. As to why he would disappear and come here, that's another matter. If he was brought here, and it wasn't John, then I have no suggestions.' Zoe takes a drink and makes a face, which suggests my coffee is not of high quality. I let her drink it while I think out loud.

'There are a few things we're not seeing here. Someone has a go at Sir Mathieson, with enough nerve and money to do it abroad. Then Balliol either comes here or is brought up here, or at least his phone is. All this in the week when we close down business and pay off the teams, it doesn't make sense. Our drivers reported seeing footprints around here yesterday, one guy he says. Might be an intruder or just a poacher, I've not seen anything since.'

We sit in silence for a few minutes, until interrupted by Eilidh.

'There's a call for you.' I follow her back to the office, telling Zoe that we'll sort out a bedroom for her when I get back.

I get in and pick up the receiver after a single ring. 'Hello'

'It's me.' John Allanton has, by the sound of it, got back to Scotland.

'Is everything OK?'

'Yes, so far. The guys have just picked us up, but it's heavy snow. What's it like there?'

I check out the window at the snowy murkiness.

'It's pretty bad. If it keeps going you might struggle to get through.' I can hear him exhale.

'No, we're in the four-wheel drives, we'll keep going. Have you got any help in?'

I tell him the limited arrangements we have for security. He doesn't criticise but I can tell he's not sure about this. He's even less sure when I tell him about Tim Balliol's phone signal and he drops the call to speak to Sir Mathieson. He calls back a few minutes later.

'We'll keep going, if the road is blocked, we'll turn back and stay somewhere anonymous. We'll either be there in a couple of hours or I'll call you later. In the meantime, work with Zoe; see if you can figure out what the hell is going on with Balliol.'

I agree and close the call, although what I can do about Balliol is something of a mystery. If he's up here, there are a limited number of places he could conceivably be staying, although this would take some systematic checking. I head down to get Zoe, but Gillian has already put her in a comfortable room with the benefit of a seriously warm coal fire. They have clearly been having a discussion, but I'm not sure of the subject, just that they stopped talking when they heard me approaching.

'I just spoke with John. We need to sort some tactics out here.'

Gillian stands and makes for the door, but I ask her to stay. We need local knowledge to find Balliol and the only actual professional we have in the house is Magnus

Gilfillan, who I have left guarding the door and whom I wouldn't trust to find his arse with both hands and a map right now. This gives me an idea and Gillian helpfully tells us that the library is a good place to start, which I really should have thought of. We head down there, back into the chill of the main hall and the only slightly better library room. Gillian checks a cupboard and finds rolls of estate maps and some of the wider area, collated by the looks of it by the previous and late Estate Manager, George Galloglas, during his period of highland expansion.

We settle on an OS map which covers part of the area around Inverannan, plus a couple of estate maps which show the proximity of the House in more detail. It appeared that George Galloglas genuinely coveted the neighbouring land and had gone to some expense to determine who owned what and how much each parcel was worth. Each of these maps was accompanied with a printed list of the owners and their contact details. A few were known to Gillian, some had changed hands in the past two years and one or two she'd never heard of. After an hour and a half, we had identified eight properties outside the village, which fitted the bill of being near Inverannan House, remote enough and who the occupants were unknown or were holiday lets. Of these, two were small, remote cottages at the end of roads on higher ground which meant we wouldn't be able to get in and, most probably, they wouldn't be able to get in or out either. The other six were near enough a main road to be theoretically accessible; that is if we took Magnus' Land Rover and the weather improved. I head along the corridor and see him looking out his office window.

125

'I've been going in and out. No signs of anyone sir.' I nod and ask him about the Land Rover. He agrees but tells me that it's still coming down and maybe by the morning no-one will be driving anywhere. I can't do anything about the weather, so I shrug and leave him to his vigil, going out for another walk around the perimeter before heating myself up at the now-active Aga, left with something cooking, ready for Sir Mathieson. The office team have all come in today despite the weather, the full complement of six needed to make sense of Magnus Gilfillan's paperwork shambles and get the resultant disputes resolved in the correct order. They are planning to leave later in a large and robust looking seven-seat Jeep which belongs to one of Eilidh's daughters, who is stuck at home unable to get to her work in Scourie due to the weather.

Half an hour later I'm relieved to see reflected lights of vehicles coming along the driveway and I walk up and outside to meet Sir Mathieson, Benny and John, with great relief. They slide out and greet me with handshakes. Sir Mathieson and Benny look the same as ever and well, John less so, no doubt concerned over this unexpected threat to his father. We get straight inside the now-busy house and, with Zoe, into the library, which is warmed by a well-stacked coal fire in the hearth. Jackets off, I fetch the three of them whiskies and prepare to have our first collective briefing since the incident on the yacht. I am as yet unable to connect the dots of the overall situation, our last week in the business, the Treasurer and the attempt on Sir Mathieson's life, all without visible cause but perhaps down to coincidences, as sometimes happen in life.

I hear the phone ring distantly in the office and my name is called; I run along the corridor into the office and am passed the handset by Eilidh who looks stressed. I hear the voice of Williams, back at London and obviously lost without the contact of those of us stranded in the western highlands. He's blabbering so I get him to slow down and try to make out what he's saying.

He grunts annoyed, frustrated at the situation and my ongoing lack of understanding of his dense South London accent. His voice becomes slower now, enunciating for my benefit.

'Is Sir Mathieson there yet? I have to speak with him urgently. It's nothing to do with that other thing'

He clearly just wants the boss rather than me, so I pass the handset back to Eilidh and ask her to transfer it to the library extension. I walk back, to see Sir Mathieson listening intently to Williams and occasionally prompting him for further details. He asks him to check the details again and closes the call, turning to us with a grimace.

'Adam, Zoe, I must thank you for your sterling efforts on my behalf.' He raises his glass to us and takes a decent swig.

'Williams has been trying to find out from every remaining source about the fire on my yacht. It looks like this was a contract allocated to someone abroad, identity as yet unknown. The other piece of information, from a reliable source in the market, is that after this failed another contract has been allocated within the UK. The good news is that we know who they are and where they are going.' He grins in my direction and I have a distinct feeling that he's about to land me with something. He finishes his malt, pours another one, and I wish he'd just fucking get on with it.

'The contract appears to have been allocated to siblings of an individual, who you apparently terminated some time ago on behalf of the business, apparently in the outer Manchester area. The brothers go by the name of Hannaway.'

I look at John and he looks at me. I remember the guy, but not his surname, he had a nickname like they all do but it evades me.

John pitches in. 'So, what is this? Are they taking the contract to get paid for some coincidental personal revenge on us?'

'So it would appear, unlikely as it seems. We already had them tagged as being one of the potential threats, and this confirms it.'

This is a serious problem. We don't have much manpower up here and have effectively disbanded our reserves. This leaves us with only a few professionals and whoever in the area we can persuade to help.

John goes on. 'So where are they heading? How many are there?'

Sir Mathieson seems to be stifling laughter. 'There are, Williams thinks, potentially four of them, probably well-armed and destined not here, but for the manse.' I know that the Allantons have the other place up here, but I'm not sure exactly where it is. Zoe looks as unclear as I am, so John clarifies matters.

'It's about six miles back south, through the village and down a single track. Empty currently. It's remote, not overlooked'. I can see he's thinking about this, maybe even got a solution.

'Perfect for an ambush' Sir Mathieson volunteered, looking my way and giving me his finest beatific smile.

14   UP, UP AND HANNAWAY

The second contract to assassinate Sir Mathieson had
been allocated to a crew of four brothers with
professional and personal reasons to despise the Allanton
crime clan. The fifth brother, rather the Alfredo
Corleone of their family, had been terminated by one of
the Allanton senior men, a young Scottish guy with a
reputation for harshness even in their business, about six
months prior in response to some minor indiscretions.
This angered the remaining relatives and, if they were on
their estate, they would have taken revenge within days
but they knew they were out of their depth, that they
couldn't touch the real bosses without the right timing
and even then, they would have to go into hiding for a
long time afterwards, which was expensive and
problematic. So, they had gathered intelligence, better
than the cops could have, asked questions and tried to
piece together who was really running the show. They
followed the Scottish guy twice, losing him the first time
in traffic, but the second time they stayed with him
through the outer London chaos, into the centre, running
red lights to stay with him until he stopped in a posh
business area. They couldn't get parked, so they left their
driver to circle around the streets and the three others
went on foot after their quarry, following him to an office
block where they could get no further. There was a
plaque on the entrance with a list of occupant companies,
so they took a photo of that and left, to restart their
enquiries; there were twelve businesses listed, so more
research was needed. It took them a few weeks to get the
information they needed on each; three were possible, all
investment organisations of one kind or another. Further
digging left them with just one, a Property Asset

Management and Investment House, which after paying a hefty sum to a contact, was found to be a global concern with a trail which suggested the owners were trying very, very hard not to be found by the general public. There were however enough threads to lead their paid expert to the Allanton family, and the realisation that their enemies were in the top-tiers of the business world.

So, they waited, despite temptation and the oft drug-induced revenge tantrums of the youngest brother. They waited and planned, just as Sir Mathieson would have, with great care and regard to the aftermath. When they were told the unexpected and sudden news that their narcotics supply was to cease, that was the catalyst for them to act. They silently accepted their pay-offs from their boss, given to him by the Scottish guy who had carried out the murder of their brother.

From that point, the planning became a reality.

The youngest of the brothers, Warren, since being discharged from the army after four years and of that, six months in its penal system, had been carrying out a series of paid assaults and murders in and around the Midlands. He gratefully accepted the down payment on a new contract which, after receiving the call, turned into an exceptional piece of good luck when he realised that he was about to be paid a six-figure sum for murdering the man he was about to kill anyway. He did not, after some consideration, decide to share this information with his older siblings, primarily as it allowed him to keep the money, but also as they had recently been making him feel like something of an arsehole. He dealt drugs, as they all did, but he took them too and in prodigious quantities which caused some heinous behaviour that even his appalling family frowned upon. A strong lad, he would get an idea into his head almost every weekend that someone or other from the estate was disrespecting him and then, then it was a problem for all of them. That week, after a seriously mind-damaging binge, he had added to his ongoing catalogue of assaults, threats, thefts and generally psychotic behaviour by almost beheading the scion of a neighbouring narcotics family who, even if they were in an inferior position, would certainly take revenge. So, the day after the partial beheading, they decanted from their flat and their business, leaving the estate forever, their pay-off from the Allanton clan already transferred by courier to Spain along with their savings from years of dealing and all their possessions not already impounded by the Police under the Proceeds of Crime Act. These possessions were shipped to the oldest brother's house outside Benidorm where his partner would prepare for their arrival, once their business in the UK was complete.

They rented an Air BnB for an overnight near Carlisle and from there, made preparations for the reprisals against the Allantons. They had weapons aplenty and, without explaining the secondary rewards of the paid contract, young Warren furnished his siblings with the information he had been given on the location and expected arrival time of their target. He simply told them that he had been doing some digging on his own and that he'd done it well, no further chat required.

They arranged for their getaway via departure flights, two of them leaving from Glasgow Airport and two from Edinburgh to the Spanish mainland, to begin an extended holiday away from the tribulations of the aftermath of their mission and any reprisals from this or the problem back at the estate. They would raid the Allanton's property, deal with the occupants quickly, ruthlessly and leave no clues, no prints and no DNA before driving south, swapping their van for two other cars they had with them, which would in turn be left on the outskirts of Glasgow and Edinburgh respectively before taxis took them the last leg of their escape from the UK. After that, a year or two in Spain would be just reward for their long-term efforts, maybe even open a nightclub, they thought. When Warren was emailed his final instructions for finding the Allantons and the second payment landed in his account; then it was time to implement their plan. They were all straight for the trip, no chances taken with this one, but Warren had a bag of high-grade coke, just in case he got nervous.

Their cars and the van each had fake plates, made in the garage which had so recently served as the front for their business. These were copied from genuine plates from similar cars, so if they were spotted by the cops, it would lead them to some innocent mug who had the misfortune to own a vehicle like theirs. Thus assured of anonymity, they set off on an icy morning for the long drive north, guns hidden under the false floor of the van and heading for Aviemore where the two cars could be left parked safely in a large and unsupervised hotel car park until needed again for the escape south.

The trip was straightforward despite the conditions; after parking the cars in nondescript locations, they met up in Aviemore's main street for some food. They were hardly likely to raise an eyebrow in a tourist town, although they did still stand out somewhat from the skiing crowd and families milling around the shops. Partly this was because they were dressed like chav gangsters in predominantly black clothing, but also because of the second oldest brother, Darren, had long since lost one of his ears back in Salford during an unsuccessful knife fight a few years before and tried to deflect from the loss by having the rest of his face tattooed with the image of a spiders web. Notwithstanding, they managed to negotiate a bakery lunch without incident, before crunching through the snow to the van and onwards to the far north. After they had driven a few miles from the town, it became apparent that the van's heating facilities had, unfortunately, ceased to function; a perfunctory check by the brothers indicated, after various disagreements, that perhaps the resistor, the valve or even the heater motor were indeed fucked. After donning the few pieces of cold-weather clothing they had brought with them, they continued north and past Inverness to the Western Highlands.

After an hour, they were free of any traffic and skidding slowly along the route they selected; inside the vehicle, the oldest brother, Geordie, drove with fingers almost blue from the sub-zero draught coming through the vents, not helped by the failure of the passenger window to completely close. Geordie, or Codheid as he was known due to an unusually angular visage and widely spaced eyes, was now opining with some loquacity, that they should have used an earlier plan which involved a trip to murder their target in London. Too cold to argue, even Warren was quiet, huddled into his jacket and wondering when he would have the first chance to sneak a couple of lines to make the experience less miserable. He was stymied in this regard as there was nowhere suitable to stop and the snow had got to the point where he wondered if they would all die up here anyway, in the icy cold of the van.

Eventually, Codheid managed to negotiate the van towards their destination, at the end of the longest road he'd ever driven. His hands were like clawed talons and the slight cold he felt back in England now felt like full-blown influenza, his throat almost closed and raspily painful. Collectively, in the fridge-like interior of the van, they scanned the map they had brought with them and agreed that they were not only on the right track, but almost there. There were very few houses in the area and after a check on the snow-covered plaque at the driveway pillars, Codheid confirmed that they had arrived at the location provided by Warren. They had planned to observe the house for an hour or two, but weather conditions and their desire to get back to the central belt was the catalyst for a group decision to just kick the door in and shoot the fuckers. So, in the driving snow and braving a wind chill of around minus 12 degrees, the Hannaway brothers gathered up their sawn-offs, a Czech sub-machine gun which they had got from a contact in London and a pistol each.

A renewed determination caught them, plus a few minutes in the cab alone gave Warren the chance to sort himself out with coke, so they were all locked and loaded by the point Codheid closed the back door of the van and gestured them to follow him. They walked slowly through the drifts at the stone-pillared entrance to the property. There were a few signs that others had walked this way recently, leading to the front door which was a solid-looking wooden job, studded with iron rivets and presenting them with their first challenge. Shushing the negativity from his brothers, Codheid gestured them to listen to him as he tried to explain that they would need to find a window to get through, maybe around the other side of the house, but to stay down so that they couldn't

135

be seen from inside. Warren watched him, heart pumping and desperate to get going, get a few shots at the bastards who had done their brother in. What puzzled Warren was that his oldest brother's head wasn't the same as it had been a moment ago. It was all over the door and there hadn't been any noise. They turned around, guns pointing into the snowy darkness. Darren fell next, then the other brother, Sammy, leaving Warren to spray the darkness with the Skorpion submachine gun until his clip was emptied. He stopped, bereft of ammunition and the ringing silence giving him hope that he'd got the bastards. This was disproved a moment later when he felt a bullet thud directly into the centre of his chest and he joined his brothers on the reddening doorstep of the former manse. A minute later, three men carrying long rifles walked over and with a few succinct prods to the splattered Hannaways, confirmed their demise. Together, they dismantled their weapons into the long backpacks specially designed to hold their expensive components, tight in the tailor-made compartments. This complete, one of them walked off alone; back to his vehicle which was parked a mile or so farther down the road, leaving the others to do the cleaning up.

Neither of these men minded the cleaning up work they were sometimes allocated by Sir Mathieson, overall, but this bit was a real pain in the arse, especially in this weather. Still, it paid well enough for them to put up with the odd bit of carcass disposal.

They walked back to fetch their four-wheel drive and got their coveralls and gloves on, having already sealed the back of the separated cab with plastic sheeting. They sorted out the correct number of body bags and left the spares, and then set to hauling the Hannaways into them and thence to the cab. The gore-strewn snow was a slight issue; however, experience always provided a solution. They shovelled the offending snow into the other six spare body bags until it just looked like someone had cleared the snow from the front door, even throwing a generous amount of rock salt down to complete the deception. Almost exactly thirty minutes since the Hannaways walked into the driveway, they were being driven back out and their van with them, to a disposal facility which the Allanton's men had used before, a few times. The Hannaways cars, back in Aviemore, were impounded by the Police some time later and, thanks to the scrupulous anonymity of their preparation, never linked to their mission or the disposal of the brothers.

Their only close living relative, the partner of the unfortunate Codheid, would quickly come to the realisation that the brothers were not coming to stay with her in the sanctuary of the Costa Blanca. Their flight missed, their mobiles dead and the lack of communication were sure signs that, whatever the pack of arseholes had been up to, it hadn't worked out. She fleetingly thought about trying to locate them, to bring closure to the mystery, but the twelve current bank accounts she managed on their behalves yielded enough motivation to remain silent on the matter and let them fade into the murky background of petty criminal history. After a decent but brief period, she sold the house near Benidorm and moved to a more upmarket location. She adroitly shifted the disparate monies a few times through her own accounts and added the brother's redundancy cash which had arrived by courier, then finally, she reactivated her little-known given surname and settled into a long, well-funded and sunshine-cheered early retirement, Codheid and the Hannaways part of her well-forgotten past.

15   AFTER THE HIT

The Hitman sat in the bar in Menorca, watching the fire
on the yacht being extinguished and drinking as much
beer and whisky as he could, as quickly as he could, to
shut out the miserable reality of his failure. People and
Police came and went, the fire became extinguished and
the billowing smoke gradually evaporated, with eventually
just a few plumes visible as they dissipated into the night
sky. He paid his bar bill, lurched back to his hotel and
arranged to stay another night, paying by cash and
dumping his rucksack in the new room before emerging
into the dusk of the resort to continue his self-pitying
bender.

It was fully light when he awakened, again uncertain how
he arrived back at his room. After being noisily sick in
the bathroom toilet, he showered and gathered up his
clothes into the rucksack. He went down to the dining
room for what he realised would be lunch and sat sadly
until he had the energy to call his erstwhile comrade back
in the UK and report his failure. It was while he sat at the
phone table in reception that he noticed the two men,
one being his actual target and the other a younger man
with dark hair and a palpable air of concern. Heart
thumping, he leaned back to the edge of the reception
desk, just behind a dividing wall and shielded from their
sight. Although he couldn't catch all of their
conversation, he did hear enough to know they were
bound for Inverness Airport and somewhere he thought
was called Inverannan or Inverarnan. There was still
hope here, if he just got more time and maybe even could
agree on a fee to cover his mistake. He didn't want to
risk being caught listening in, so as the two men rose, he

ducked down low and rushed upstairs to quit his room to start a new, better plan.

After one more extremely uncomfortable phone call to the UK, he was back on the mission. It took some convincing and some bullshit he made up about the target moving after the arrangements were made; the kind of situation, he told his contact, which could happen to anyone who tried an assassination in a public place. The call ended on a sourer note, however. This was a high-level gig, he already knew from the remuneration, but there was a strong implicit threat that a second bungled attempt could result in not only a failure to pay him but also a highly displeased customer who may take punitive action. There were a lot of unexpected words for him to process, but he knew a threat when he heard it and with a promise to deal with it as soon as possible, he rallied and prepared for a flight to Scotland.

A quick check online at the hotel showed no flights that day to Inverness or Aberdeen from Menorca; he cursed himself at the realisation that his target would be on a private charter. He bought a one-way ticket to Edinburgh Airport for late that evening and, booking out of the hotel again, got a taxi to Mahon to wait for it to come round. He needn't have bothered rushing, a two-hour delay meant that he emerged into the late winter chill of the early hours at Edinburgh Airport, dressed in clothing which was fine for the Mediterranean but not so much for the biting winds in the east of Scotland. He caught a taxi into the centre of Edinburgh, only then realising that as well as being one of the most expensive places to get a hotel room in the country, that the chances of getting into one without booking at 2am was virtually a non-starter.

Eventually, and after much expense and advice from the taxi driver, he found an establishment willing to take a poorly dressed blue-faced gentleman of ample proportions, and spent the last hours of darkness thawing out in a boutique hotel room which cost more than his flight. The next morning, turning down the option of an eye-wateringly expensive breakfast and opting for a cheaper McDonald's version instead, he sat mentally planning his next sortie. There were two place names to research, so a visit to a library would help there. He had no weaponry; consequently he would have to improvise. This would mean buying a knife at least, a simple thing he knew but he needed the right thing. A serrated one if he could get it, ideally suited to what he had in mind and similar to his own one which was probably still in the blue sports bag in thirty feet of water in Menorca. He wasn't going to give up all that money just because of some bad luck though. It kept repeating in his mind, the disaster at the marina. The two main things that bounced around in his head; firstly when he swung the bag around and the weight of the Semtex made it heavy at one end, making it fall into the water; secondly, his failure to recognise the target. He had been sent to assassinate Sir Mathieson Allanton but had failed to kill even the wrong target. At least he'd bluffed his way out of that situation, but the only way back was to keep going after the old bugger and take him down properly. He blamed it on the waiting he had to endure, making him fill the time with beer which always did rob him of his focus.

Other than the shame and possible threats of failure for this mission, his main underlying motivation was to get out of this with the money. He had initially retired to Mallorca with his wife, with plans of idyllic days in the sun and evenings out on the balcony with a glass of wine.

They bought a villa with a small pool and he just felt like a winner, back at the start. The first winter though, she got bored and joined a Learn Conversational Spanish group at an ex-pat friend's house. It really seemed to perk her up, until she announced that she didn't love him anymore, well she loved him but wasn't *in* love with him anymore. He'd been told some harsh words in his life, but those words were like the death of his soul. She left to go and live in Malaga with the Conversational Spanish tutor and, via her bloody lawyer, took half the villa and a dispiritingly large chunk of his army pension. Back then he had thought about ending his life, there in his shitty little apartment in Mallorca, but he came through it on his own, damaged but maybe inherently stronger and he knew that, if he could come through that, he could do anything.

Fired up by these memories and with the determination of the serial loser, the rest of that day was productive for him, as he prepared for his second attempt on the life of Sir Mathieson Allanton. He threw money to the wind and equipped himself with the right camouflage gear from an army surplus store he located just outside the city centre. He told them he was finishing up his arrangements for a fishing trip up north and bought a lock knife as if it were on the spur of the moment. With the cost of the gear, tent, rucksack, rations, binoculars, sleeping bag and boots, he spent almost 700 pounds on his credit card, which, added to the financial pain caused by the Menorca debacle, his flight and the Edinburgh hotel, meant that he really, really, needed the contract payment after this. The Hitman knew, literally, that he could not afford to fail this time. He bought a fishing rod and equipment in another shop, more for appearances than any intent to use them.

A series of online searches at the Central Library identified Sir Mathieson Allanton as a retired military man, who some time ago left a distinguished career for a quiet life in the west highlands of Scotland. Putting the descriptions together, it was 100% clear that Inverannan was the destination. Further searching on news items revealed that Inverannan House was the only big place up there, some kind of former corporate hunting and shooting lodge. He figured that this would be the type of place someone like Allanton would go live in, which was confirmed by an old news story about his target being knighted for services to military charities and which included an interview quote where he offered the helpful and perhaps unwisely-shared information that he was about to be part of a project to reinvigorate a highland estate with some former comrades. He could see why the old man would retreat there for safety, but he knew that safety was never assured, that he had to complete this mission regardless of how remote or difficult it would prove to be. With a reversal of his bad luck in Menorca, the Hitman knew it was still within his abilities to complete the operation this time around. Exhausted from lack of sleep and exertion, he sorted his travel arrangements for the next day and booked into a budget hotel for the night. A late trip to a bookshop provided an Ordnance Survey map for the Inverannan area and then he devoured a pizza in a cheap café before settling into his hotel for the night. He would not drink any booze on this trip; he felt embarrassed at his prior conduct and knew deep down that was the reason he blew the mission in Menorca. Tired from the previous day's efforts and without the impediment of alcohol, he fell into a blissfully deep sleep before his alarm wakened him for the long journey north.

It took him two trains, then an appallingly rattling bus journey in poor conditions and a long walk in the snow to get him to his off-road approach to Inverannan and the start of his final insurgence. He'd spent much of his time on the expedition examining the map in close detail, selecting the most appropriate points where he could reach Inverannan House and commence surveillance. He noted wooded areas, ruins and any other points where he would either avoid or perhaps seek shelter. No Bed and Breakfasts on this one, he thought, this is just me back at army training, Hampstead Heath and all that, pissing down with rain and surviving it, loving it even, at times. He was older now and a few stones heavier, but that would be OK.

There was absolutely no-one around when he left the bus, just snow, wind and the cold, biting at his face. There were no cars and the sound of the wind was all that he could hear, except the creaking newness of his jacket and the pounding of his heart as he crossed a fence and set off for the valley between two hills which protected Inverannan from the south-east. There was an outline route, of sorts, to follow but it took him longer than he hoped to trek the three miles to the beginning of the valley, the snow up to his knees but deeper in some places. It was on a gradual rise and the daylight was getting away from him, so he found a flat spot to set up his tent under some covering trees in the sheltered forest floor, protected from the worst of the snow. Momentarily wishing he had brought a bottle of whisky with him, he started on his rations and water, before trying to sleep despite the cacophony of creaking forest branches, bird and animal sounds which seemed never to cease.

His sleep was broken a few times by sudden loud wailing noises, foxes he thought and a number of other indistinguishable rackets from above and around the tent. He eventually rose with the daylight and ate some more rations, staying in his sleeping bag until he summoned the willpower to get his boots on and stow the tent and kit. It was a grey, dry morning but bad weather didn't seem too far away. He also knew that, in this remote and unforgiving place of snow and few strangers, he would have to be doubly careful to approach his target without warning. He reckoned that it would be another good six miles until he reached the house, doable on a track but tricky through snow-covered heather and the dips and folds of this terrain. This proved a fairly decent prediction, especially as his own weight combined with the rucksack made him somewhat clumsy and top-heavy. He tripped and fell a couple of times, but his inner strength kept him going. By late lunchtime, he had emerged from the valley and had his first view of the estate where his quarry waited.

It was a rather grand sight to behold, the house itself a confection of turrets and granite, surrounded on the two sides he could see by tiered, walled gardens and circled by a mixture of forest and snow-smoothed clear land. What was less cheering was the number of staff moving around the grounds. It looked like a hard place to approach unseen, a busy estate with a number of vehicles and workers coming and going, including a fair few heading out by van. This meant that any surveillance he was going to carry out would need to be started after they all left for the day, whatever time that might be. If he had to use the cover of early evening darkness, it would limit him to a start around perhaps 6.30 pm at this time of year, this far north. So, he settled down in a copse of trees and bushes with a good view of the house in the distance, settling on a route which appeared to be well enough hidden until he was near it. He nodded off for a short time, wakening up to see that there were fewer vehicles parked at the house and those left were mainly four-wheel drives, not the vans and pickups of the estate workers. This looked like the time to begin his approach to the target and commence close surveillance.

The first part of the journey towards the house had the tremendous advantage of being predominantly downhill. He had wearied badly through the valley but now felt some progress was achievable with the assistance of gravity and the motivational impact of nearing his objective. He was some way away from the road on his left and Inverannan village itself was also a fair distance away in that direction, so he was unlikely to be spotted by someone unless they were off the estate roads too. Still, he took the cautious approach from his army days, stopping regularly and ensuring that he was not making noise or leaving obvious tracks, a tricky task for his frame, the hefty rucksack he carried and the snow-covered hillside.

Another half-hour took him to a point where he could get a close look at Inverannan House, so he climbed upwards through a line of prominent conifers on his right-hand side to gain a better view of the windows. He had sight of a couple of storage buildings and a solitary cottage or bothy but hadn't seen anyone on the grounds during his approach. Cautiously, he made his way to the last trees on the edge of the snowy approach, giving him a view into the windows of the building, just as the daylight faded. He crouched for around half an hour, only seeing shadows passing the windows on the second floor and figuring that, at this time, the occupants may be either at dinner or in some kind of lounge. The side door opened and a tall, rangy man emerged unsteadily and lit a cigarette. The fellow appeared slightly drunk and, before he ventured back inside, spent a long moment looking upwards to the sky. Thicker, heavier flakes of snow started falling and he decided to retrace his steps and get his tent up, just in case. It was noticeably colder since he had stopped walking and the sweat he had generated had left him soaked and shivering. It took another hour to find somewhere suitably hidden and make camp, the snow falling constantly now but soon he was inside the tent and sleeping bag, asleep in no time after his labours took their toll.

It was bright and cold when Tim awakened in the cottage, the cover having fallen off his body while he slept leaving him numb and shivering. He stood up, pulling the duvet around him and wandered around the cottage looking for some form of central heating until he realised that there were no radiators and that the building was indeed not equipped with that facility. There was a fireplace however he didn't fancy being caught as a result of sending smoke signals to the enemy. In the kitchen cupboards, he discovered a hot water bottle and, after using a kettle to fill it and then figuring out how to operate the stove, made some hot soup from a tin he found in the cupboard. He had been so focused on his escape that he hadn't realised that he hadn't eaten in twenty-six hours, far from his normal four-hour maximum gap between meals. He cleaned up the dishes and looked at his pile of clothes, a mass of mud, blood and holes, but they were all he had. There was a washing machine of sorts in the kitchen, which after some deliberation he successfully managed to operate it, shoving all his clothes into what he hoped would be the correct wash setting to make them clean again. He also found a small hotel-style sewing kit in the kitchen, left no doubt with all the rest of it for tenants of this rustic holiday home. There were brochures on a table near the door, which after a quick perusal, showed him that he was in a real off-grid part of the west highlands of Scotland, almost at the coast. There weren't any actual towns nearby, just a couple of what looked like hamlets or villages, one just a few miles away.

Tim knew that contacting the Police was not an option for him. Being kidnapped from his job as an accountant for one gang of criminals by what might well be the previous gang of criminals who employed him was unlikely to end well for him. He was an office-dweller and did not relish at all the thought of jail time, especially if they found out that he was the accountant for vast mob fortunes and he was the only bloke who knew where the money was. He'd be tortured for the information and dead inside a week.

Instead, Tim understood that he had to use a more self-reliant method to make good his escape and reach his destination. In a facility just outside Knightsbridge, he had a safety deposit box holding, with the utmost security and reliability, his passport, another false passport, genuine and fake birth certificates to match, his qualification certificates, eighteen thousand pounds sterling and three hundred and sixty-five thousand euros in a mixture of hard cash and a scatter of global accounts in his real and assumed names. It was Tim's bug-out bag, set up for a time when everything would go wrong for him, full of the monies skimmed unnoticed from each of his employers; some of it had been written off as fees and bribes to contacts who only occasionally received their full payment and other amounts just plain stolen from those who were foolish enough to trust him. To get to Knightsbridge from here was now his challenge and one which he would not shirk. He knew that he had been watched 24/7 while working for Allanton, but now he wasn't and they wouldn't have a way of knowing about his safety deposit box arrangement. They would have searched his hotel room, even from the start, and maybe wondered where his passport was, but there was not one shred of information that would tell anyone about his nest egg and the Knightsbridge plan.

Tim nodded off after all that thinking, his mind calmed by the thought of retiring to a rented apartment in rural Portugal for a couple of years and consigning his current predicament to history. He was capable of communicating, or nearly so, in Portuguese as a result of a six-month sojourn there as part of his mixed-subject degree. He had loved it there, the limitations of his language having the fortunate impact of limiting his verbal capacity to piss people off. In short, the people he'd met in Portugal seemed to like Tim more than anyone he'd met since leaving university and he really, really wanted to go back there. He also knew that he could make money anywhere with a laptop, a few bank accounts and an internet connection, virtually anonymously and keeping the individual amounts low enough to remain unnoticed but high enough to enable a decent lifestyle.

First though, Tim had to escape his current predicament. He awoke after perhaps an hour of sleep and found that the washing machine had successfully done its job. The shirt was a bit grey after being washed in with the suit, but that was fine; at least the blood had mostly come out. He hung the clothes up on a hanging frame arrangement which was suspended from the kitchen ceiling and took some dexterity to keep horizontal, however by lighting the oven and leaving its door open, he managed to heat the kitchen to a point where his clothes would be dry enough to wear in a few hours. It would be the next day before he'd set out anyway, so long as no-one visited the cottage in the meantime and threw him out. He reviewed the visitor's glossies and from a tourist map, found the likely roads he'd need to take to get back south. His former captors would almost certainly be looking for him, so he'd need to be careful about hitching a lift or even stealing a car, whatever presented first, Tim thought. He had done enough walking to last him, and his legs ached like buggery as well as the various lacerations, which he daubed again with the foul pink antiseptic. He slept that night on the bed, this time more comfortably and woke to a new day, the day of his escape back to London. He'd forgotten that he'd left the oven on and the kitchen was stifling, so he turned it off and searched the cupboards for sustenance. There was very little left to eat, but he settled on a tin of potted meat and returned to the warmth of the bed to eat it, falling asleep afterwards until the nagging worry that he may get caught in this house forced him back to reality.

When he finally emerged from bed, he went to retrieve his clothes and found that the kitchen was still extraordinarily hot and the clothes were not only dry but rather crispy. He pulled the rigid clothing down from the pulley and, after carrying out some rudimentary stitching to the torn sections, donned what he realised was an uncomfortable and significantly shrunken version of his wool blend suit. He couldn't close the waist buttons, having to use the belt to keep them in place and the legs were a good three inches shorter than before. Still, it was clean and barring a few glances, would be passable enough to let him blend in. He had an outline plan to hitch a ride on an HGV or a delivery lorry south, not something he had any experience of, but without funds, his options were limited. He could try and steal money from a house or something, but the risk of getting caught was perhaps not worth it.

So, fully clothed except for the three inches above his shoes, Tim tidied the cottage to the point where it would be hard to judge if he'd ever been there with the exception of blood and pink antiseptic stains on the underside of the bedcovers. The afternoon was cold as hell and snowing again, which was not ideal. He'd found a scarf in the cottage, left by the owners or some renter, so had this around his face and mouth partly as a disguise but mainly to help with the intense cold. The knee-deep track from the cottage took some twenty minutes to negotiate, leading to another broader, fence-lined single track which was increasingly hard to walk on as the snow drove in his face and drifted in parts. Eventually, he reached a cattle grid and a T-junction with an old road sign, faded white with black lettering and border, showing Inverannan to be three miles on his left and what looked like Kinloch-something the other way, the distance rubbed off by the years. The weather was desolate, wind and snow-swept and the road did not seem to offer much to Tim in regards a hitchhike south or indeed the possibility of pinching a vehicle. Closer inspection of the road sign showed that Kinloch thingy was four times farther away than Inverannan, so deciding to walk the shorter distance to a populated place and with no idea where his captors might be, he strode as quickly as possible along the least-deep parts of the snowy road and towards his closest village, only passing a couple of houses on the way, each of them set back from the road by some distance and barely visible in the snowstorm. Tim decided against seeking shelter, better to focus on a more rapid escape to London.

It took the best part of two hours to get to Inverannan village, Tim frozen to his black office brogues and having been passed by just two vehicles the whole time. The relative silence of the snowy breeze meant that he could hear them coming, but on both occasions, there was nowhere to hide so he had to watch them pass. Both seemed to be farm-type all-terrain vehicles and neither driver, other than a vaguely suspicious glance, seemed interested in picking him up. They were both heading in the opposite direction anyway, so that was not a problem except it did give him second thoughts about the course he'd chosen. His almost complete disorientation after escaping the bothy initially meant that his subsequent choices were largely guesswork, although he had a hopeful feeling that he was heading homewards, in general. The village sign at Inverannan was a pleasant sight, followed by his even more welcome arrival at a genuinely populated village.

Tim found himself outside a rather pretty B&B, which also reminded him sharply that he had no way of paying for anything, his property having been removed by those dreadful kidnappers. In theory this would only be an issue the next morning, however, Tim knew that would just delay and increase his problems rather than helping solve them. He knocked at the door and was faced by the landlady, who after a friendly smile then regarded him with a degree of suspicion. A cheerfully energetic dog, Tim thought perhaps a Cockapoo, ran around her feet before a man's voice from inside called on him, "Fergus!" and the merry canine loped off to find his master.

'Will you be needing a room?' the landlady had an accent as soft as the snow itself and Tim indeed wanted nothing more to stay there and be fed and rested.

'No, not at present, thanks; I wondered if you know of any way I could get a lift. My car is stuck in the snow and I need to get back south urgently.' This was fairly unconvincing stuff, but apart from the world of creative accounting, Tim did not generally excel on the quick-thinking front.

She looked at him with thoughtful uncertainty. 'Well, the estate vans go up and down all the time, that's your best bet. I don't think they will be running in this weather though but you could always ask I suppose. It's a fair distance to walk to the estate in this weather – that way about half an hour – have you not got a coat?'

Tim shook his head and thanked her. She seemed about to say something but turned and closed the door as the snow thickened again in the air around him. He walked back down the path and in the direction she indicated. After an hour of walking, he reached both the entrance to the estate and the realisation that she had seriously underestimated the time needed to reach the sodding place. There was a four-wheel drive parked at the entrance, but the occupant appeared to be fast asleep. Tim had a moment's indecision about wakening him up to confirm directions but instead decided to keep going, starting another long walk in the darkened light through a snow-deepened avenue which unwittingly took him to his destination, the impressive Inverannan House, the focal point of the Estate and Highland home of his employer's father, Sir Mathieson Allanton.

17 ADAM AND ZOE GO ON AN ADVENTURE

I shoulder my rifle, leaving the manse and marching as quickly as I can back to Magnus' Land Rover, which has to be cleared of a few inches of snow before I can drive. My two colleagues for the ambush, formerly Sir Mathieson's military comrades then later his ghillies, know well what they were doing with the disposal of the bodies and can take it from here, while I head back to Inverannan. It had taken four hours to prepare, wait for them to arrive and then less than ten seconds for the three of us to kill the Hannaways. I check my watch and it's just before eight pm, I am freezing cold and want to get away from this, this shit I thought I was finished with.

The killing of my two allocated targets, the first and last of the Hannaways to enter the driveway and stand at the door, was both simple and without any associated emotion. I was far enough away not to be at risk, so my adrenalin levels were minimal, but close enough to see their faces clearly with the night sights. I recognised one of them immediately, Codheid Hannaway, his nickname and his fascinatingly piscine face. He was present at two or three of my meetings down south, but I didn't know that it was his brother I had shot that day, for theft, fraud, disloyalty or, to roll these misdemeanours together with his others, his utter pointlessness as a member of both the human race and our organisation. Partly because of this well-deserved elimination, I hadn't put him down as someone whose family might seek revenge, unlike others. Still, you never can underestimate family loyalty, I suppose.

It takes me ages to drive back to Inverannan village, which is completely blocked by snow at the far side. I consider heading to the B&B for an overnight, but I have a high-powered and decidedly illegal rifle with me which I'd prefer neither to leave in the car nor take into the Mrs MacEachen's house. The access road is impassable, so I park the four-wheel drive at the roadside and, with my gun rucksack on my back, embark on a long walk to Inverannan House. It's at least well lit by the reflective snow and I get back eventually, chilled to the bones but otherwise fine. I get in the side door past Magnus, guarding the door with more dedication than I would expect. He also appears slightly drunk, but I am too cold to care, so I leave him there, smoking, and get into his office to get changed out of my camouflage gear, lent to me along with the weapon by John's guys. I open the rucksack to clean the weapon, which I almost finish when the door opens and in comes Zoe, who must have seen me arrive.

'How did it go?' She walks over and looks at the rifle, still wet from the snow and with two fewer bullets in the clip, a Hannaway each.

'No problems. The guys are cleaning the site and they'll be back once that's done. I recognised one of the Hannaways, a guy from the Manchester area if I'm remembering correctly, odd looking bloke.'

Zoe seems relieved. 'Better get into the library and brief the boss. He'll be glad that the pressure is off, but we need to talk about who's paying the contracts.' I nod and gesture at my clothes, Zoe takes the hint that I need to get dressed and leaves me to get on with it.

Five minutes later, I'm a deal warmer and dressed in my dry jeans and shirt, heading out of Magnus' office for the library. He's waiting to get in, and I strongly suspect that he has a bottle or two of whisky secreted somewhere in there. I guess it doesn't matter now, the threat is over and he's here as a favour anyway.

Sir Mathieson, John and Zoe are waiting for me in the library. A gleaming smile from Sir Mathieson, the two men join to congratulate me on a job well done.

'We had a bet, Adam, how many rounds did it take?' Sir Mathieson is in good humour for sure, beaming at me like an adoring grandfather.

'Four. One per target.'

Sir Mathieson claps his hands once and reaches out to his son, who takes a note from his wallet and places it on his father's palm. The older man turns and, in an instant, reverts back to his military demeanour.

'Now, we have to turn our thoughts to the originator of these atrocities. Williams has been working diligently as ever on our behalf and although he has provided a deal of intelligence to Zoe, this has left us something of a puzzle.' I'm fascinated now, but I can't read Zoe's expression. Sir Mathieson continues.

'We have no reliable information on the source of the contracts as yet. They are being allocated through a third party, whom we may have circumstantially identified, although not his current whereabouts. It is possible that our investigations have already alerted him and that he will disappear for a period of time to prevent our resources from discussing this matter with him.'

John looks intense, like he's still worried as hell about the situation.

Sir Mathieson continues 'We have people actively pursuing this character; however I feel that it's unlikely that he will break cover to place another contract. This does not mean that further assassins will not be commissioned, just not from this source. We must, therefore, seek to identify the malefactor, a tricky proposition in our – former – line of business.' He walks over to the fireplace and looks to me and Zoe.

'We also have a slight problem, perhaps of my own making. I acted unilaterally, while waiting for John's arrival in Menorca, to extricate and question the chap Balliol who, as it turns out appears to have stolen quite a large sum from my personal funds, which although separate from the Portfolio, he accessed through our composite account network.'

This explains the disappearance of that little shite Balliol, but I'm still missing something, or even many things. I also notice that John isn't looking in our direction.

'I didn't disclose this to anyone else as the situation was somewhat chaotic at that point. I found myself in a position where, for which I must apologise, I had cause to take a rather defensive approach which I understand may come across as a failure on my part to trust you. I did not inform John until today, partly to prevent him from taking any actions until I could establish the exact method by which Balliol accessed a set of accounts which he had neither the security permissions nor the password required. This would have placed both of you on the list of suspects here, as you do have the security levels and I assume Balliol may have had methods of bypassing the passwords.'

Zoe looks instantly furious now and I finally understand why John has looked awkward from the moment I arrived, hardly speaking and taking an uncharacteristic back seat in the meeting. He shakes his head slightly, looking offended at the lack of trust his father placed in us, and perhaps more importantly, him. I can understand though, I might have kept things tight too in his place, assuming that anyone could be betraying him for money, the god of all business. Not telling his son though, that might be harder to forgive.

Sir Mathieson, perhaps ruffled by the silence in the room, cleared his throat and went on.

'I regret that I took this course of action and I do extend my apologies.' John nods back at him and I tell him, no problem. Zoe nods too and he looks less annoyed, ready to move on.

'Your excellent work in resolving the immediate problem of the Hannaways is doubly appreciated under the circumstances. That said, I fear there is another problem which we have to deal with in the morning. Young master Balliol has unfortunately loosed his shackles and trotted off into the snow. Our focus on my own security here at Inverannan and the Hannaway problem left me with no option but to leave him temporarily unguarded, and unfortunately, I seem to have underestimated his abilities somewhat. My men confirmed that he had escaped through the roof of the building he was placed, possibly trying to reach a road and make his escape from the area. Since we are in a rather remote location, and given the weather and the paucity of vehicles, this may be something we can resolve.

Zoe can't hold it in any more. 'So in the middle of this mess, your trained monkeys kidnapped Balliol, wasted a bloody load of my time, all because you didn't trust your principal Security Officer with the actual security of the business? This is ridiculous.' She turns and heads out the door, slamming it as she leaves. She's right to be pissed off, but I prefer to stay calm, reminding myself of how many men Sir Mathieson has had killed during his career for crossing him.

'I'll speak to her', says John, following her and possibly with the same thoughts I had, for her own safety. Old man though Sir Mathieson may be, he's still a cold-blooded former gang boss who has just had his yacht incinerated and a large an amount of his money stolen, so best not to get in his way at present, if ever.

Sir Mathieson turns to see John and Zoe re-enter the room. She still looks angry, but sits down and seems prepared to tolerate the masculine ineptitude she quite rightly considers him to demonstrate. John seems set to take part now and starts on whatever plans he is about to reveal.

John takes out one of the maps we used earlier and shows us where he was being kept. 'We need, as a matter of priority, to find Balliol, ideally alive to get him to return the missing funds, but if he's out in this weather, a corpse might be the realistic outcome. First thing, we need to try and locate him, starting from here.' He points to a place which means nothing to me, but looks a long way from the main road. It is, however, apparent that any searching will be on foot, as even the main roads are snowbound, never mind some bloody wilderness at the arse end of the estate.

Zoe reaches into the desk drawer and takes out the list and map which Gillian provided earlier and we compare the two. Balliol had been left in a bothy, one of the foresters shelters, just off a remote track on the west side of the estate; we matched the other houses we identified within reasonable walking distance, which meant that whoever had the misfortune to be sent out in the snow had four cottages to check. We sit back after our mapping task is over and Sir Mathieson asks Zoe what time she will be heading out in the morning. Zoe looks at him with barely concealed fury, which almost makes me laugh out loud until I realise from his glance that I'll be going with her.

All too soon it's six thirty a.m. and we're ready to set off. The snow helps reflect the morning light enough for us to see our way out of Inverannan House and towards the western perimeter of the estate to search for the redoubtable Balliol. I have the hunting rifle with me; John gave it a proper clean last night, its cartridges renewed ready for Balliol after its unquestionable effectiveness on Codheid Hannaway. We trudge steadily forwards into the gloom, the compass and map keeping us in a fairly direct route. Zoe is dressed, like me, in layers of fleece and Gore-tex, some of which we accumulated by raiding the garage where the guys still had their gear stowed. It took a while to discern which items were the most inoffensive in terms of odour, but we got there and eventually donned the least malodorous items. We're now an eclectic mix of colours and brands, certainly not of a camouflaged nature.

161

It takes an hour and forty minutes of slow going to reach the bothy, left unlocked after the two Allanton men found the building empty and a hole in the ceiling where Balliol had made his escape. Too much snow has fallen to leave any tracks, although we can see the trail from the roof, slates askew and the inside with more than a dusting thanks to the Balliol-sized aperture. How he got through that small space amazes me, I couldn't get my leg through that gap.

We decide on a sweep around the nearest cottages where he may be hiding, from the first one directly west, then the three others on the way back. It'll take the best part of the available daylight, so we don't delay any longer, Zoe taking the lead and me following, both of us checking for any signs of a frozen Tim Balliol as we go. Another two hours of mainly uphill struggling and we're at a cottage, pretty enough but definitely no-one home. We check inside and there's no initial sign of Tim Balliol, but perhaps a few hints that someone has been here. The bedroom stinks of antiseptic, there's still a slight heat from the cooker and, after a search of the rooms, Zoe finds a recently-opened can of tomato soup. It looks like Tim is not only alive but on the move, rested and fed.

After checking the area around the cottage and finding nothing, we set out along what, if it weren't for the snow, be a single track dirt road. Thankfully, we can still see the very top of the wire fence which edges it, so follow that as the snow falls heavily again, the light dimming as a dark grey cloud sits directly over us. We reach the main road, where the snow is easier to walk on, although even the compacted tyre tracks are well covered by the new snow.

The next building we come to sits a couple of hundred metres back from the road, another detached cottage which according to Gillian's notes, belongs to an artist who decamped a while back and now sits unattended. We traipse up to the front door, there's no sign of anyone inside either and it's securely locked. I walk around the rear, but the snow has drifted to almost three-quarters of the way up the back door, so no-one has gone in there recently. We peer in the windows and with nothing to show, go back down to the road.

'What if we don't find him?' Zoe asks. 'He might have hitched a lift and be in Inverness by now, or heading south in a lorry.'

I think about what I would do in his place. A lift in a van would be possible, but at this time of year, in this weather and other than the Inverannan vans, there isn't much going to be on the road up here apart from tractors and the sturdiest of four-wheel drives.

'Not a chance, he's still on foot. We've not seen a vehicle yet, this road is more or less closed for traffic. I don't know the area, but if it's like where I was brought up, the adults just made sure all the old biddies were alright and then settled indoors with as much booze as they could get until the snow melted.'

Zoe laughs, ringing out in the silence of the countryside.

I don't know that much about her, other than our chats in the office, so I guess I should find out.

'You've been in the services – come across much weather like this?' I can't see her face, like mines it is obscured by the hoods of our parkas.

'Yeah, I did a lot of cross-country skiing in Norway when I was in the army, cold as hell there too. I grew up in Kent though, so I'm more used to rainy winters than this arctic weather.' I thought her accent suggested that kind of area, no hint of any common glottal stops though, middle class all the way.

Zoe stops and looks at me. 'What do you think about this whole thing with Balliol? We had him monitored every moment he was online at the office. How would he even know that account was the only one that was separate from the business accounts, the only one with no alerts on it? If Sir Mathieson hadn't checked his own accounts after the yacht fire, or if he'd been killed, it would have been weeks, maybe months before we realised what had happened. '

Some of this is news to me, I hadn't realised that the account was any different from the others, but this isn't really my area of expertise.

She goes on, animated now. 'So maybe, he's smarter than we thought and perhaps bolder too. One thing is for sure, he must have acted alone. Our London team is solid, all vetted and trained to report any problems to us, straight away.'

Zoe tells me that she constantly updates all our fraud training, each staff member has their own accounts monitored as a condition of employment too, not a 100% guarantee but as near as you'll get.

I tell her that I agree; they are a trustworthy lot.

'I know, but some risk is always there. Someone getting into trouble with gambling, or threatened by an outsider, nothing is absolute when people are involved.'

'Does that include me?' I ask to see what she comes up with. She stops walking and turns to me.

'No, you are in the lowest risk category. You don't have the access passwords, the knowledge or the training to use the system in that way unless you've been hiding it well.' I follow her, feeling rather slighted but partly relieved as she walks away.

'What about you?' I call after her.

She pauses without turning and says 'No, I'm far too aware of what people like you do for a living.'

With that, we walk in silence through the deepening snow to the next destination.

The blizzard is just about as bad as it has ever been when we reach the next one, a two-storey house, two windows on each side of the front elevation and a door in the centre, the traditional style up here. We struggle through the drifts to get to the door and this time we are not alone. Lights are on inside and I knock the door, standing back and to the side, my revolver ready inside my coat pocket as I've left the rifle back at the gate, not needed at close quarters. A man curses as the door opens inwards and a foot of snow cascades inside. He peers out at us and, without prompting, gruffly tells us to get inside. We had a script ready for this scenario, so Zoe tells him that we are heading to Inverannan village after our car got stuck, but our friend went on ahead, we wondered if he had seen him. A loose description of Tim elicits a silent but ambiguous response as we are beckoned further inside to escape from the cold. It's initially good to get out of the chill but the stench inside is soon worse than the low temperature. The entire house reeks of pungent decay and long-term hygiene negligence, along with what smells like a recent dish of some kind of overcooked fish meal. I can't hold my breath, but try to inhale using the left side of my anorak hood as an air filter.

We are offered a hot drink, which even in our odour-pressured situation we accept as we need to talk more, the absolutely overpowering smell in the house a temporary sacrifice if we are to find some indication of where Balliol has got to. A few minutes later, the fellow hands us hot chocolate drinks and introduces himself as Owen, no surname given. We exchange the same level of information and I'm already I'm extremely wary of this guy. He's heavy-set, clean-shaven but shabby as hell, tartan work shirt on top and what was once a pair of blue jeans below; at a guess, he's a labourer, he has the look of a manual worker but the gut of a big eater.

'So, do you work up here?' I ask, seeing if my estimation is going to be accurate.

'Aye, I do some forestry labouring when they need me, and some beating on the moors in the season. Pay is shite but it gets me by, you know.' I nod and sip the drink, which tastes more like heated mud than chocolate, so I just let the mug warm my hands. He's looking at Zoe a bit too much, she is ignoring it but I'm thinking he's been up here alone for too long and we'd better get out before his hormones make him try something he'll regret.

'We're looking for our pal, he might have passed by here a while back, we're just making sure he didn't stop anywhere before the village. Have you seen him, slim guy, and darkish hair, a bit pale?'

Owen nods, 'Aye, well I couldnae tell you what he looked like, but a fella walked by the house a while back, heading to the village I reckoned.' I ask him if the passerby was alone and if he seemed OK.

'He looked like he wasn't dressed for the weather – the snow wasn't as heavy then, he was on his own but he looked all right to me.'

I glimpse at Zoe to see if she needs to ask anything else before we get out of this dreadful stench, but she seems happy just to get out, much as I do.

Owen starts the chat up again. 'Are you two working up here or just visiting?' I tell him that we're just passing through, didn't think the weather would have been this bad and we'll get back to the village to let the storm pass and wait till we can get our car moving again. He nods, but for a taciturn-seeming bloke, he's trying desperately to engage us in conversation, keep us around as long as possible.

'There's a B&B in the village.' He offers.

'Yeah, I think we passed it, we'll get back there and settle in.' I go to stand, but bloody hell he's started talking again, so I sit.

'I tried to get work down there, at the village. Most of the men have jobs doing the driving or on the land, up at the estate at the big house. I got an interview up there once, but I didn't get the job. I've been in trouble you see, when I was younger.' He takes a long drink from what I now notice is a mug of whisky. I thought he was a bit odd as soon as we walked in the door, but now I'm thinking he's been on his own up here way, way too long.

He gets to rambling on again. 'That's where everyone makes the big money, up there, I tell you. The whole village makes money off that place except me.' I turn to

Zoe who makes a gesture for us to get the hell away from the guy, which I most certainly agree with. When I turn back, he's hunched forward on his chair and is staring at Zoe; he seems to have noticed her motioning for me to leave and taken it personally, which to be honest we could really do without in the circumstances.

'That's the same thing everyone does to me. Rude, that is, after I've given you a drink. Why don't you go and you stay?' I realise that this madman is actually trying to get me out and Zoe to remain. He takes another gulp of the whisky and turns his face to me, trying to stare me down.

I break his concentrated gaze by standing. 'Thanks for the drink mate. We should be going.' We turn and head for the door, Zoe first. He stands too, but I'm keeping a sideways eye on him, so I catch a glint of something at his right hand and turn to face him. Suddenly I'm looking at a double-bladed knife, backing away but he's following me, now he's got a hammer in his other hand and I'm in the hall, retreating to where I guess Zoe is and wondering why she's not shooting the crazy bastard.

'My guns stuck!' I hear Zoe behind me and Owen's looking past me, confused as to why a gun is involved but looking like he's ready to skewer me. This distraction does, however, give me time to slide my revolver out of my pocket and put a bullet quite neatly into his throat, a decent shot from a low angle, while in hurry and facing a knife-wielding lunatic.

He's on the floor and gurgling, not dead but having dropped his weapons to prioritise trying to stem the blood spurting from what seems to be a severed artery in his throat. He's no threat now, but I'm pretty annoyed, so I fire a bullet from close range into the side of his forehead and end both his misery and the annoying noise he is making. Rather inconsiderately, he has now spurted blood onto my clothes and face, so Zoe is looking at me as if it's I who am insane. She puts her unused revolver back into her pocket and stands beside me, a look of disgust on her face although I'm not sure if it's for me or what remains of Owen.

'What the fuck.' She says with more disgust than I could ever have mustered.

'Look around, see if this maniac is living alone.' We check the downstairs first, a cursory look at the foul kitchen, then upstairs. The situation is made somewhat more surreal by the discovery of an elderly man, or so it appears to have been, decomposing badly in a bedroom at the back of the house. We slam the bedroom door behind us and head downstairs at a run. We walk back into the kitchen, a sanctuary from rooms with corpses in them and try to figure out what to do.

'It's Pyscho, but with an all-male household.' I tell her while trying not to laugh. Zoe breaks into a snigger too, but after we've finished with my immature moment, we try and see how we clear up this new problem.

'I favour closing the door and leaving the whole thing for someone else.' I smile.

Zoe looks at me like a proper professional and tells me that isn't an option. 'Well we can't exactly hide the body, its white snow outside and he, if you hadn't noticed, has lost quite a lot of blood, about three-quarters of what he had by the looks of it.' We look through the door at the recumbent Owen and it certainly looks that my initial choice of a throat shot and the subsequent bullet to the side of his head means that the area around the body is not going to be easily cleaned.

'Should we try and bury him? She asks me.

The point of trying to hide the body, and not a light one despite the blood loss, is lost to me. As I have shot him twice at close range, it is more realistic that I leave the untraceable pistol in his hand and let the authorities puzzle over the two corpses, one of which shows initial signs of a thumb-fired pistol suicide. I'm not sure why, but I enjoy wondering about what the forensic team would make of it, if they get here before Sir Mathieson's clean-up squad.

Zoe acquiesces wearily and, after turning off the lights and heating and wiping anything which might have had our fingerprints on it, we set off again on the hunt for Tim Balliol. She tells me that we'll try and get the guys out to do a clear-up when the road is clear, although god knows when that will be. I just hope no good Samaritans turn up to see if the old man is alright and finds Owen before we get a chance to have him disappeared.

After about another half-mile, I use the snow to clear my face, hands and jacket of the blood from Owen; it's bloody freezing, literally, but the method works well enough after a few goes. Zoe checks me over and can't see any of his blood on my face at least, so we're fine to approach the next property. Closer to the road than the last one, but the access track is deeper with drift, so we take a route a little farther on and head back to the front of the cottage through what is probably a field underneath. It's an older house, low like a blackhouse but modernised, or so it seems. There are lights on here too, unfortunately, and I have to remind myself that Tim

Balliol could be inside, even with a weapon if he could find one. We get to the door and stand, readying ourselves.

'Let's see what's behind door number three!'

Zoe just looks at me.

She knocks the door and, after a wait, we see the face of an elderly woman at the window. She opens the door slightly, nervously and peers at us through what looks rather fortunately like a haze of cataracts. Zoe does the talking. She gives her the same story about the car and our lost friend but the lady hasn't seen anyone for two days. I try to find out a little more about the recent debacle.

'Who are your neighbours dear?' I ask, talking loudly after seeing her hearing aid.

'Mister Ludlow and his son live on their own back up that way.' She then points in the direction we were heading. 'Down towards the village, it's a new family, the Mackenzie's. They are from Paisley; don't know what they were thinking about moving up here.' We agree with her, it's not an easy life up here and Zoe thanks her, tells her to get inside and get warmed up, we'll be down at the village and safe soon, out of the cold. We struggle back the way we came, our footprints already starting to fade as the wind drives the snow into every crevice.

Back at the road, we are guided now only by the snow marker poles; spaced at intervals to show snowploughs where they should be clearing. We're tiring, especially me it seems.

'Can we give the next one a miss? All we are doing is letting people see our faces, if the Police find the remains of Owen before our guys can get out and do a clean-up, we'll be in trouble. Christ knows if Owen killed poor Mister Ludlow but the cops won't take long to figure out that Owen wasn't a suicide.'

She agrees with my summation of our predicament and we walk straight past the last house on our list and along a steady, vacant descent along to the loch and the village. We check a disused and empty wooden shed in case Tim has sheltered inside, but to no avail. The short cut we had intended to use back into the estate is impassable, so we keep going towards the proper entrance to Inverannan House. The snow has drifted to near waist height in places, so we can hardly get through, but use the last of our energy reserves and determination to keep going.

It's dark now and we've covered the round trip of about ten miles, including a couple of stops and one accidental murder, in just over eleven hours. All we've had to eat are two cereal bars each and a sip of appalling hot chocolate. Owen didn't even offer us a biscuit.

So, we are hungry, cold and utterly exhausted when we get into the side door of Inverannan House, still guarded in the dark by a drunk Gilfillan who can't seem to focus on us when we arrive, which gives him quite a flap until he hears my voice, telling him to calm the fuck down. Dumping our gear in his office, we trudge upstairs to our bedrooms, nodding to Sir Mathieson's man guarding the hallway and consciously ignoring the sounds of music and laughter from the library. Gilfillan, trying to be helpful no doubt, shouts after us that the staff are staying the night because of the weather, which due my exhaustion and the fact that I can no longer feel my extremities, does not interest me a great deal. Inside my room, finally, I pull my soaking wet clothes off, dump them in the bathroom and get into the shower, first turning it down to help gradually bring my body temperature back to normal. I get the expected pins and needles in my hands and feet, but this lessens as the water takes effect and my colour returns. I dry myself and put on clean boxer shorts before lying down and letting the fatigue turn to sleep, our failure to find the elusive Balliol not giving me even one, solitary fuck.

Tim trudged past a few vehicles at the parking area of Inverannan House before noticing some estate-liveried vans at the open door of a large garage on the far side of the mansion. He walked around towards it, past the main door to the House and to what looked like a loading operation, no workers at this late part of the day, but a few mid-sized delivery vans. He strolled confidently over to them, planning to ask for a lift to wherever farthest south they go, hoping that their highland generosity would extend far enough to help him. A rather impressive-looking man in a dark puffer jacket was standing at a small, basic office just inside the garage and Tim decided he was likely the man in charge, the best fellow to ask for help. It was only when he stood in front of the man that he realised that he was talking to John Allanton.

'What the fuck,' said John Allanton with some feeling, to the wide-eyed and astonished face of Tim Balliol. John looked at Tim's blue-faced and frozen visage, his snow-covered clothes with ice clinging to the ill-fitting hems of his trousers. He looked fit to cry and for once, John Allanton felt a fleeting pang of sympathy, mixed rather oddly with a strong sense of déjà vu.

'Let's get you inside.' He smiled, leading the stunned, frozen and dispirited Tim inside the office to where two rather unpleasant men sat. He thrust the squeaking and wriggling Tim towards the two men, giving them with instructions to get him up to the House and keep this clown quiet and out of the way. Tim tried to put up a fight, briefly and painfully for himself as he found himself being punched almost insensible and dragged out to the main house, up some stairs, then a corridor, then up another couple of flights until he was flung onto a single bed in what appeared to be the old staff quarters of this damnable country house. One of the men, whose voice he recognised from his kidnapping, told him the consequences of trying to leave the room or make noise, which were both appalling and anatomically damaging in equal measure.

He lay on the bed and wept; his escape plan bust and with the realisation that whatever these bastards had been planning to do to him when he was first taken, it was likely to be worse now. Tim took off his icy, soaked clothes and lay on the bed, eventually crying himself to sleep.

A few hours later, Tim wakened and, for a confused but blissful moment, lay lost in a fog of disorientation after failing to recognise the room. When it all dawned on him in, he curled into a foetal position and entered something akin to a mental shutdown, where his normally reliable psyche seemed to have had enough, refusing to enter the logical phase and help calculate his situation. He didn't look round when the door opened, simply allowed himself to be pulled up from the bed and turned to face the now distinctly unsmiling face of John Allanton.

John Allanton, for his part, did not want Tim to be there either. His father's left-field suggestion that Tim could not only be guilty of stealing a large quantity of money from Sir Mathieson, but also be part of a plot linked to the incinerating of the yacht, seemed implausible although possible. John was therefore in the unpleasant situation of potentially having hired, albeit without realising, a thieving spy who now has access to, or at least knowledge of, their most intimate financial secrets. This scenario,

John knew, would have to be resolved and, considering that the money in question could already be moving farther from their grasp, done quickly. John didn't like that he, Zoe and Adam had been kept in the dark, but accepted that one of Sir Mathieson's tenets was often proven true, that trust must not be extended any further than absolutely necessary.

His father's original plan was to follow normal protocols and have Tim questioned somewhere remote, where his screams could not be heard and his carcass disposed of by his most trusted subordinates. Now, John found himself in a house with rather too many other witnesses for his normal type of noisy interrogation, but Tim was there to be pressured to the point where he would be unable to keep secrets from his inquisitors, so other, quieter means would be needed.

'Do you know why you are here Tim?' John lowered himself to the level of Tim's lolling head.

'You seem to have broken some of our little rules, the ones we discussed when you joined up, remember?' Tim made no noise and stayed inside his bubble of denial.

A resounding slap on the side of his head woke him from this reverie.

Tim felt like he'd been hit by the flat side of a hammer. He struggled to remain conscious, fighting the dizziness from the thump on his ear and the taste of blood filling his mouth.

'I haven't done anything wrong.' Tim spluttered. Another whanging blow suggested that his response was not what John was looking for. The two other men came into the room, and it didn't look like they were here to rescue poor Tim, who was drooling saliva, blood and two teeth onto the worn carpet.

'Please, I honestly haven't. I did what you asked, the transfer and everything. I really don't know what you mean.' He looked from John to the other two men and hoped for all he was worth that they were going to believe him.

John Allanton moved away from Tim and ushered him to stay sitting on the bed while he pulled out the only chair to sit across from him. 'You know Tim, you sound genuine, but my father's accountants, who I trust a fuckload more than you, have reliably informed me that just over £12 million has now somehow evaporated during your brief employment with us. Also, it would appear that you have a few personal accounts which have recently become significantly heavier and I am suspicious that if I have full access to these, I might find that a similar amount now resides in them? What would your thoughts be on this situation Tim? What would you expect me to do now?' John Allanton was face-to-face with Tim and appeared that he was about to rip his head from his shoulders.

Tim thought and thought quickly. He hadn't stolen any money, but unless John Allanton was misinformed, someone had and he didn't know why.

'I can find out, please. It wasn't me, but I can sit with you and find out what happened, probably even who did it. I've been set up, I promise!' Tim kept on babbling until John stood and contemplated his options. He turned back to Tim, who immediately stopped telling John about algorithmic investment predictions and prepared for a punch, which thankfully for him, didn't arrive.

'Can I check Tim, that you are asking me for access to these accounts again, which will let you examine what happened while sitting with me, your boss - someone who knows close to fuck-all about online banking?' Tim started to offer assurances before the punch arrived, cutting off his suggestion and his consciousness simultaneously.

'Fuck sake', said John, with some feeling.

'Right, when he gets up, fill him with that stuff until he admits whatever he's done.' John gestured to a black case which one of his men had set on the small bedside table. With that, he exhaled loudly and putting this episode behind him, left to join his father downstairs.

Tim wakened a few minutes later, the sides of his face numb where the first punches had landed and his nose bleeding from the last one. He was back in cable ties now and had a dreadful awareness that he was in very great trouble, before the sharp and specific feeling of having a syringe painfully thrust into his upper arm. Almost immediately, the combination of benzodiazepine and sodium thiopental gave Tim a feeling of exquisite relaxation, followed by a feeling of slight nausea.

Tim could do nothing now about his chemically-enhanced inclination to tell the truth. The two men asked a series of questions, prepared by Cheryl and Williams back in London, and supplemented by Zoe, John and Sir Mathieson Allanton. Unable to resist, Tim told all about his previous transfers, his petty skimming from each employer including his current post and finally, about his plan to escape to Portugal with the contents of his safety deposit box. He just couldn't stop talking, poor Tim, not a secret could remain while under the detached influence of the narcotic cocktail used by these thugs. However, despite much encouragement, Tim could say nothing of the Allanton's missing twelve million. Finally, the effects reached their limits, his head keeled backwards and they packed up their medical kit, taking his cable ties off before laying him on the bed and departing to make their report.

They found John Allanton in the lounge downstairs, hosting an impromptu party with the office staff, stranded at Inverannan House because of the weather and taking the opportunity to nosh into as much free booze as they could. They gestured for him to follow them into the next-door library where Sir Mathieson waited, half asleep on the leather Chesterfield beside the fireplace. He stirred when his son and his trusted men entered, and asked them for their thoughts on Tim.

'Well, he's a smart little fucker, that's for sure. Been ripping off everyone he's ever worked for, but not your twelve million.'

The second man, Jim, was equally puzzled by the interrogation outcome and hesitated before speaking to his superiors.

'He's got a stash in a deposit box, which we knew about, but he really doesn't know about these other accounts, and he was completely gone with the gear. He doesn't know anything about the yacht, nothing about a contract, nothing. Waste of time boss.' He threw up his hands in frustration at not being able to get what his officer had asked of him.

'That's OK Jim, we'll keep going. If it wasn't him, we'll move our sights elsewhere.'

John looked pensive for a moment. 'We need to decide what to do with him. Make sure he stays in that room and keeps quiet while the office team are here. Also, take care that he doesn't react after having that shit in his veins; keep him alive and locked up until further orders.' Sir Mathieson thanked the two men and set them to their guard duties. John lowered himself into a chair across from his father and they exchanged glances. Sir Mathieson spoke in a low voice, although the shrieks and laughter from next door would have covered anything under a shout.

'If this is correct, we now need to look towards other suspects, sadly all of whom are our permanent employees.' John nodded, his father unfortunately correct in his assumption. Despite how hard it was for him to take, it looked now like Balliol could have been set up, perhaps someone taking the opportunity of his temporary employment to use him as cover for their theft of Sir Mathieson's retirement fund. They sat back and considered, and planned. Their mystery had not yet been solved, although at least Tim Balliol was not cleared of suspicion.

Tim's innocence had been established, however not without significant detriment to his health. Unknown to the Allantons, poor Tim's heart rate was at that time dropping gradually but steadily as he lay comatose upstairs. It was a couple of hours later when one of Sir Mathieson's men again checked on Tim. By then, his condition had worsened and a pulse had been difficult to find. Unwilling to draw his colleague away from his guard duties, Charlie took a unilateral decision to follow orders and keep him alive by firing some cocaine solution into Tim's system. He wasn't particularly comfortable with the use of pharmaceuticals in these situations, having spent his post-military career using the more traditional strong-arm methods, which had rarely failed and were something of his speciality. However, when situations like this required quiet and urgent responses, he knew they had their place. Charlie had only one rudimentary piece of medical knowledge to help an overdose of benzodiazepine and that was to get the motors running again with a strong whack of coke.

He also knew that a serious number of things could also go wrong after firing the cocaine solution into Tim. However, in the circumstances he really couldn't give a fuck about any of them. It was far from the first time he'd overstepped the mark and could reasonably defend any mistakes as a genuine attempt to reverse the effect of the earlier overdose and follow John's orders. So, placing him on his side in case Tim was sick and then loading a generous amount into the mix, he filled the syringe, tapped a bubble out and then injected his captive with enough coke to start a decent sized party. There was a moment where nothing happened, and then Tim inhaled deeply and sat up with staring eyes and started shaking like a leaf.

'Welcome back.' Charlie told Tim as he left him sitting bolt upright, vibrating, but very much back in the land of the living. He closed the door and left Tim to deal with the building adrenalin-judder that the cocaine was starting to cause.

Tim felt like he'd just burst out of a grave, then within minutes his mind was buzzing uncontrollably and he could feel the energy rising through his battered body. He knew that he was now going to have a great day and no mistake. He bounced up from the bed and leapt to

181

the door, which was locked from the outside. No problem to Tim, it was a weak internal door which was loose and would soon be incapable of resisting his determination.

He put his shoes back on and stood back from the door frame, ready to give the lock a thump with the sole of his foot. It opened after three kicks and Tim stood on the threshold of his revenge, of his escape and retribution against those who had disrespected and mistreated him. He knew he was a titan of accountancy, a god of banking and that no moronic gangster would be standing between him and his safety deposit box in London. He knew who they were, and he would kill all the bastards for this. Tim, the coke-energised synapses of his brain firing a thousand little rockets of information around his mind, knew it was time for him to realise his potential and throw off the shackles of profit and loss and become the Accountant from Hell.

He stepped out into the corridor, heard some noises below and set off downstairs to confront his enemies, wasting no time except to arm himself from the arsenal on the walls of the hallway. After equipping himself with a replica claymore and dirk from a wall display, he stopped moments later at a glass cabinet with the title "Game Hunting at Inverannan" and a picture of the former owner of Inverannan House, a chap named Galloglas, pictured smiling with two ghillies over the corpse of an unfortunate stag. Aside from the helpful information on the development of hunting shotguns since the late 19th century, there were eight fine examples of their kind on horizontal display, each with their respective cartridges to demonstrate their corresponding progress. Hardly a safe way to store dangerous weapons, but this was the highlands and for Tim, a rather fortunate find.

After using the claymore to prise open the delicate lock, the glass front swung open and Tim contemplated his options with a maniacal grin. He'd been required to attend only one corporate team-building day in his entire life, an appalling experience at the time, but clay pigeon shooting had left him with a rudimentary understanding of how to load and use a shotgun, albeit not how to hit the target. Reading the plaques, he fancied the ornate early Boss Over-Under which looked perfectly serviceable but if the cartridges were of the same era, they might well fail on him. Scanning the more modern alternatives, his eyes lit and his smile widened as he looked upon exactly what he needed. He read no more, just picked up the hefty 10-gauge Zabala weapon, which was complete with a box of twelve cartridges and looked simple enough even for Tim to use effectively. What Tim did not know was that Galloglas had bought this weapon after using a similar version on an illegal big-game hunting expedition in central Africa some years before, intending to store it in a collection at Inverannan as it was not really suited for hunting the mammals of Britain. It was, in short, not quite the shotgun Tim had popped at his clay pigeons that rainy day in Hampshire.

Tim loaded the heavy and longer than expected shotgun as efficiently as his heart-pounding condition would allow. Hefting it into a shooting position to his shoulder, he walked gun-first along the corridor and then down the flight of stairs towards what he thought was the first-floor landing. His first sight of an opponent was one of those bastard kidnappers looking directly up at the double barrels of his shotgun in disbelief, unsure what to do and rather surprised that the mousy accountant had the nerve to go on the offensive. His indecision did not prove to be the best course of action as Tim, fuelled by narcotics and suppressed rage, let him have both barrels.

The weapon made a noise greater than Tim had ever heard indoors. With a boom of unbelievable extravagance and the instant recoil in his shoulder, Tim was flung backwards onto the carpeted floor, momentarily unaware of the outcome of his attack. He left the shotgun on the floor and peered down to see what had happened. The guard lay spread-eagled, his body complete with the exception of the crucial part of his head above his lower teeth, that portion now distributed in an impressively symmetrical and widening pattern, starting from its origin and ending at the edge of the staircase some eight feet behind where his body lay inert.

Tim knew that no-one could have missed the explosion and now, he had to keep going. His adrenalin was pumping so hard in his veins that it felt like a snare drum-roll, an accompaniment to a battle he would surely win. He reloaded the weapon, taking longer as his hands were now shaking even more violently. Taking the tartan-carpeted stairs down, he was aware of figures below him and to the left. This time, he held the butt of the weapon closer, descended the last few steps, turned and fired.

Tim was flung back again, not as far as before but still enough to make him fall heavily. He looked up at the roughly circular hole his shot had made above a corridor door and the figures now running away at the end of it, some of whom appeared to be women. Tim didn't want to engage with anyone innocent, so he was glad he'd missed whoever had been standing there, even felt sorry that he'd fired without looking. He promised himself he wouldn't do that again, he just wanted that Allanton bastard and his cronies, ideally the rest of his captors and that Scottish guy, he was definitely on Tim's list. The coke was driving him on, relentless energy keeping him in full-on rampage mode. He reloaded and set off after the fleeing women whom he hoped would lead him to the real targets.

A few minutes of searching left Tim with little idea where they had all got to in the appalling labyrinth of this Highland mansion. He felt that he had missed a section, a bit where a smaller staircase might have allowed them to get back to the upper floors and he was right, a backtrack confirmed that he should have followed that route. Gun to the fore, Tim ascended to the first floor again, this time with no noise for him to follow. An explosion rang out to his left, almost giving him a heart attack and making him jump backwards when he thought a bullet had been fired at him. Thankfully whatever it was had missed, but he was in no mood to mess about so turned his weapon into the corridor and returned fire at a figure at the end of the corridor, this time keeping his feet at the powerful recoil of the shotgun.

He glanced round to see what damage he had done this time. There was another hole in the wall but otherwise, he'd just done peripheral harm to some wall coverings and a lamp, no bodies to show this time. He reloaded and crept along, hoping to reach his quarry while avoiding whoever had fired at him. The buzzing in Tim's ears from the shotgun blasts was excruciating now, preventing him from hearing any assailants even if they were making noise. As he walked past one of the doors, he caught a glimpse of it opening behind him. He tried to turn and shoot, however, the 32-inch barrel made turning impossible, something that his assailants noticed a moment before he did. The next few minutes were a flurry of pain and confusion to Tim as first, a series of plant pots and ceramics were thrown at very short range at his face and head. Then a number of enraged women attacked him directly, punching, kicking and slapping him as he was forced along the corridor away from these harpies. He had no idea what fluids were running down his face, however, a mixture of his blood, water from plant pots and what felt like wine from bottles bouncing off of his forehead would be his best guess. Miraculously, and possibly due to the numbing effect of the cocaine, he managed to stay upright through the onslaught, turn and break into a run, still feeling projectiles hitting him as he went. He turned the corner and used the pause in the attack to wipe his eyes clear and the wideness of the corner to turn the shotgun back on the women assailing him so grievously. A volley of screams and makeshift missiles hit him as he turned, but he pulled the trigger, firing two cartridges into the wall on his left. They fled shrieking at the explosion of the shotgun, racing back along the corridor and down the stairs he had come up when searching for his enemies, to whom he now added this heinous hen party.

Tim reloaded, shouting, 'you'd better run, you utter bastards' to keep them warned of his imminent vengeance. His head was in agony, he had cuts front and back from the barrage of pots, bottles and vases.

He heard a shouted response from the women along the corridor, which despite the shotgun-induced tinnitus, sounded entirely aggressive. This coupled with the capacity which they seemed to have to launch a frenzied attack on the heavily armed Tim, made him decide that he would leave them alone for the moment and refocus his search for John Allanton. He looked around for some indication of where his quarry might be. The staircase to his right had a more luxurious carpet and, his premise being that Allanton's room might be in the best part of the mansion, Tim pointed his shotgun in that direction and limped along behind it.

There was a faint sound ahead of him, but the damn tinnitus prevented him from detecting what was going on. Aware of some noise, perhaps even conflict ahead, Tim carefully trod his way forward to another bedroom door. Resting the end of the shotgun on the joint between the door and the frame, he turned the handle and opened it enough to see inside. Unfortunately, the door gave a bit of a creak, probably warning those inside of his presence, although some loud voices may have covered it. Tim pushed the handle and with the confidence of having the shotgun, coupled with the massive and still-active cocaine dose, he propelled himself forward. Jumping into the room, his finger instinctively compressed the trigger, firing both barrels into the back of a darkly clad figure and doing Tim's tinnitus no help at all. Tim fell back onto the wall, but quickly regained his footing, picking up the rifle and cracking it open to reload while ignoring whatever else was going on the room. His impeded hearing meant that he was not fully aware of what was occurring, but Tim was determined to get his weapon reloaded. He rose as quickly as his lacerations would allow and pointed the shotgun at whoever was in the room.

What was immediately apparent was that his blind shot into the room had struck some targets. What appeared to

be a soldier was lying face down on the floor, his back a
mess of shotgum-blasted rucksack and tattered clothing.
Two elderly gentlemen on the other side of the room had
been on the periphery of the cartridge's spread and were
sitting with shocked expressions. Despite some shot
hitting them they were relatively unharmed, unlike the
other occupant of the room, John Allanton. He was
recumbent beside the window and Tim, for the life of
him, couldn't figure out how he had managed to shoot
him too. Perhaps a ricochet, he thought. Regardless, he
was on the floor and bleeding from a shoulder wound,
unconscious and not presenting a threat. Tim turned to
the old men and realised, through his pounding heartbeat
and screaming ears, that he had just shot the scion of the
Allanton clan, the fabled Sir Mathieson Allanton.

The old man was trying to talk to Tim, but his hearing
was now at a stage where conversation was virtually
impossible. His vision had been blurred by sweat and
various fluids over the past ten minutes, so Tim Balliol
was in no position to converse with anyone, even a figure
so mythical as the patriarch Sir Mathieson himself. Tim
knew that he had to keep going, that if he just kept killing
everyone then no-one would be left to shoot him, so
operating on that principle, he raised the gun, shouting at
the old man to sit the fuck down and then screaming at
him, telling the old bastard not to mess with Tim Balliol, a
man who deserves respect. He struggled to keep the
heavy shotgun steady but managed to find the strength to
raise it ready to discharge it straight at the grey-haired
figures. Then Tim felt something hitting him in the face,
like a punch only much, much worse. He collapsed and
looked up at the blood on the door beside him and
turned the other way to the window at the dark figure
approaching him. A boot went back and forward towards

him and then, the bone-smashing impact threw Tim to the floor once more. The coke was wearing off, but it still his heart pounded strongly and Tim hadn't quite lost consciousness. Even the excruciating pain kept his senses alert enough to force him back up after a moment, trying to get the heavy weapon up and pointed at his assailant in front of him. He just couldn't do it though. Tim felt the gun being taken from him, then the agony of being shot in the knee finally doused his coke-sparked synapses and he was rendered inert.

He awakened to an exceptionally cold tent, even for one
pitched in the Highlands of Scotland. Hauling himself
forward, he started to open the zip of the tent, only to
find snow drifted up to its height at the front, perhaps
three feet in depth.

'Fuck' he told himself. He hadn't checked the weather
forecast, assuming that late March in Scotland would
perhaps be rainy, but that snow and storms would not be
on the menu. Unfortunately for him, that was indeed the
case, and it looked like there was plenty more on the way.
As the wind whipped the snow around the tent in gusts,
he took his only option and closed the zip to stay inside
and see out the storm. For the whole of the day, he was
stuck in there, the snow covering his tent even more
deeply amidst the relentless cacophony of thrashing trees
around him. He could hear branches rending in the
weight of the snow, hoping all the while that the dreadful
weather would subside and let him get on with his job.

It did, however, give him an opportunity to plan his
eventual escape. He had no transport and no chance to
hide from those at Inverannan once he had killed the old
man. Rather, he decided to carry out the mission quickly
then take the keys for one of the vehicles and drive down
the only road which his map showed him, leading
through the village and thence south-east. He'd need to
drive like a madman, which fortunately he could, and rely
on some good luck, for which he figured he was long
overdue. It would be tricky, but if he could get a head
start, he would back himself to drive to Inverness without
being overtaken and once there, disappear before finding
his way to an airport and home to Mallorca. For a few

minutes, he allowed himself to reheat his dream about having enough money to buy another villa, one with a balcony and access to a pool. Maybe he'd lose some weight and get a girlfriend once he had the money, instead of scrubbing around alone trying to eke out his pathetic pension.

It was night-time before the wind dropped and he pushed his way out and up through the drifted snow to see what the weather had inflicted. It was at least bright in the moonlit sky however the complete white-out was now a definite obstacle to him reaching the house. There were drifts all over the area, some really deep ones near him too and he thanked his dumb luck that he'd pitched his tent in this hollowed dip under the broad tree, chosen to avoid detection but inadvertently keeping him from being buried even deeper. He did, however, have a few pressing problems which occupied his thoughts; he had no food or drinks left whatsoever and felt distinctly like was coming down with the cold. Through these trials, he lay considering his options. He knew that if he went anywhere close to Inverannan House in daylight, he would leave obvious tracks which would give away his surveillance location, or indeed lead them to his tent. All this meant that he had to stay put, eating freshly fallen snow to keep hydrated and wishing to god that he had bought more cereal bars.

So, he lay in the tent all that day, eating snow from a billy-can with a spoon and trying to stave off the cold by putting all his clothes on, or over him. Thankfully the sleeping bag was living up to its high price and, by zipping it right up to his face, he could stay warm enough inside to tolerate the cold and wait until the light faded and he could finish his mission. He knew that the target would

191

have to die that night, that he couldn't handle another day in the tent, in the cold, hungry, waiting. So, when the light dimmed, he packed everything he would need in his rucksack and struggled from the near-buried tent. He left his sleeping bag and the rest of his redundant kit inside the tent, underneath the snow covered tree and left his sanctuary to resume his function as Hitman, extraordinaire.

The cold was however even more unpleasant than the frozen immobility of the tent, as he found when he struggled through the snow back to Inverannan House. His discomfort worsened as his boots filled with ice, every step letting more in until all feeling had gone from his feet. He kept going though, falling a few times into the snowy depth, the recovery from which drew his swears and, almost, his tears. Inner determination kept him going though, telling himself that his week-long debacle would be over that night and he'd have at least an outside chance of making it back to Mallorca and safety. After much effort, he was in a position to see through the windows of Inverannan House again and make ready for his sortie. If he could gain access to the building unseen, he could locate the old man, in his bedroom ideally, he could get him on his own. If not, he'd improvise and just handle each situation as it came along. Hardly a grand plan but without much weaponry and reaching the end of his tether, it was just the best he could do now. He'd always banged on in army training sessions about the need to be agile, to deal with changing circumstances and have the wherewithal to trust one's instincts and abilities to get the job done. Right now, that was exactly where he was.

The curtains were drawn on almost all the windows on his side of the house. Instead of being able to assess the situation, he was left without any clue as to how best to approach the building. If he walked across to it, his footsteps would be visible in the snow for a while, at least. Better to use the same path to the door as the others and then see if a window of one of the darkened rooms could be levered open. His knife would be ideal for that, slim and strong with a hefty rubberised grip. The door which had been used by the smoker the previous night had a window just round a corner from it, maybe an office or something but there had been no light in it, so a good candidate. It couldn't be seen from the side where the smoker was and his footprints would mix with others, except a quick hop round to the window.

He moved in as carefully a manner as his frame allowed, crouching as he went to the door, eyes fixed on it in case it opened. He had his serrated knife in hand, ready for action. An ungainly hop to the right and a couple of lurching paces took him to below the window. Placing his knife between the seam of the upper and lower window frames, he pulled the latch across which should let him lever the window. Unfortunately, a few coats of paint had been applied since the last time that window had opened, so he toiled with his knife for over ten minutes until every inch of the frame edge had been scratched clean. He heaved at his knife, levering the window till eventually, a gap appeared. He got his fingers into the space and hefted it up a few inches until it would move no more. After using his knife some more, his fingers now bleeding, the window moved a little more. He shoved his rucksack inside, then poked his head and shoulders into the open window and strained with his trapped chest muscles to shift the window open, maybe eighteen inches and enough to get through, with a struggle. He wriggled and hefted himself inside; pushing a table away to avoid any more noise. Finally, he lay on the floor of the small office, panting and listening to his heart trying to burst out of his ribcage. He rose, sweating and dazed but with enough sense to pull the window down, which it did with surprising and annoying ease.

He jumped at the sound of footsteps approaching, clear on the parquet flooring of the hallway outside. The door of the room was open and looked straight into the hall, so he crouched behind a chair and hoped not to be noticed. The figure unlocked the external door and stood at the entrance, lighting a cigarette, it seemed to be the bloke who had been there for the same reason last night. After five minutes, the man closed the door and lurched unsteadily back along the hallway, leaving it in silence apart from the sound of a clock, ticking its way just past eight o'clock. He sat for a few minutes until his breathing had normalised and the sweating abated slightly.

He made his way along the corridor, moving slowly to keep his boots silent on the floor as he passed offices and a meeting room or two. Every door was open, so he knew that he was alone in that section of the building. There was some noise ahead, which sounded like laughter but might have been screaming. Perhaps his inner tension made it so, but he wasn't sure at all who was inside the house. If the old man was well guarded, he might face a real problem, if they were armed or in force, he didn't have a back-up plan so he just had to wait and see, keep quiet and not be discovered until as late as possible, ideally after he'd driven away. To try and get that one task completed, he glanced into each room to see if any car keys had been left lying around, but to no avail.

194

The search continued, as he walked slowly towards where the noise came from, up ahead but not clear yet whether a party was going on, or some kind of darker event. Either way, the screams were intermittent and piercing. He approached a doorway to what looked like the main hall and paused, flattening himself as best he could against the wall. He could see the shadow of the smoker and what seemed to be two other men. Harsh words were being spoken.

'So, on a scale of one to ten, how pissed are you right now?' An English voice, but not strong in accent.

'I'm fine. Been up and down to the side door umpteen times, I've told ye. Naebody there.' This sounded like the smoker, who was closest to the hallway and had his back to him.

'Well, all you have to do is watch the staff corridor and back door. Shout if there's a problem, or better yet come and get me. I can't hear a fucking thing over the racket in there. Have you got a weapon?' He asked pointedly and with more than a hint of condescension.

'No sir, I haven't. After the duck thing, I've been telt tae touch nothing.'

'Fuck me. Give him the Taurus.' He seemed to be addressing a third man, who as yet hadn't spoken. 'It's loaded so don't shoot yourself and if I find out you are pissed, I will personally take it off you and beat you to death with it. Clear?'

'Aye.'

'So, get back down there, make sure the side door is kept locked and if anyone comes into the corridor, shoot either them or yourself, because if they reach me I will kill you myself'. It didn't sound much like he liked the smoker, but it also sounded like he knew what he was doing. The difficulty of getting to the target suddenly seemed much tougher than the innocent times of an hour ago.

He slipped back a few metres and into an office with "Factor" in gold lettering on the door, taking the key from the lock first. He found an alcove on his right and pressed himself, with the exception of the last couple of inches of his stomach, into the recess. He heard the sound of the smoker stumbling towards the room, perhaps glancing in, and then a click as the door closed over. The smoker's steps could be heard moving along the corridor and towards the side door, wisely following the directions of the other man. His problem now was that he was in a corridor with a guard at either end, both ready for intruders and, worst of all, armed. His only option now was to wait; he lay down out of sight behind a desk, making a pillow of his rucksack and straining to listen for sounds from the main part of the house. He wasn't sure if these had fully subsided as the closed door muted the overall noise, however, this was rendered immaterial as he fell asleep some ten minutes later; the warmth of the radiator beside him overcoming any residual adrenalin.

It was just before midnight when his uncomfortable position on the floor caused him to stir. He almost immediately descended into panicking anxiety when his situation dawned on him. Gradually, his thought processes worked through each aspect of his situation, providing a degree of comfort that his nap had worked out for the best. At this time of night, whatever party or whatever had been going on earlier must surely be finished by now; also, the guards had a few hours of inactivity to dull their attentiveness, maybe even enough to sneak past them and find the old guy. He expected bedrooms to be on the upper floors, maybe it would be possible to check a couple of doors and hit it lucky. A quick in-and-out, the knife across the target's throat and his job would be done, not even discovered until morning. A set of car keys was the other result he needed, letting him escape and head for Inverness, dump the car or whatever and keep his head down until he could get away further. One step at a time, he knew, that was the trick.

He got up, put his rucksack on and opened the door one tiny inch; no movement or noise from either side. He drew his knife and opened the door enough to glance out, back along the corridor. There was a chair there, the smoker on it with his back to the Hitman and with one hand to the side. Clearly, he had fallen asleep and hopefully, if he had taken strong drink earlier, unlikely to wake up at a creak or a footstep.

Easing himself through the door, he crept along to the main hall; a couple of steps up and he was on the side of the dimly lit foyer, the main entrance door to his right and a flight of stairs to his left. There were spears, animal heads, shields and swords covering every surface of the wall, which he considered for a moment as an upgrade to his knife. His gaze lowered for a moment towards a man slumped on the stairs, sleeping as soundly as he himself had been just a few minutes ago. He was a tough-looking guy, probably the one who was giving orders to the smoker earlier and who, unfortunately for him, was now in a rather vulnerable position.

He had little option at this point, other than to commence the mission proper. The adrenalin surged through him just like in his younger days, giving him the impetus to take the initiative and deal with the guard. He ran, albeit in a somewhat unathletic manner, straight at the sleeping man. His vague and panicked intention was to drive the knife deep into him, ideally his heart. The knife did indeed penetrate the skin, but his bumbling last lurch towards the guard meant that the strike was higher than intended, just inside his right shoulder. The serrated knife embedded deeply into the skin and gristle of the guard, who awakened with a gasp of pain, understandable given the sudden penetration of his shoulder and the heft of the large and looming assailant. The guard squirmed instinctively to his side, causing the Hitman to lose balance as he tried to grab at the knife handle; they tussled more a few moments, the guard impeded by his wound and the Hitman wrestling as much as his girth allowed him to.

The Hitman broke away first, trying to get space to punch the guard down. This did not go the way he thought. The guard started shouting, the noise of which was drowned out by what sounded like a shotgun fired somewhere in the house. The boom of the gunfire made him instinctively dive to the floor giving the guard time to start off upstairs, the knife still sticking out of his shoulder and an extraordinary amount of blood spurting over the stair carpet and wall. Moments later, another explosion went off, again high up and out of sight, causing him to involuntarily throw himself to the floor again while the injured man escaped. He looked at the foot of the stairs where, at the start of the bloody trail, was a black handgun, accidentally but fortunately dropped by the guard during the brief frenzy. He picked it up, thinking that although he had lost the benefit of surprise and silence, he now probably had 10 rounds to take care of the target or anyone who got in his way. He had always loved the feel of a gun, mainly the confidence it gave him and now a surge of power took hold of him as he pursued the wounded guard upstairs. Maybe with luck, he'd be able to follow the guard, if he was heading to the old guy's room to warn him, follow the breadcrumb trail of blood.

At the top of the stairs, a carpeted hallway went in both directions, however to the right a bright new trail oozed along and into one of the rooms. He was heading slowly in that direction when another figure passed by the end of the corridor, holding what appeared to be a full-size shotgun and trying to reload it clumsily. He considered shooting him as the figure briefly stayed in his view; however, it was not immediately apparent who this new player was. If he was a guard, why not come towards him, or even shout for help? There were screams now from further along the corridor, so there was obviously something else going on here. If it was someone else sent to kill the old man, that was understandable, he'd wondered about that a couple of times on the trip here. Since it looked like an even bigger clusterfuck than his own mission so far, and in the absence of an explanation, he decided to treat it as a diversion and focus on his own mission.

He stood outside the door where the trail of blood led and tried to control his breathing. A quick check at the door handle proved that he wasn't getting through the solid oak quickly or quietly. A momentary feeling of panic made him turn round and look down to the main hall. If the smoker had wakened at all this noise, he was still armed and could come at him from that direction. The Hitman had to deal with him first, and quickly. He ran back downstairs and into the corridor, faced by the smoker rising blearily from the chair while trying to retrieve his pistol from his tweed jacket pocket. The Hitman raised his gun and fired twice, hitting the man in the chest and dropping him noiselessly, flat backwards to the floor. Walking to where he lay inert, he picked up a small black handgun and put it in his own pocket. He felt a deep and genuine elation, now having both the firepower advantage and having put the first obstacles down without a scratch. Time for the old man, he thought.

Once he had got back to the upper floor of the entrance foyer, it was immediately apparent that his was not the only fracas underway in the building. Various shrieks and the sound of persons unknown running around caused him to pause and again assess his situation. There were, he reckoned, some twenty bedrooms in Inverannan House and the commensurate number of public rooms, staff quarters and stairways. This and the Victorian architecture which seemed to favour turrets, corners and multiple layers meant that a labyrinth of uncertainty lay ahead for anyone like him who had little clue of the layout. He therefore trod carefully, along the corridor at a slow pace, trying each door handle as he went and glancing in, handgun ready. In one, there appeared to be a sleeping woman, so that was all well enough but no help.

The next four rooms he tried were either locked or vacant, so he figured that there must be a series of occupied rooms somewhere ahead and up another half-floor. Climbing the partial staircase he could hardly fail to see some significant and recent damage to potted plants and wall coverings, at least some of which looked like pellet damage from a heavy weapon.

It looked to him that he was following in the footsteps of the shotgun guy, who he now thought definitely to be another assassin, perhaps his contact had lost confidence in him after all and sent along a new man. That wouldn't be a surprise, but he'd be fucked if he had come this far to let some tool with a shotgun get the payday. No, the shotgun guy was going down too, even if he got to the target first.

He had to continue to be systematic though, that was the only way he could work his way through the jumble of corridors and stairs and fucking portraits of stags. He planned to mark each door with his knife, a single stroke if it was open and checked and an x if locked. He'd force his way in after he'd checked the open ones, door by blasted door.

The Hitman now found himself in a more brightly lit corridor which also showed recent evidence of a fire-fight in its twenty or so metres. It was strewn with shoes, a stick or two and some broken pots and wine bottles, not to mention the pellet-marked wall coverings. Inhaling deeply, he turned the doorknob of the first door on the left side, holding his handgun in his right hand and swinging round to look into the room. He was faced with an exceptionally angry-looking young woman, who, rather than back away from the gun he pointed at her, chose to spray something at him. Pepper, or anti-rape, or whatever it was, he had never felt such agony in his eyes. He shot one round blindly into the room, hearing the door close as he stumbled back and sat down on the glass-strewn carpet, swearing and rubbing at his face.

It took a few minutes for the absolute worst of the burning sensation to subside and to even start to see shapes again through the tears and swelling. He knew that it wasn't a direct hit on his eyes; just the edge of the spray had caught him as he reeled back but it was still enough to leave him with a bubbling feeling around his right eye in particular and a horrible choking sensation in general. He tried to keep the handgun pointed up in case they tried to get him while he was down, but no such attack came.

Once he had enough capability to stop coughing and have at least a rudimentary return to usable eyesight, he made his way to the next two doors, both of which were locked. He could hear nothing from the rooms, but now realised that any dangers could lurk behind them, so made a tactical decision to kick them in, abandoning his previously more stealthy approach. The first was empty, however as the second door was flung inwards, he was aware of a simultaneous movement both ahead of him and back in the corridor.

The old guy he had thought shot dead at the side door was clearly not as deceased as he'd assumed. From the corridor behind him, a crossbow bolt was fired with some accuracy at his head, only slightly deviated by an impact with the wall corner which he jumped behind. The point of the bolt made it through the wall plaster and into his left ear, just above where one would normally expect an ear to be pierced, albeit not with half an inch wide of pointed steel. He screamed as he pulled away from the embedded bolt, leaving a bloody section of his ear behind on the viciously-tipped hunting arrowhead. Although he had been extremely lucky that it hadn't just hit him in the side of the head instead of spending most of its energy pushing itself through the plaster, it certainly didn't feel lucky right then.

He turned as the man was pulling the crossbow string back to use again, this time he ignored the pain enough to point the handgun at where the blurry figure stood. He loosed off two rounds which knocked the man over, however, he couldn't be sure he was dead without going back to him and finishing him off at close range. This was however impeded by an attack from behind, as the occupants of the room took the opportunity when he turned his back to throw what felt like a heavy paperweight at him, followed by a medium-sized vase. Given that the front of his face was somewhat sensitive after the application of whatever pepper spray he'd been inflicted with a few minutes earlier, followed by the partial loss of his left ear and associated damage to the surrounding skin, the last thing he needed was two hefty scuds to the back of his head. He fell forward after the second impact, not unconscious but just dazed from the attack. He turned after landing on the carpet and loosed off three rounds at no-one in particular, mainly to dissuade his attackers from sending more ornaments in.

He lay on his right side and hazily stared at the base of the wall facing him. Feeling like weeping at the comprehensive cranial wounds he had sustained, nevertheless, he knew he had to continue. There were perhaps three rounds left in one handgun and hopefully another nine in his unused weapon. In the minus column, he only had sight in one eye and hearing in one ear and was rather dizzy from the concussion caused by a quick-fire glass paperweight and a reproduction Rennie Mackintosh ceramic vase. He hauled himself to his feet and wiped his eyes with his sleeve, which didn't help at all as some residue from the pepper spray was still lingering on the fabric.

The doors all appeared closed again and he had no energy to go back and check that the guard was actually dead this time. Three bullets should be enough, he thought and now he just wanted for it all to be over, to kill this old bastard who seemed to be guarded by all the pain in the world.

He stumbled forward, deciding to ignore the rest of the rooms here and trust that he'd come across the correct one further on. Maybe this entire corridor was some kind of booby trap arrangement, and if it was, he'd just skip the rest thank you very much. Turning left onto a rather more serene hallway also lined with portraits and plants, he lurched forwards, trying to listen for voices as he went. Stopping his stealthy approach at the third door, voices could be heard from inside. The door was insulating the lowered voices but he was damn sure it was an old guy's voice, so he steadied himself and kicked the door in with all the force his weight could muster.

He panickingly fired off two rounds at the figure facing him, a youngish guy with dark hair who tried to reach his own weapon when the door was flung open. The man fell sideways to the floor, bullets taking him somewhere in the blurry upper torso. The Hitman turned to the other occupants of the room, what appeared to be two older men and pointed the handgun at them.

'Whatever you are being paid, it will be doubled if you put down that weapon now'. A voice came from one of the indistinct figures.

'Too late.' His voice croaked far more than he himself expected, not realising the pepper spray was still playing havoc with his respiratory system. 'Got car keys?'

The blurry man on the left held out a set of keys and walked over, handing it to him at arm's length.

'What car – colour?' The Hitman knew that this was the final opportunity, the big one. A successful hit and make off with an escape vehicle, although he was heavily dependent on the fuller return of his ocular faculties before a night drive could be considered viable.

'It…it's a black Range Rover. Parked outside' the old man added rather pointlessly. His accent sounded Scottish, clipped tones, he thought. That meant that the old guy on the right was probably his man. He'd kill them both anyway, no point leaving the place without making as sure as he could.

The pain in his eyes hadn't subsided, but the vision in his right eye had improved enough to be fairly confident of hitting the target, so he took aim at the first of his victims, only prevented in completing his mission by the momentary feeling of something extremely painful hitting his back, through the rucksack and into his jacket, piercing his skin and projecting him forwards, unconscious to the carpeted floor, his trigger pulled, but the bullet lodging neatly into the eye of the stuffed wildcat sitting on a chest of drawers behind the two old men.

It may have been a few minutes, or just moments before he wakened again. A bang had echoed around the room and stirred him. He lay on the carpet and his eyes, painful but working, just, fell on the revolver just beside his right hand. A figure walked past him and, as he did, the

Hitman pulled his fingers around the butt of the pistol and rolled around, taking aim at the figure standing in front of him. He fired as the other man moved aside, hitting him somewhere but he couldn't be sure, lower than he wanted, but he felt a bullet impact his own arm, driving it downwards and making him drop the weapon. Trying to reclaim it with his left hand, he saw the figure loom above him and as he lifted his head to see who it was, a bullet hit him in the upper shoulder, then another exploded right beside it. Dropping the pistol and stunned by the impacts, he looked down to see the carpet coming towards him, again.

My dreams are more vivid than usual; perhaps the shooting of crazy Owen is stirring my mind a little, so when I wake all I can hear is explosions and crashes, then silence and I nod off again. I'm not sure how long goes past, but I'm wakened properly this time by another explosion, definitely a firearm which sounds off near my door. I look round in a panic but my revolver is downstairs, still in the pocket of the blood-smeared parka in Gilfillan's office, where the rifle is also stored with the shotguns. I pull on jeans, a jumper and boots and open the door a crack to see what the hell is going on. I immediately fear that another contract has been accepted for Sir Mathieson, or John, or maybe me too. There's some noise from downstairs now and whoever passed this corridor seems to have moved on.

I peek out carefully and there's a hole in the wall at the end of my corridor, plus a table and vase have been trashed. The noise continues downstairs and I suppose I should follow it, despite being not only being unarmed but also still completely knackered from the hunt for Tim Balliol. There are a few other noises, which sound like they are from another part of the house, but I guess whoever is in the building has made the rest flee. I wish that I'd spoke to whoever was in the library before I went upstairs, at least then I would know who is in Inverannan and maybe what I am facing.

The corridor is strewn with glass and plaster, so I try to avoid treading on it and stay quiet. I glance around the corner, no sign of anyone there, so I follow down to the first floor. Here's a scene though; bottles, ornaments, blood and signs of a shotgun having been fired at least once but probably more. A woman's discarded shoe lies outside a closed door; I check the room but its empty, just a double bedroom with signs of recent habitation. Another cautious look round the corner down to the first floor and there lies the first casualty, one of Sir Mathieson's guys, can't quite recognise him without the top two-thirds of his head though. Quite a blood spray too, whatever shotgun the assassin is using isn't of the lightweight variety, so my priority is to get armed. I head along the corridor to Gilfillan's office; however, he's lying in the corridor beside a chair, either drunk or dead by the look of it. I don't have the time to delay, but I feel guilty if I don't check if he's alive. Turning back from his office door, I get to him and kneel down, turning to see what's happened. There's no blood, but he's out cold; I pull the front of his tweed jacket open and the smell of whisky hits me, he's saturated in the stuff. I nearly crap myself as Gilfillan inhales suddenly, the rasping gurgle reverberating along the corridor and he grips my forearm reflexively, eyes open and gaping at me. His hand goes to his chest, then into his inside pocket, pulling out a mangled hip flask with a bullet embedded right in the centre of what was a nameplate with a thistle emblem below it. He sits up and looks at his jacket in disbelief, there's another hole in it where a bullet went through the material at the side and seems to have missed Gilfillan completely. He's OK apart from a bruised chest I guess, so he's had his luck for the day.

'Who did this Magnus? How many were there?'

He looks up at me, seeming to return from wherever his dazed aftermath had taken him. He shakes his head.

'One sir, that's all I saw. A pistol I think, he shot me from the end of the corridor. I was watching the door so he must have got in somewhere else.' This suggests that there may even be two assailants on the go, pistol man and shotgun man.

I help him up and back into his office. He opens a filing cabinet and pulls a bottle from behind the file boxes in the wall cabinet. His hands are shaking, but after a long swig from the bottle, he seems to find a more Zen-like place and sits back. I can't waste any more time with him, so retrieve my pistol and check it.

'Stay here Magnus. I'm going to see what the fuck is going on.' I head for the door, but decide Magnus probably should get ready to defend himself.

'Keep out of the way Magnus, but maybe get a weapon in case this guy comes back before I do.'

I leave him to it, whether he understands me or not I cannot say. I walk back to the ground floor, there's still no change there and no sign of life. I open the library door, crouching as I go but it's empty, well, of people anyway. The room has, recently, been host to a rather messy party. There's bottles, glasses, plates and food all over, which seems to have been abandoned in something of a hurry. Drinks nearly full, plates of snacks and what looks like a pitcher of cocktails sitting on the mantelpiece, fruit floating at the top. I check around the rest of the ground floor but no sign of life. At that, I see Magnus standing in his corridor, a crossbow loaded and held with the manner of an expert, albeit a drunken one. He gives me a thumbs-up and I return it, thinking that I would be extra cautious next time I walk towards him as he's more than likely to prang the first person to hove into sight unless he falls asleep first.

There's another salvo of gunshots somewhere in the floor above and to the left, maybe the direction I have just came from. I don't have time to check on anything else, I need to get to John and Sir Mathieson; sure as hell they are the targets. Before I get up to that floor, I hear running from the next corridor of this bloody building, although the steps could be echoing from the floor above. If it's the gunman, I need to keep out of sight, but now it sounds like more than one person, all running. I turn the next corner and I'm looking at Zoe, Gillian, Niamh and the rest of the office team, armed with a selection of fireside irons, a short sword and ready to chuck various items at me.

'It's me!' I shout in some panic as I see hands going back into the throwing position.

'Adam, what the fuck is going on?' Zoe is no doubt right to inquire, although she's asking the wrong one here.

'Fuck knows. I woke up to the sounds of chaos and I'm none the wiser after creeping around for ten minutes. Someone, at least one person, is probably here to kill Sir Mathieson, so that is where I'm heading unless you can tell me different?'

Zoe shakes her head at me. I'm not sure who these guys are, but they are checking in all the rooms, looking for the Allantons. We pepper sprayed one of them and had a real go at another one, but we had to run - he's got a bloody shotgun and he was firing it all over the place.' I realise now that they are all in a significantly drunk condition, especially when Gillian comes over and gives me a rather passionate kiss. She breaks off and we have a moment of looking at each other before I remember that we're in a stately home with two heavily armed assassins.

'Look, get into this room and lock the door. I'll try and get the Allantons and join you. Then we'll barricade ourselves in and wait for reinforcements, OK?' A shite plan possibly, but I'm under pressure and should probably prioritise getting along to help guard my employers.

I leave them as they take cover in this spare room with a lockable door, then head towards Sir Mathieson's room at a jog, glancing around each corner as I go. I have an impression that I've arrived too late, and feel distinctly panicky and out of control now. I stop at the first-floor corridor of the east wing. There's a fleeting thought now, sneaked into my mind, that my future success might not be fully dependant on Sir Mathieson and John surviving. If they get killed here, what are the chances of me still getting a pay-off like the others, or even taking over the UK Portfolio? This unsettling dichotomy now in place, I'm less sure about jumping into what looks like an assassination attempt by at least one unknown perpetrator who is quite probably more professional and capable than me. Perhaps I should just be careful here, I think. My continued existence is the one critical aspect which I must ensure; the rest may be mere happenstance.

Two rounds ring out ahead, in the corridor around the corner from me, quite probably from Sir Mathieson's room. Moments later, a shotgun discharges and I shake at the sudden explosion, flattening myself to the wall and readying the pistol in case the gunmen are going to escape my way. Moments pass and nothing else happens, so I walk slowly along the corridor and hear the door of Sir Mathieson's bedroom closing with a slam, I hear some voices behind it, but can't quite catch who is talking. I pass by the door and turn the handle of the next room which opens silently, dark and empty inside. There's no connecting door, so I open the sash window and lean out, trying to get sight of whoever is in the next room. Snow whooshes in, I still can't get an angle to see without going out onto the balcony. Its bloody freezing and I'm without a jacket but need to go farther to see what's going on. I wipe the snow from the edge of the parapet and get my right boot up. I take what I suddenly think of as a lowp from there, across perhaps a three-foot gap, onto the balcony outside the room of Sir Mathieson, missing the equivalent parapet there and landing face-first, flat but safely into a deep and thankfully cushioning layer of snow. Inside the room, all hell breaks loose, a cacophony of explosions and yells and I decide to stay in my snow pile until it calms.

My heart is pumping and I wait a moment until I look up. The snow dampened any sound I would have made, along with the gunfire and howling wind which hasn't calmed any since I got back from my trek around the Inverannan area, looking unsuccessfully for the escapee accountant.

So, it's a fair surprise when I kneel up and see the little bastard himself, Tim Balliol, standing side-on to the door and pointing a huge hunting shotgun at whoever is in the room. There's a moment of panic when he glances towards me, but I immediately lean backwards, hiding my upper half from his view. This position lets me see part of the rest of the room, including a pair of recumbent legs projecting from behind a cabinet to the right of my window. These are John's, I'm sure and from a first glance it seems certain that he's been shot. I can't figure for the life of me how Balliol got here, or why he is pointing a weapon at my employers, but now, because it's him, I really need to get involved. I shuffle closer to the window pane to get a better view.

Balliol looks insane, covered in cuts to his face and his eyes are popping out of his head. I then realise that this lunatic tableau has more to it than I first thought. There's another figure, dressed in army fatigues, on the floor with his arms forward and not in a great state. Further along, although I can't see them all, it looks like Sir Mathieson, possibly McGowan and maybe someone else are the subjects of Balliol's ire. He is having a stream-of-consciousness rant by the sound of it, his normally dusty demeanour shaken off and replaced by this new psycho version of the timid accountant. He also looks like he's going to pull the trigger at any moment, so I'd better get on with it. I pull the revolver from my jeans pocket and check its ready; a slow lean back to get a good position and wait for a moment when his shotgun isn't pointed at my boss. He spits something vitriolic at Sir Mathieson; the shotgun leans up and with a squeeze of my trigger, Tim Balliol reels back as the bullet hits him, not where I aimed but straight through the right side of his face, a spurt of his blood and possibly teeth spraying onto the door.

I pull up the window with little difficulty. Balliol has sort of sat down and is still holding the shotgun, but looking at the door as if wondering why it's all red. He turns to me as I pull myself through the small opening I've managed at the window, cutting myself on the hand while I go, then walk over and land a seriously angry kick to Balliol's already damaged head. He is thrown over and lies in the doorway, silently and ideally permanently. Sir Mathieson and Benny are sitting down on the other side of the room so I walk over to them and try to see how injured they both are, it looks like the shotgun has been fired near them and some pellets have grazed them. As I do so, the guy who was lying down, at first appearance I wrongly assumed dead, makes a grab for a gun, which I hadn't noticed, lying a foot or so from him. I fall to one side to try and avoid his bullet, to get my aim sorted before the army chap gets up and shoots properly. Simultaneously, we fire at each other and both shots find their mark. I feel like I've been punched on the leg, but I know it's a bullet, and it's really, really, fucking painful. I let out a yelp and look over to my assailant, who is trying to pick up his pistol in his other hand, my lucky bullet having hit him on the right forearm. Limping over till I'm directly above him, I shoot him twice, despite hearing what sounds like Sir Mathieson telling me not to kill him. I now see Balliol stirring, even after being shot and kicked; the little shite is trying to get his shotgun up and pointed at me. I lurch up and over to him now, pushing his shotgun barrel downwards with my left hand, away from me and shooting him in the knee at the same time. He wails and I take the shotgun over to Sir Mathieson, handing him it before I sit down on the bed and, my work necessarily complete for the evening, collapse unconscious.

The Hitman woke up, lying on a white, raised metal bed, in tremendous pain and with an acute sense of his own impending mortality. To his left, separated partially by a white cabinet of the sort found in hospitals, another figure appeared to be in a similar state. He also realised that this was not actually a hospital and that they were lying on trolleys, not beds. The room itself was roughly constructed, stone walled without plaster and heated by a log fire in a rudimentary hearth, directly across from him. He couldn't raise his head fully, but after a few moments of checking, as he was trained to do in the army, he was more than relieved that all his limbs, hands, feet and other treasured attachments were still functioning and visibly attached to his torso. His complete body, however, was giving him pain like never before, especially his upper arm, back and shoulder, not to mention the headache, earache and raw eyes; he became aware of the agony more now, the feeling that front and back, he'd sustained a fair bit of damage.

There was no memory of how he'd ended up in this state; he tried to remember the last moments, his walk around that appallingly chaotic house trying to find and kill the old man. He recalled objects hitting him, not sure at what intervals, but after standing in the room, facing his target and the end of his mission, well, that was absent from his memory bank.

Looking around, his neck stiff, he could see no method of requesting help, so emitted a gargling noise which he hoped would attract someone's attention. No luck with the first, he tried again, louder and longer this time until a door opened and a medical person stood beside him.

Another one joined in, female this time and questions were asked, although his responses were perfunctory grunts. An injection into his arm later, he was wheeled from the room, out into an ante-chamber where he then lay, silent and increasingly nervous, for what seemed an eternity. Finally, a surge of icy air announced the arrival of others, men who were soon to dismiss the medical staff and sit either side of him. He opened his eyes to see the pair of elderly gentlemen whom, the last time he was conscious, were on the other side of his pistol. He let out an involuntary whimper.

'Good afternoon. I assume you know who I am?'

The voice, clipped, Scottish, frightening like the officers of long ago, scary as hell and beside him, right there. He nodded, only slightly.

'I need to ask some questions of you, which I understand will be difficult, however my staff assure me that your vocal capacities should be unaffected by your wounds. Do you understand?'

This time, he replies, a soft but distinct 'yes'.

'Excellent. I, well we, require information on who you are, who paid you to commit this crime and any other information which you have on the matter. I am ambivalent as to your future, so I strongly suggest that you co-operate fully.' The words were spoken as if they were the terms and conditions of a bloody salesman, and the Hitman felt from that, all things considered, he would best tell them what he knew and see if he could get out of the awful place alive. Ten minutes later, he had convinced Sir Mathieson and Benny that he knew little more than the name of his old comrade who had hired him and the details of Sir Mathieson's whereabouts.

216

Accepting the coincidence of overhearing the Allanton's conversation at their Menorcan hotel, they were confident that no more could be gleaned from him.

Sir Mathieson patted the arm of the Hitman, rising and leaving the bothy to step out into the cold air, warm cap back in place over his receding grey hair. He gestured to two of his men, standing at a cluster of four-wheel drives, dressed in winter army gear and carrying bags, to come over. A single muffled gunshot sounded inside and moments later, Benny McGowan emerged and the body removal crew replaced him inside, their work commencing as Benny's finished. The two old men got into the back seats of the closest vehicle and were driven back to Inverannan House, the roads still snow-covered but after being ploughed, at least accessible.

Sir Mathieson turned to his friend. 'Better now?'

'Aye' Came the unreadable response from his long-time subordinate, friend and occasionally, when needed, advisor. Benny never liked risk and preferred his and his master's opponents to be dead, if at all possible, along with anyone who could cause future problems. In this case, Sir Mathieson had to agree. They weren't quite in a position to research the Hitman; however premature death is an occupational hazard of such a man. After trying twice to murder Sir Mathieson, he was most unlikely to be allowed to maintain his position in the land of the living. The other one, the Balliol chap, could still be of use, for a time at least. Some of this hadn't been his fault, but some had and for that, he would have to make redress, although he had inadvertently started on that process by painfully losing part of his lower jaw and some peripheral damage courtesy of Sir Mathieson's own young protégé, Adam Darnow.

Benny McGowan and Sir Mathieson settled into the library on their arrival at Inverannan. The place was still busy with workers, much of the repairs to the fabric of the building being carried out by former employees from the village, happy to lend a hand for a generous reward. Some were rightly annoyed that their wives and daughters had been caught up in the frantic mess of the insurgent evening, however calm discussions with Sir Mathieson and the deployment of large sums of compensation soon drew their ire to an acceptable conclusion. At least no-one outside the Allanton professional ranks had been hurt, with the exception of Magnus Gilfillan, who with some luck would recover fully and perhaps use the entire experience as a catalyst to discontinue his daily alcohol abuse. In the meantime, Sir Mathieson and Benny, who had been through so much together, concocted the bones of a plan, while their colleagues rested, soon to be given their orders.

I've been drowsy for a while, not sure what has been happening; then I wake up with a sickening feeling in my stomach and a piercing agony in my leg. My eyes open, a crust on my eyelids suggesting that either I fell asleep crying or I've been asleep for a long time, or both. My mouth is dry, my left hand has a mitten-like bandage around it and when I move my other arm towards the glass of water on the bedside table, I'm inhibited by the drip that I realise is attached to the back of that hand. My head is lifted from behind and a glass is raised slowly to my lips, I'm in pain again as the water rushes over my arid tongue and throat. I lie back and realise that it's Gillian, so I smile at her and she hugs me, long and with feeling.

She sits back and I look down, my left leg bandaged but thankfully still attached, and no other signs of any new damage.

'How are you feeling?'

'Fantastic.' I croak. 'Someone appears to have shot me.'

Gillian snorts with laughter, a good sign that my condition is otherwise healthy enough.

'You should see the other guys.' She looks serious now. I make a face to tell her that I need a bit more of an update than that.

'They are both alive, Sir Mathieson has had them taken to another property though; his men got here after the snow ploughs got going. John is OK; he's next door with the doctor. They had to take two bullets out of his shoulder. Yours was what they apparently call a "through and through", but they still had to work on you a fair bit, so they just kept you sedated.' I nod and ask about Sir Mathieson.

'He's fine, just sort of angry now. I don't know what is going on; Zoe is doing most of the organising. I just said I'd help with you.' She is holding my hand and I can now see tears dripping down her face.

Gillian shakes her head, trying to keep her voice going. 'Magnus got shot twice in the back and Jim and Charlie are both dead.'

There's a moment when I don't wrap my head around this, I left Magnus safe, holding a crossbow and a half-full bottle of whisky. That must have been the shots I heard before I got to Sir Mathieson's room. Gillian gives me a kiss and heads out to tell them I'm awake.

Five minutes later, the door opens and Zoe comes in with Sir Mathieson, who has a few slim plasters on his face and neck which must have been the work of either Balliol or the other guy. He shakes my hand and looks concerned, with a distinct hint of anger. I ask what the hell happened and Zoe takes the lead.

'It was a total shambles. This apparently was the guy who set the fire on the yacht, contracted by someone we are trying to find and funded by an as-yet-unknown party. Balliol was just a bloody disaster; He'd turned up here uninvited yesterday, looking for a lift home no less. It looks like he was struggling after being questioned, Charlie or Jim shot him full of coke to keep him alive and, well, you saw what happened.'

Sir Mathieson replied. 'Then, they both ended up in my room. Thankfully you got there in time before it got any worse.'

Right now, I'm having a slightly giddy feeling again, like I often do in situations where insanity and chaos have taken precedence over sense. Sir Mathieson pats my arm. I tell him I still don't get it, ask if John is OK.

'He's recovering well. This so-called assassin shot him in the shoulder before Balliol hove into sight and blew the bugger's rucksack right off his back with that bloody shotgun. A damn shit-show and no mistake.' He looked close to tears too, but his expression hardened before they could take hold.

'We brought in some private medical staff by helicopter after the storm passed. The Inverannan team worked wonders until then, we are very appreciative of their efforts.' Sir Mathieson walks over to the window. 'We have also brought in reserve officers. John's chaps had been working with Williams in London, however, this rather unexpected intrusion warranted a re-prioritisation of our tasks. Should have done it sooner, but there's nothing can be done about that now.'

I sit up a little, which stretches the bandage on my leg, causing some discomfort and a brief period of muted swearing.

'So we settle in here until the situation becomes clearer?' I ask.

Zoe nods. 'We have investigations underway into a number of subjects. There is a further issue which you and I were not aware of.' She glances towards Sir Mathieson, who continues to stare out of the window.

'The intrusion to Sir Mathieson's personal account was not what it seemed. A series of large sums were taken, apparently, or so it was thought, by Balliol. We - or the team back at base anyway, are still attempting to trace the funds and the method, but it wasn't Balliol as far as we can tell.' Zoe looks frazzled, I realise, and if she is, the rest of us must be worse.

'Neither have we been able to determine who paid for the contracts, although we believe we know who the facilitator was.' This is new to me; I've never been involved in contracts or anything criminal outside of the Portfolio, which seems to have quickly diverted from near legitimacy to a state of military-level action. Sir Mathieson walks over to me and Zoe squeezes my hand before leaving, perhaps intuiting that the old man wants some time alone with me.

'Get some rest for a while, Adam. I will not forget what you did for me and my son. We reward loyalty well. Neither I nor John would still be alive without the actions of Zoe, the staff here and most crucially, your own.' I am lost for words, so I nod at him before he turns and leaves. I realise that I still don't have a full picture of the events of what was either last night or perhaps two nights ago.

Two days of boredom and opiates pass before I can dress and get out of the bedroom, walking with a bandaged leg, straight as possible to keep the stitches in place. John had already dropped in on me a couple of visits and we'd arranged to meet in the library for lunch, where I could stretch out on the chaise-longue. He looks pale but otherwise fine, having only a shoulder-strapping to show that he had so recently been close to being killed. Sir Mathieson is there to help me when I enter, my five-minute solo struggle to negotiate the downwards journey on the staircase having taken a bit out of me, not helped by the giant bandage mitt which is still needed to pad the taped cuts on the palm of my hand. Sir Mathieson has a few pellet grazes on his face, which I hadn't noticed before. The bruising and swelling around it has purpled now, however, he does not seem like a victim at all, his vitality staring out of him and stirring me to feel less sorry for myself. He makes coffee for me and sits down, joining John on the leather Chesterfield. He starts to tell us his update.

'We have, as of this morning, been able to communicate with the redoubtable Tim Balliol. Despite some vocal difficulties' He looks to me with a smirk. 'He has been capable of telling us some more, at least of the financial issue. It appears that, despite being a wilfully consistent fraudster and thief, young master Balliol is adamant that he has committed no such acts since joining our employment. We presented him with the facts and our findings so far and he has, rather helpfully, provided us with a scenario which may lead us to the scoundrel who perpetrated this theft.' He stops and helps himself to a sandwich from a table beside him, offering me the plate afterwards. I demur.

'His hypothesis, which I will qualify has in no way been tested, is that another of our employees had gained access to my own account and set up another in the name of Balliol. He or she would transfer funds through these after Balliol and possibly all of us were terminated. Far-fetched, I agree, but a scenario which almost occurred.'

John is shaking his head, looking either annoyed or frustrated. 'Not possible. Our staff have been with us for years, decades in some cases. All checked and monitored, all locked down and their passwords kept separate, not one single person know the details needed for that to work.'

Sir Mathieson looked straight at him. 'Perhaps, if some of our trusted staff were given the responsibility to monitor and oversee the work of Balliol, what then? Could they have collected the passwords, the keys needed to access these accounts, piece by piece?'

'No. Williams is the accounts administrator. Cheryl and four in her team have access to the general accounts under his supervision; in addition, Zoe makes them change passwords on a cyclic basis, each of the team having their own identifiers, part of which is given to her in case something like this happens.'

Sir Mathieson placed his cup on the table and looked to both of us in turn, then lowered his voice.

'I know. However, if more than one of those staff whom you have mentioned collude with each other, then somehow gain wider access through Balliol's work, then what?'

John sits back and stares at the ceiling. 'Bugger' is all he says.

We finish our lunch, our plans and our timetables for the work we are required to do. Once complete, I stand stiffly and limp over to the window. The worst of the weather has passed since I last looked outside, but still lies deep and with piles of ploughed snow at the sides of the car park. Someone has obviously done a fair bit of work with the snow plough, a tad late to avoid all the shambles we endured but at least we can drive now, or in my case be driven away from Inverannan House if need be. I'm processing the information from Sir Mathieson, but I need to watch what I say to him. The last thing I need is to be implicated with whatever kind of internal group fraud this may be.

Turning to John, I tell him 'This still doesn't add up. Our guys could have been coerced, blackmailed or just plain greedy, but they must have known that this was a risky gamble. Balliol's premise is that, if they reckoned we'd all be dead, that no-one would go back in, go deep enough to trace them and they would be off, away with Sir Mathieson's money and whatever else? It doesn't make sense. There's something we're not seeing yet.' John looks pensive but nods agreement while Sir Mathieson continues.

'Our next steps require some caution. You will both return to London by car, tomorrow if you are well enough to travel.' Fuck me, I can't even bend my leg yet and I've got to sit in a car for a full day. Sympathy is suspended now that he's back looking for revenge, and of course his money.

He leaves us, off to arrange our transport.

'Zoe not involved in this?' I ask John.

'No. Dad doesn't know how, or if she's involved, so he has tasked her with the clear-up here, for now. Most of my guys will stay here to make sure no other problems pop up.' His glance suggests that the discussion about Zoe's involvement is something he does not wish to discuss further, so I leave it at that and lurch off to get some clean clothes on and see how best to pack up for London.

Three hours later, I get some dinner sent up; one of John's men brings it and asks how I'm doing. I recognise him, largely because he looks a bit like someone off the telly, although I can't remember the name I'm looking for. He also tells me that he's our driver for tomorrow, early start as he hopes to be down in London by nightfall.

I really can't be arsed going anywhere yet, but I nod and tell him I'll be there. After packing and not with the opportunity to see anyone else before I go, I fall asleep, codeine doing its stuff with my bullet wound and cuts. With the aid of a rather juddering alarm clock, I wake at six a.m. for my journey.

It's milder than before, but as I walk to the car I feel that my recuperation might have better taken place over a few more days. I've taken off the bandages on my hand and left the wounds open to help them dry a little, although partially this is because I'm fed up wearing a gigantic mitten. I sit beside John in the rear passenger seat, extending my leg and resting it on the centre console when needed. He seems brighter now, his colour returning more to normal and no longer using his arm sling. He passes me some tablets and, whatever they are, I fall asleep way before we've even reached the border, only awakening when darkness falls and we're leaving the Midlands. John seems to have been on his phone a fair bit, although he chooses not to share whatever messages he's received. The traffic is light, for London, and we're soon at our office building, surrounded by quiet streets as the worst of the rush hour traffic has passed, here at least. The underground car park has a lift to our floor which I'm really glad of, my leg has stiffened up after the long journey and I reckon that another few days are needed before I can walk without my stick.

Williams is waiting for us, no doubt on Sir Mathieson's request. He shakes our hands and takes the lift up with us, exchanging pleasantries as if we're arriving for a sociable coffee. I have spent some time with Williams, here, and found him to be a rather deep-natured, professional type. Around mid-forties, dark hair turning grey and his stature slim, perhaps even gaunt. When I started with the Allantons, he initially seemed to me the epitome of a sensible, reliable operative although I later learned that he was something of a night owl, a casino man if you would believe. Hardly likely to betray his employer, although that, well that will be examined.

We enter the long, typical London office board room, anonymous in decor due to our line of business. I smile slightly as I imagine portraits of the Allanton family on the wall, holding bags of cash and with plaques commemorating their years in the narcotics business. The thought gone, I return to the work in hand and dismiss my juvenile daydreams.

John sits Williams between us, with our driver behind him. He sets out what has happened, chronologically, up to the point where Balliol's supposition ends. Williams looks like he's been insulted, but after a last panicked denial from him, John's driver grabs him by the hair and spins him out of the chair to the floor and stands over him. A few moments of punching and kicking ensues, before Williams is returned forcibly to his chair, hair now rather out of place as is his nose and a front tooth. He is held by his neck and I still have an odd feeling that the driver looks like someone famous. I lean towards Williams and his head is steered round to look at me. We're looking at each other now, except for his left eye which is closing after our driver's ministrations.

'You have exactly ten seconds to start telling me what you have done and who you were working with. If you do, we will let you live. If you don't, you will be dead after that time. Go.' I look at my watch for effect, a device I have used a few times since my employment commenced with the Allantons. It doesn't take half that time for

Williams to start to talk. During which, John Allanton has placed his phone on the table to record the voice of the battered Williams, who will not, as I promised, survive this situation. With a few intermittent prompts, he blubbers on for a few minutes, enough to incriminate Zoe and the rest of his subordinates at the Portfolio, more or less validating that part of Balliol's theory.

He's weeping while talking and looking at me with pleading eyes. I wonder if he really expects me to save him. After we have no questions left, I nod and the driver deals with him quickly and without mess. He fetches a body bag for Williams and as he leaves, I ask his name. A glance at John Allanton, who confirms to him that it's OK, and he tells me it's Donnie. He's dragging the bag out through the door when I get the epiphany. I click my fingers and point at him.

'Sean Bean, the actor.'

He smiles at me. 'Get that all the time.' With that, the door swings shut and Williams is off to be incinerated.

John is already on the phone to Sir Mathieson and I limp over for some water, handing a glass to John first. I'm glad I slept on the way down south; it looks like tonight might be the night of the long knives, for some. He closes his call after five minutes and we sit in silence. I know John and he'll be considering deeply our next few moves, seeing what variations on the outline plan are required.

'My men will bring the rest of them in. I will call each of them, tell them a car is waiting and they need to come in urgently. Unfortunately, unlike Williams, the rest of them have partners or families who will miss them so our approach must be more business-like.' I agree with him

228

and, getting my stick, head out and along to my office, leaving John to make his calls and initiate the next phase of our plan.

The building is, as I always thought, an austere and sterile place to work. There are no photos, nothing on desks, just workstations and chairs. There is no paperwork for investigators to trail through, no personal items to associate us with our desks and crucially, no hint that our business is anything more than a property investment house. Our website holds all that needs be in the public domain and our lawyers hold copies of anything else. It is wiped clean daily, seashore if you like, the tide receding leaving no trace of us for any to find. My office is the same as all others, only more tucked away, my preferred low profile even more secretive than the others. From the outset, I have avoided any unnecessary social contact with lower-level colleagues. Apart from there being no real point anyway, my guarded conduct has always been driven by the thought that, if we were to be investigated, that I would just be described as aloof, not joining in much and with only the already-vetted few aware of my role in the business. Aware enough to provide any actual evidence, that is.

The next hour or so passes in silence, with me carrying out the tasks allotted and waiting for the staff to arrive, along with a number of John's men. I hear the lift opening and closing a few times and I ready myself.

It takes most of the night to interrogate the staff and reach our conclusions; only one of them tried to resist for any meaningful time, and even then nothing that threats could not overcome. We had something on everyone; that was the key. That's why I didn't want Balliol, although this intrusion was not of his making. John and I gathered the facts, the passwords and accounts, and, given that we had nobody else left to trust, spent the whole of the next working day reversing the transfers, the thefts and the damage that had been done. We brought the rather dishevelled Cheryl through to explain how to do some of the banking work. Neither I nor John was capable of navigating all of the systems in use or the methods used to move the contents. By 7pm, almost all of the funds were back, or we were pending approvals for them to be released into their original accounts. It was then that our misbehaving employees were sent home, with instructions to tell their relatives that the systems had crashed and their presence had been needed overnight to fix the problem. They were also, of course, reminded of the parlous situation they were in and the consequences of further miscommunication; for now, though, we leave it there. Other fish and all that.

We sit in John's office and drink coffee, my eyes are sore with the lack of sleep and the glare of long hours looking at the laptop screen. John Allanton looks as knackered as I've ever seen him and I realise, despite my general lack of emotional empathy, that he's taken the betrayals of his personnel worse than anyone. Me, I'm immune from this type of sentiment as I generally don't trust anyone, especially not here in London.

'You OK?' I ask.

'Yeah, been a long few days. I'm missing the kids too.' He looks at me and reaches out to shake my hand. 'Thanks for doing all this. Too few people I can trust now.' I smile and drink my coffee.

He rises and puts on his jacket. 'Get home for some sleep mate. We'll meet here at 8am?' I nod but I really want a bath, food and to sleep for at least 12 hours. Still, this won't be forever, I know.

We head out the front door, a couple of John's guys leaving at the same time and it suddenly looks like I'm part of a group of city boys leaving the office late, instead of a team of rather highly-focused criminals taking a break from progressing their revenge plan. How well we seem to blend into the rest of the office staff milling around, their late shifts complete and a few heading for the bars down near the river, pressure off and time for a drink. For us though, another regroup and we start again, the next day and for a time afterwards until we are restored.

My silent taxi takes me all the way back to Knightsbridge, the apartment warm as I'd left the heating on a timer while I was away. Taking a shower, I remove the dressings on my leg and the strips from my hand, all of which seem to have been super-glued to the skin. Swearing and gradually teasing the dressings off my leg to reveal some clumsy looking stitches, I manage to get my first look at the exit wound on the back of my leg. It's bigger than the one at the front and considerably harder to get the new dressing on. I get some microwave food from the freezer and, despite it tasting like plastic and deeply unlike its promised tasty and spicy flavour I finish it and head for bed. It seems like moments later when my phone alarm buzzes and I can't deny that it's time to get up. I can't be bothered showering again and getting my dressing and plasters wet, so I wash in the sink, dress and, stopping at the door to retrieve my spare revolver and holster, take the waiting car back to the office. It's Donnie, who gives me a couple of messages from John, but I just listen, I need some coffee and painkillers before I'm ready to communicate.

I sort both of those out in my office, then meet John in his. Donnie joins us, with another guy whom I vaguely recognise and I think works here too, not a soldier type, perhaps an IT guy. They both leave us after an initial briefing, then John and I finish and check the most recent reverted transactions. Sir Mathieson now has almost £12 million back in his accounts and this part of the Portfolio looks like it is expected to. Two hours have passed and our financial problems are resolved. Another half an hour and passwords and administrator details have all been changed and thank god we're finished with all that stuff.

'Now Phase Three' he tells me, rising and expecting me to follow. Tim Balliol is sitting alone in the main office, in a wheelchair, with his face bandaged up to just below his nose and with his leg in a blue plastic splint projecting onto a framed support. He has a breathing tube projecting from where I think the right side of his mouth should be and is looking at me with teary hatred.

'Good Morning Tim!' John welcomes him cheerily.

A whistle comes through Tim's breathing tube and I have to turn to avoid collapsing with laughter. John has his hands on his hips and seems to be back in management mode, although this may be entirely ironic for all I know.

'Tim is going for an operation this afternoon Adam. He's going to get his jaw all realigned and then they will have a look at what has to be done to his knee after that unfortunate accident. He's going to be staying in London until he's finished his little plan for the future of our finances, aren't you?' John grins happily at him.

Tim nods, painfully and another comical little whistle comes down his breathing tube. 'First of all Tim, we need your skills to help trace a couple of things. Will you do that, Tim?' Another single whistle, which I now realise means yes. John wheels him forward to the table and laptop, and Tim starts to tap the keyboard. John and I exchange a glance as we watch Tim, asking him to note some information as he navigates the systems and takes us into the end of our search for our elusive malefactor. Tim is indeed a genius at navigating financial systems and after a short while provides the name of the organisation which paid the unsuccessful assassins. A series of financial and company checks leads to some searches of electoral and phone systems, which quickly confirm the addresses we seek and, after saying cheerio to the clinic-bound Tim, we leave with our colleagues to pay our respects and ask some questions of the individuals in question. Our Range Rovers take less than an hour to reach the address in Ilford, where we park around the corner and watch four of our party, dressed as Police Officers, commence the intervention. Driving to the front gate, they knock and arrest the two men inside, quickly and without any fuss or fighting. Placing them in separate vehicles, the men are bound and their mobile phones removed, to be passed to our IT officer for further examination. We have a facility thirty miles farther, which we recently used for disposal purposes, so our questioning of these individuals will be most convenient there.

After arriving and divesting themselves of their uniforms, our colleagues set the two individuals on chairs in the building, an unused furniture factory of archaic design. We have to wait for them to get more agitated, during which time we get a chance to get a coffee from our thoughtful driver, who gets the piss taken out of him for bringing a picnic. I don't participate in the banter as I'm massively hungry and he's brought sandwiches, of which I demolish more than my share. I feel much better now and my various injuries aren't as bad as they were even a day or so ago. We finish our coffees and with our two visitors simmering, we get back over to them for some discussion. I take the lead.

They are both solidly ex-military, maybe around fifty but look terrified of us. They are glancing from face to face and, although I have no long-term history with John's guys, it looks like these two have recognised some of them and don't relish their presence. That said, it's me they really need to worry about. We establish which of them is which and this is confirmed by Donnie, who has managed to do some background checks on them. They've been making a decent living by, amongst other things, acting as middle-men in a few strong-arm jobs and hits, of which we have become embroiled. They start with some bravado about who they have in their corner but I discharge blank rounds from my revolver beside their ears a couple of times, tell them what I'll be doing next with live rounds and where it will hurt them, and we instantly get the information we need, no further fucking about. Donnie tells them that we'll be keeping them here for a bit and with that we're off, leaving them with a couple of guys and some leftover sandwiches.

John, who had left that whole thing to me, finally lets me know what he's thinking of doing. 'We'll hold onto them for a couple of days, and then let them go. The guys will tell them that their business is in liquidation permanently and if they make any moves or contact anyone, they will be in the same situation.' This seems very lenient to me, but I guess John might be reaching his limit with the whole mess. We'd been so close to leading a normal business, then this turnaround; I must admit I enjoyed parts of the past few days, getting shot admittedly being the lowest point.

Soon we're back in London and in the office. John puts the names on a whiteboard and, with Donnie away organising flights for both of us, we plan our next phase of work.

Back at Inverannan two days before, Tim had wakened
from his sedation, back to a world of pain and horror.
Strapped into a hospital trolley bed, he looked around the
room without any movement of his head, which was
tightly held in place by a neck brace and some metal rods,
which seemed to be attached higher on the structure. His
face, which was the main source of agony and, without
being able to raise his hands, felt from the inside that it
had been most grievously assaulted, although he couldn't
remember what had happened. It took a few hours
before the memory of the incident came back, partially,
into his traumatised mind, and only then after a
discussion with a pleasant elderly gentleman, despite Tim
not understanding who he was through the painkillers,
seemed intent to help him recover from his injuries in
return for his assistance. Tim was glad to help, although
this was impossible as the only sound he could make was
a somewhat asthmatic whistle through his breathing tube.
He was also completely off his tits on morphine and at
least three other liquid additives to his drip, so his
judgement on who to trust, or not, may not have been
wholly reliable at that point.

He was, after the next discussion with the old man,
allowed to reply using a small laptop, which was placed
on his lap and his wrist ties removed by a nurse. From
his uncomfortable position, not quite looking straight at
the laptop screen, he answered questions on the word
processing application when asked. He was also given
some other, different medicine which made him even
more helpful, although it did make him rather nauseous.
The old man, who he now recognised slightly but not

specifically, asked him first about his life, general stuff which he answered honestly and helpfully, although why anyone would be interested in his personal life evaded him completely. Still, it was nice that someone was taking an interest in him.

The questions then moved into his work, the things he did for a living. Tim loved accountancy, loved the simplicity and the logic of its form and above all, loved that he was the best at it, the best he'd ever heard of. When he was young, he quickly understood that he wasn't a sportsman, or good-looking, or talented, or sociable, or artistic, or musical. He tried all sorts of activities and hobbies, he exerted himself, he tried, many times at many things, but Tim, well Tim was shite at everything. Everything except accountancy, that is. So when he was asked to tell this indulgent pensioner about his favourite subject, how he did it all, the clever stuff, well for Tim it was just Christmas. He gave examples, of everywhere he had worked, what he did and what he learned and why he left, which was always their fault.

After he had a rest and they had a nice chat about the types of weather they both liked, the old man asked about his most recent employment, and what he did there. So, Tim, his blood saturated with morphine and a steady low drip of sodium thiopental, launched his typed confession of all that he did, knew and was about to do, for the good of the company. Occasional prompts kept him going, a few denials made, which confused Tim as he was asked about stealing money, which he hadn't really. He hadn't worked with anyone else either, not to do anything wrong anyway. It was all exhausting and Tim, his mind a jumble of synaptic misfires, eventually passed out for the day.

The next morning, Tim had awakened to the same experience, his pain receding in the haze of strong opiates and barbiturates making him pliable as he lay inert with his laptop. With Sir Mathieson Allanton beside him, he completed his input to the old man's plan. An hour and a half of questions and tapping on the keyboard proved that Tim, despite his many, many flaws was innocent of any misconduct against the Allanton family. He even started to take an unexpected lead on some of the analysis, as his drugged but reliable auditor's thought processes comprehended the situation and offered some suggestions, some scenarios where such thefts could have conceivably been carried out. Tim remembered the long days in the London office, monitored and shadowed by a small team of inferior accountants who had to keep asking him what he was doing, why he was doing it and even then, only just keeping up with his strategy and methods. He knew now that they could have worked together, taken notes of passwords, account numbers, keys and names, organisations and contacts. They could, with a bit of effort and a lot of disloyalty to their employer, moved the money through accounts until it ended up somewhere secret, making it look all the while like poor Tim had done it all. Well, for professional honour if nothing else, Tim was not having that, not one bit.

The old man was very, very pleased with Tim and gave him a beaming smile at the end of their chat. He passed the laptop to another old man, who Tim had seen beside him, sometimes. That man told Tim that they would take him to the hospital soon, to London, to get his wounds fixed and then all would be fine. He told Tim that the medical staff had checked his knee and that the bullet had just grazed the important bones, and that even his jaw would be fine after a couple of operations, except for a bit of scarring. Tim cried then, tears of joy and sadness and he wished, so deeply, that the man was telling the truth.

Tim slept then, for a long time. He was in pain, hungry and confused when he finally awoke, the vehicle in which he travelled less than smooth as it hurtled southwards. He was alone in the back the whole way, looking around at the cabinets, the fire extinguisher and paraphernalia of an ambulance, private it seemed. He was strapped in tight, lying on his back but not flat, propped up enough so that he wouldn't choke, perhaps. Tim tried to speak, but his jaw was padded inside and out, taped up too and with only his breathing tube to make a noise with. He tried to whistle with it, and made quite a decent job of "Land of Hope and Glory", much to the amusement of the driver and nurse who watched and listened on the CCTV pointing at Tim from the ceiling. They were going to check on him, but the journey was long and they were under orders to get Tim back to London for first thing in the morning. Tim slept again, after his whistling, until the ambulance stopped in an enclosed car park and his helpers transferred him into a wheelchair with a leg extension and, via a lift, up to the office he recognised as the hub of the Allanton operation, the Portfolio.

He was left in an office for a while, his wrists thankfully freed and only his condition and fear preventing flight. Hunger was clawing at his stomach, but he knew that it would be a while before his mouth is in any state to chew food. Nobody had told him specifically what was wrong with it, but he could feel with his tongue that all was not well and gaps were there, where they weren't before. Still, he was alive and if the old man was telling the truth, maybe they weren't going to kill him, maybe even help him, well that would be just great. His problem was that, as his capacity to think returned as the barbiturates faded, so did his fear grow. If the old man was John Allanton's father, however, then he would have told his son not to kill poor Tim, that it wasn't his fault at all, none of it.

So Tim hoped anyway, as John Allanton and that monstrous Scotsman entered the room where he sat. Allanton seemed to be acting decently, although Tim knew, after working with a fair few maniacs, that a smile does not always mean that someone is about to be nice to someone. Quite the opposite with that Scottish guy anyway, his eyes were like dark portals to hell, so Tim thought anyway. He'd seen him in action and if anything frightened Tim, it was this distant, unreadable bastard who he tried to avoid at all costs and was now, unfortunately, sitting across from him. He broke away from his sphincter-tightening terror to look at John Allanton, who was asking him to do something, so Tim nodded as best he could and tried to listen, a laptop placed on the table for him to work on, and work he did. It didn't take long for the now nearly-lucid Tim to trace a few payments, transferred to cover companies whose names failed to conceal the owners and their addresses. When he reached the end of the trail, Tim turned the laptop to the two men and, avoiding their gaze, waited for their reaction. Instead of a partially-expected bullet, John Allanton thanked Tim instead and told him that he was destined for a clinic, there to commence the repair of his fragmented jaw. They left a drained Tim to watch the door close, then moments later he was wheeled back to his ambulance and thence to a private clinic, where Tim rested, recovered and thanked the gods of accountancy for his continued existence.

The last leg of John's flight took him to Melbourne, arriving on an autumnal day with a fair bit of the summer heat enduring. Fetching his case from the carousel, he took a taxi to the hotel just before noon. His room looked down onto the muddy Yarra River, which despite the pleasant sunny day, still looked like a flow of slurry meandering through the city. He checked his phone and realised he'd missed a call from his wife, so he tried the home number but it made an odd sound, not connecting. He took his jacket off and felt pleased that his shoulder was no longer giving him any great pain, even after the flight. It had been a busy week, a week of working and planning, and now acting on those plans.

Balliol was proven right, the unpleasant little turd, that a group of his co-workers were responsible for taking the money. It was all about the theft of the Portfolio funds; a cabal of greedy bastards working in the London office of the Portfolio who wanted their share of the wealth. They were well paid, but London is an expensive place to enjoy and to John's embarrassment they realised that his managerial disinterest in the financial side of the business left a gap which they could, with some cunning, take great advantage of. Gradually, increasingly, they siphoned off income to a series of linked accounts before extracting the money, usually offshore which could then be accessed anonymously.

When Tim Balliol arrived, it gave them an opportunity not only to blame someone new in the business for their activities, but also to steal a larger amount, this time belonging to Sir Mathieson Allanton instead of the business itself. Tim had moved the Portfolio money along so many clever, intricate paths so all they really had to do was copy him, make it look like he did it, which was easy once they knew his methods. Cheryl kept notes of exactly how and who Tim used to filter the money, so she along with Williams could repeat the process and make the stolen millions move through these same untraceable waters.

At the end of it all, they would put most of the funds into accounts in the name of Tim Balliol, letting him take the entire blame while they took a portion of the total. The missing two million or so would never be found, Balliol would be killed by the Allantons for his betrayal and, if Sir Mathieson got back nine or ten million of his stolen funds, the whole saga would end there. All they had to do was sacrifice Tim Balliol, who despite being an expert in shifting money globally was naïve in the ways of the real world, never thinking that his bravado, his show of accounting genius could have been repeated and used to implicate him in this massive fraud.

John, through Tim's later analysis, knew that they as a group intended to leave the Portfolio accounts so labyrinthine that Tim would have sole ownership of the problem. Cheryl and Williams had vocally expressed their admiration for his genius and their bafflement at how he managed to do it all.

They gambled that this would happen, and lost.

The matter of the attempts on the life of Sir Mathieson Allanton was just a coincidence to their activities. Williams, Cheryl and the others had no doubt hoped that the owners of the Portfolio would be victims of assassination, making their own crimes less likely to be scrutinised by the extended Allanton family.

Zoe had been named as the mastermind by Williams before he died and in turn, Cheryl confirmed that Williams had taken the lead as far as she was concerned. Those in Cheryl's team admitted under little pressure that she herself had persuaded them to take part in the scheme, so that was it, despite her protestations.

It had taken some acceptance, but John knew that all the evidence pointed to Zoe and, as head of the business, he dealt with her himself before he left for Australia. Adam seemed glad that he was spared that one, he had seemed fond of Zoe and well, sometimes these things just have to be done by the boss.

After the terminations of Williams and Zoe, the rest of the staff involved had been merely dismissed from the Portfolio office, although financial reparations were required as a token of their situation.

John met with Sasha and her father in a private room of a downtown fusion restaurant, the kind that made him wonder if it was great food his palate didn't appreciate or just a chef trying to make money by being faux-clever. Sasha looked as effortlessly beautiful as every other time he'd seen her. Her father, Paul Verattis, is a rotund but nevertheless tough-looking character with the permanently deep tan of the antipodean golf fanatic that he was.

'So what the fuck happened up there?' he growled at John, belaying any small talk. John gave him a potted version of the events of the past week and he seemed, albeit with a fair amount of criticism of John's security arrangements, to accept the situation. Sasha exuded a cool detachment from the minutiae of business, her expression blankly covering her intent, a gift that few possess.

She listened while he finished explaining the rather bizarre circumstances of their situation and then watched with amusement as he politely let his uncle exhaust his reserves of constructive criticism. When the older man had finished his last expletive-strewn opinions on his security arrangements, John Allanton moved the discussion towards his main objective.

'I do have to discuss something with you both, which may seem, well, rather presumptuous.' He told them.

They both looked at John expectantly, and he put them out of their misery. 'I want to permanently withdraw from my position as head of the Portfolio.' There was a moment of mutual silence and Paul Verratis looked even redder than before.

'Why the fuck would you do that? Just because some arsehole put a contract on your dad? C'mon, we're tougher than that!'

John had anticipated this response, so told him that he and his father are still maintaining high security until the situation is under control. Verratis calmed slightly and nodded, trying to think through the situation no doubt. John Allanton got to his next point without delay.

'We would support a member of your family if either is prepared to head up the overall Portfolio in my place.' Again, an uncomfortable silence took over the room and Verratis senior looked stunned.

Sasha asked softly 'What are your real reasons, John?'

'Without wanting to sound all pathetic, I want to spend time with my family. We were almost legitimate. Then this shambles landed on us, and after the nonsense at Inverannan, now my staff are almost all gone - part of a whole fucking conspiracy against us. I've had enough of all that shit, I've got enough money to do whatever I want and to stay safe, and that's what I'm going to do. One of my guys is going to head up the Portfolio in the UK and after that, I'm not much more than a shareholder, watching my money come in every year without working for it. What's not to like?'

Verratis senior snorted. 'Fucking retirement, you'll be bored in two weeks and wanting back.'

John Allanton looked straight at the older man and shook his head. He was tired, fed up of being at the fore of it all, ill at ease with the relentless violence and, after his betrayal by some of his most trusted staff, without the energy to rebuild the business. He had known for many years that he was fundamentally unsuited to leadership, especially after his father retired. It just wasn't his nature, even in the army he wanted just to be a soldier instead of an officer, most of the time anyway. Since he'd taken over the Portfolio, he had sent Adam Darnow out to do work that he should have been doing, to negotiate with teams instead of him. John had instead left the office early to spend time at home, his daughters and his wife meaning a million times more than all that crap his father left him as a business inheritance. It felt like he'd never left the pressure of the military, all those years abroad, travelling, fighting and when he got back, it was somehow even worse, illegal business instead of duty, still missing out on the promise of real life. In the past couple of weeks, he'd been shot, his father had nearly been killed, his men had died guarding them and he'd been forced to terminate some of his most trusted staff. In short, John Allanton was done and done for good with it all.

It took little more discussion but after their meal, Paul and Sasha Verratis left him outside the restaurant, after agreeing to meet at 10 am the next day to hear their response. John, pleased that this hurdle had been passed without a flat refusal, headed back to the hotel for a long, deep sleep. He awakened at 8 am, readied himself for the day to come and took a taxi to meet his relatives again at their office in the banking district of Melbourne. It felt distinctly alien for John to be in a hot day in a city environment, although London does get the odd good summer, it almost never feels so hot that it's a relief to get inside and to the air-conditioned sanctuary of their reception area.

An hour later, John stepped back out into the blinding light and arid warmth of the late autumn heatwave. The meeting went well, the last check on whether he meant what he had said and then fifty minutes of coffee and arrangements, the whole thing to be ratified at a proper family business meeting one month hence. There would be little opposition to the proposal, John and Sir Mathieson's steering views on the best business decisions likely to be largely unquestioned by the others. There were some who would perhaps dislike Verratis heading the business, primarily because of his overly assertive nature, but also partly because of a history of being something of a loose cannon. Still, with his votes and Sasha's, plus John and Sir Mathieson, even one or two dissenters would not be enough to prevent the changes and enable his early retirement from the most senior post. That done, he would gladly delegate most of the duties to Adam, with his new team supporting him to move properties and land deals along, make their capital do the work while John just sat back. That's the way of the world, and John knew that now, no point working like a fool when all you have to do is watch the profits roll in. He knew that after the army that he didn't want to work, but wanted to help his dad when he was getting too old to run it all, and John Allanton wanted to be rich too, for his family. He didn't let the immorality of the business get in the way of just doing it, following his father's orders instead of his C.O.

It was all for his family, really. He wanted his dad to be safe, to be retired, but it was really for his wife and children that he had kept his involvement. It was uncomfortable, to be the guy who burned poppy fields in Afghanistan, and then be the guy who brings tons of the same shit into the UK for money; but since he never had to see the consequences of the import, John was comfortably removed from it. That was the other reason why he sent Adam into the cities, John wanted to feel that he was better than those drug dealing shits, wanted to be a high-value importer and strategic director instead of just a drug-dealing money grabber, which, deep down, he knew he was. At the end of it all, he wanted more than anyone to turn all the bad money into good money, which could pass through property deals and it would come out even larger, more for him to help his family, their fabulous holidays, their wonderful houses and them, so pure and never knowing what him and their grandfather did to earn it all.

John Allanton walked in the searing heat along, past the towering, mirrored buildings which shaded him from the sun. He kept going although he didn't know if he was going the right way, probably wasn't but he wanted to

247

look at Melbourne, look well as he might not ever be back here. There was a central street, perhaps the entertainment hub for Melbourne, restaurants and bottle shops mostly closed at that time but it looked like it would be lively at night time, at weekends. There were shoppers and students, going about their business and heading to classes. Some of the kids had Monash t-shirts and he guessed that was the name of their university, he envied them their innocence and wished that he had had the chance to go to further education, with friends and maybe just to have fun. He had gone straight from school into the army, had John. Well, he'd been to Sandhurst, but not for that long and although it was worthwhile, it was still like an institution for him, not a rounded experience like real university seemed to be. He had to put these regretful thoughts from his mind, he couldn't turn the clock back and opt out of it all, he'd done what he'd done and liked most of it, especially the army bit, even later on when he was an officer and had a great bunch of guys around him. John drank a coffee in a cool, dark Italian café while he checked his phone and found the route back to his hotel. He'd gone almost exactly the opposite direction he should have, so it would be another long walk back. He booked himself a flight for that evening back to the UK, via a one-night stopover in Tokyo, sorted a hotel for himself after a moment's doubt about what the date would be for the booking and headed back to rest and pack, his business in the antipodes all but complete.

His journey was longer than he would have preferred, the stopover taking about fifteen hours but helped by a good hotel and the second leg of the flights to London in business class. John ached to see his family again, for good now, he wouldn't even go into London unless he had to, not after he'd seen Adam and told him what was going on. Adam, the last honest bugger left in the Allanton office and only his army men left who were also loyal to him. He thought of Charlie and Jim, who would have been missed if they were still in the narcotics business. Except they wouldn't have been needed much now anyway, which seemed a bit cold to John after he'd thought it. Neither were family men, so they were disposed of in the same way as the Hannaways, unfortunately, but there it is, John and Sir Mathieson couldn't risk any questions or investigations and the lads, if they were alive and could have been asked, would most certainly have agreed. Their flats were both company-owned, so would be cleared and sold by Adam as part of his new duties as head of the Portfolio, Property Investment only, no narcotics now incorporated.

John had jetted off first, to Australia and a meeting with Paul and probably Sasha Verratis and I am, for the first time, left in temporary sole charge of the business. I've been asked, by John and Sir Mathieson, to fix the office arrangements after the recent unpleasantness. I start by immediately hiring a few younger professionals from an agency; then I need to get someone who can finish off the more sensitive aspects of our transition to respectability. So, after a period of consideration and because I also find it funny, I decide to re-hire Tim. I'm going to offer him a two-week contract, to be paid £2k a day to set us on the right track and to train our new staff on how to answer any probing questions in the future.

He limps into my office, helped by a confused looking Donnie, who shakes his head as he leaves us. Perhaps my sense of humour is not fully appreciated here. Tim sits down with some difficulty, his knee may well still be troubling him after the surgery, but it seems crass for me to ask how it is healing after causing the damage. He still has a bandage on the left side of his face and has a despondent look of a man desperate to not be here.

I'm trying to find the right words, so settle on something anodyne to break the ice.

'How's the new apartment, Tim?'

'Fine, thanks.' His voice is slightly guttural, soft too but I can hear him well enough.

'Getting in and out OK after the operation?'

'Yes, thanks.'

'Great. What were you going to do with the money in the safety deposit box?

Tim looks up at me and I realise that his face is swollen and bruised after his operations.

He answers me in a wearily pleading tone. 'It was just a back-up, there's no plan.'

'But you had passports, real and fake. You must have had a plan.'

'I didn't, not really.'

'Bullshit Tim, you don't go to all that trouble and have no idea what you would do. Where were you going?'

'Nowhere, really.'

'Don't fucking lie to me Tim, I can tell when people do, you know. And you're doing it now.'

'I'm not.' I put my face up to his and look straight into his eyes. He turns his head to look away, but I move it back to look at me, bandages and all.

'I swear. It was just in case I had to get away, I got it ready ages ago before I worked here.'

'Do you want your face to be taken apart again? If you keep lying to me, I will do it, right fucking now and there are no Allantons left here to get you fixed up.'

Unfortunately for him, I'm still at least partly a journalist and Tim can't keep the pretence going after these pointed questions and more probably, my threats. He wails, tears falling down to be absorbed by the bandages on the left and past the stitched scar on the right side of his face.

'I was going to Portugal.' He blubbers; the admission almost seems like a relief.

'What's in Portugal? You got a house there?'

'No, nothing like that, just a safe place away from this.'

'Away from me?'

'Not you when I started, but now yes.'

'So, what are you going to do in Portugal Tim, start a bar?'

'No, just stay there. Stay away from you and from being scared.' More tears flow and I'm feeling slightly sorry for Tim, but it's not my job to be sympathetic, not here.

'How are you going to live? Money doesn't last forever Tim.'

'I can trade online, make money easy, enough to live.' I don't doubt this for a moment, he's one smart guy, but I still need him, before he emigrates.

'OK Tim, here's my proposal. I'll keep you on for two weeks or near that, you will do what you need to do for our investments and train a couple of new people. After that, if you've done a good job, I'll give you a bonus and you can fuck off to the sun. How does that sound?'

'You'll just kill me.'

'I won't, I promise Tim. Scouts honour.' I raise my hand in an approximation of a scout salute and smile.

Tim cries again, but this time seems less desolate.

'When you are finished, however long that takes, I promise that you can take your deposit box contents, the money I will pay you and go off without any problem, from me or John or anyone else. OK?'

He nods, the tears dripping intermittently from his chin.

'When you get to Portugal, or wherever you end up, you need to stay away from me, the Portfolio and everything, forever. Do you understand?' Tim nods, but it doesn't look like he wholly believes me.

He sniffs and tells me in his soft voice, 'None of this was my fault, Adam. I acted in good faith.'

'Yes Tim, but when you shot the shit out of the boss's house, you gave yourself a problem and this is the only way to repay it, to help us and after that, just be glad you are getting away. Not everyone did, you know.'

'I know.'

'OK, head to the office and get started. A car will take you up and down from your flat until your work is finished, we'll sort out flights and all that at the end, and we'll never hear from you again when you leave. Agreed?' Tim agrees with a nod and a faint rictus smile, his options long ago exhausted.

After I re-engage Tim and have a laugh at Donnie's expression of puzzled astonishment on the way out of the office, I take a taxi straight to the airport. I then endure two long and uncomfortable flights to get to Thailand, a long way to go but I want to do this. I need to finish it, the last action of this chaotic episode to be securely and discreetly mine. It takes me another two days to find out exactly where the target is, not at home but getting treatment for cancer, the poor sod. His right-hand man, this guy Roghan, is the way I found him. He'd paid the idiots in Ilford for the hit from an account which our resident savant Tim Balliol tracked to him, through the authorisation of one of his employees, but easily traced to the source.

I first follow Roghan from his office, driven by a couple of minders but they leave him off at his house, an imposing and bright condo in what looks like an expensive street. My driver and I wait for a while and I am just going to wait to go for him when it gets dark, but he comes out with what I assume is his son, dressed in a rugby kit and going to practice or perhaps to a game. A short drive later, we are parked near him at an open field, watching as he stands with the other parents, chatting while their kids bounce clumsily around the floodlit pitch. I'm not much of an expert on this type of intervention, but my driver seems to be. A surreptitious crawl under his car disables the starter motor and after a while we watch as the parents, coaches and children leave, our guy and his son stranded, their battery flattening as the frustration rises in the car.

I amble over and asked if he needs a hand and he gladly accepts. Once the hood is up, I turn to him and tell him the situation and he, an intelligent man and protective parent, gives up the name and location of my target without a moment's hesitation. I must admit that I am glad that no-one is there to witness my lack of surprise at this name, this wayward brother of the late George Galloglas turning out to be the sponsor of the contract on my employer's life. We have a good chat about him, the two of us, standing in the lonely car park. Having given me the information, I explain my concern that he may try to warn Galloglas that his identity has been revealed, however when he tells me that my target is near death anyway, it's not a far leap for him to become disengaged from the situation and agree to eschew any communication with him. He tells me that I would probably be doing Galloglas a favour if I kill him and I agree, but I'd given my word to Sir Mathieson that I'd do this, and a man's word is his bond, after all. I ask him about how it all came about and he tells me one thing that I already knew, that Big Jim Galloglas found out from his investigators and one thing which I did not, that their report was now in Roghan's possession.

I sit in the front of the car beside Roghan after my driver helpfully reconnects the starter. First dropping his son at home, we drive back to the city to pick up the file from his office safe and into my own keeping, although the contents must necessarily be destroyed at the first opportunity. I give Roghan a clear and undoubtedly graphic set of instructions on the need for confidentiality and the specific consequences of breaching the arrangement. He and his family being permitted to continue living is however the positive side of my motivational speech.

I leave Roghan to figure out how best to find himself replacement trousers after our discussion, then head down to the waiting car for a short trip to visit Galloglas in hospital, a late night visit to be sure, but one which would certainly prove palliative, for him and me.

~

Big Jim Galloglas lay on his bed, the drip coursing more numbing opiate fluids into his system, trying to blunt the cancer whilst knowing he was beaten. He had long past reached the weary point where he'd had enough of this protracted dying. His morphine dreams recalled his glorious youth, his friends in the all-white school playing their cricket when all was sunshine, superiority, good health and laughter. He'd captained the school team at cricket, winning trophies against the other city sides in Johannesburg and even a regional competition, his most glorious sporting moment and the medal still framed in his lounge.

He dreamed a memory about the day he played a charity golf event in South Africa with the prime minister and his father, the three of them with another man tagging along, a security officer he thought. Galloglas father knew all sorts of famous people through his business affairs, and this day was one of the fruits of those contacts. His father was a fair golfer, but let the famous man win to avoid any negative feeling between them, even winking at his son after hitting a drive into the rough. They had servants there too, willing to risk a snake bite or worse by retrieving the player's misdirected golf balls from the long grass and even into the water hazards. After they finished their round, they sat in the public lounge with other friends, the Prime Minister regaling them with anecdotes and making them laugh heartily, although young Galloglas didn't always understand the jokes.

Before they left the clubhouse, his father spoke privately, briefly with the famous man. As they were driving home, his father told him that he'd won a government contract that day and that all would be grand after this, and so it was, while it lasted. They got home and he told his little brother how he'd hit some great golf shots that day, but when Big Jim Galloglas wakened from his dream, he wasn't in South Africa and he wasn't young, he was just himself again, at night, alone in the hospital and tears fell from his eyes.

He wiped his face with the edge of the bedclothes as he became aware of a tall, dark-clad figure entering his room, closing the door softly and approaching him on silent feet.

'Who the fuck are you?' he wheezed, trying to focus his blurred eyes at the man looming over him.

'None of your fucking business.' He whispered in a light Scottish accent, pulling the trigger of the silenced pistol and drawing Galloglas treatment to a close.

So, Tim got back to work. Back in familiar territory, with two new students of the art of financial wizardry to impress, he took on the role of the injured genius, the man they couldn't do without. His new colleagues, both young men of serious manner, worked assiduously with him, just as Cheryl had when he started with the Allantons. He relaxed as his work became his focus, he enjoyed himself again, giving up his crutches as soon as his injury allowed, then on to just one stick and, according to the doctor, he'd only need that for a few months until the healing was finished and he could walk normally again, perhaps with a slight limp if he didn't follow his exercises.

The investments of the Portfolio were now many, various and expanding. John Allanton had all but retired, hadn't been in his office, or certainly, Tim hadn't seen him. He kept out of Adam's way too, leaving him daily reports of his transactions and responses to Adams requests for money to be moved into whatever accounts he needed for the property deals. These funds were sent mainly to and from global funds now, major investments, even more significant returns and the narcotics business buried and lost forever in their bright new corporate financial world. In under two weeks, Tim made the Portfolio unrecognisable, placed Adam Darnow at the top of the financial food chain and finished his work, the two apprentices now capable of moving the clean money anywhere they needed to and in the enviable position of being innocent of all previous dealings.

Tim became anxious in his last week. He thought that, if anything were to happen to him, it would happen soon, just after he'd finished working, but before he made his Faro flight. He spent his nights dreaming up possible escapes, alternative locations like Uruguay, where maybe he could move his money into dollars first and then use that to hide, somewhere rural maybe until they forgot about him. The nagging feeling was that you couldn't really hide from these men, these awful people that he wished he'd never went near. Days and nights of exploring options of escape and anonymity, of flight and freedom, came to nothing. For Tim knew that any escape would make them come after him and, even if he made it away, they'd get him eventually and all the while he would be in fear for this life. Better if he walked tall while he was leaving and if they let him go, that would tell him that they were genuine.

It was a pleasantly warm Thursday in London when he closed the last transaction and shook hands with his colleagues. Naturally awkward and having wisely shunned all social contact between them, little else was said as Tim prepared to leave the office for the last time. Left alone in his office to tidy his desk and put the laptop in one of the wall cabinets as always, his heart sank when the door opened and Adam Darnow greeted him with his awful faux-pleasant smile.

'Hi Tim, how are you today?'

'I'm fine. Thanks.'

Adam Darnow looked around the empty office as if ensuring that there were no witnesses present. Tim closed the cabinet and watched him, almost fearing that he'd pull out a gun, right here in the midst of other staffed offices and kill him, so crazy that it was plausible, after all that Tim had witnessed. Instead, Darnow sat down at the top of the long desk and gestured for Tim to sit beside him. Shaking perceptibly, Tim's hands grasped the edge of the desk and he lowered himself slowly to the chair.

'You've done a terrific job Tim, all that has been asked of you.'

'Thanks.'

'All the new transactions too, great work, even without John being here. I really appreciate your support.' Tim wondered if Darnow was taking the piss, as sometimes people did and Tim didn't pick up on it.

'There's a flight tomorrow morning Tim, Heathrow to Faro. Gives you the rest of the day to get your belongings together and ready for the off, maybe time to update your wardrobe too? Can't wear those wool suits in Portugal, can you?'

Tim shook his head.

'Anyway, thanks again for all the hard work and I'm sorry about your injuries. Your face is much better now though.' Adam looks closely at his scarred jaw and cheek. 'Makes you look tough too, women love all that Tim, or so I've heard.'

Tim couldn't smile properly, largely because he was terrified but also because the muscles in his cheeks were permanently damaged after being shot by this bastard. He made a "Mibbe" face, although he would have to check in a mirror later to see if the expressions had had previously taken for granted were still visibly recognisable.

Adam Darnow stood suddenly, scaring the already nervous Tim badly. Offering his hand to Tim, Adam looked him straight in the eyes and said, with not a hint of irony, 'Goodbye and good luck Tim.'

Tim, after trying his best to refrain from trembling during their discussion, replied in kind then went to the toilet to vomit, shit his brains out and, after cleaning himself up, walked the solitary corridor to the lift, down to the main entrance and out, free as a bird into the busy London street. He was feeling invigorated now, the anxious walk out of the office completed without harm and after being sick, Tim felt much, much better. The driver, that big rough-looking man who was never clean-shaved, gestured him into the car and he was driven home, hopefully, for the last time, Tim thought. He was doubly relieved that the car drew away and left him to enter his apartment alone, to pack and to take the taxi to fetch his passports and money. He dropped into a nearby electrical store and bought a new laptop and a phone, setting them up while he was still there and with his purchases stowed in a solid backpack, went home for his last night in the apartment.

When he got home, an envelope waited for him on the doormat. He sat on the end of the bed and tore it open, finding his airline tickets and a bank card, with a statement noting that the account contained just over £15,000, the equivalent of £2,000 per day and a fifty per cent bonus for Tim's work. He stopped shaking and smiled, knowing that Adam Darnow was as good as his word, this time. Tim went online with his old laptop, messaging his oft-searched Portuguese real estate office with an urgent request for a rental, and receiving a positive reply soon afterwards. He transferred some files to a USB stick and did a factory reset on his old laptop, then removed and disassembled the hard drive before using his laundry iron to smash its components beyond

261

use. Tim did not, could not, let the contents of that particular laptop remain at large, not if he wanted to do so too, or at least be placed on some dreadful register. He would upload his USB files to the new laptop when he got to Portugal. Tim then packed up, leaving all his business clothes and shoes in the wardrobe and taking a pair of scissors to the paperwork he didn't need, before setting his clock and falling into a troubled sleep.

28 MANIPULATION INC.

It had taken me a brief few days after my return to the UK to ensure that the London office was robust, effective and operational. Tim Balliol was off in Portugal, my guys were now in charge of all things budgetary and no trace of any illegal finances were to be found anywhere in the Portfolio, not any more. We have a strong investment plan and, apart from John or me turning up at meetings to shake hands and sign papers, we are pretty hands-off from this point onwards. Our assets are many and various, ethical – well much more ethical than before anyway – and as productive as we need them to be. John has given me a stratospheric salary and a bonus structure which would make a Premiership footballer's eyes water, plus a new apartment in my personal ownership, the balcony looking straight at Tower Bridge close by. I don't like the area as much as Knightsbridge, but maybe I'm being picky. Maybe I'll move every year or so, make some money on the way and keep ahead of the game, although that may require more effort and trips to London than I would prefer.

I am, if I'm being honest, a little discontented after all the excitement. Perhaps this is also because Sasha is about to marry that inbred Euro-twat she tried to hide from me, plus she's now a newly-fledged master of the global Portfolio and therefore unlikely to ever deign to see me again. Paul Verratis is in charge, in name, but Sasha is the driving force as she probably always was.

No-one, well no-one important, got hurt along the way and some of it was just me and her just fucking about, seeing what would happen if we introduced chaos to the stability of the Portfolio. John would never have resigned from the main role without some prodding; that was Sasha's problem and she, like me, is easily bored at times and has an inherent urge to destabilise, to see what would happen and to roll along with it all. I had initially mentioned a few times to John that it was piss-easy to make money once someone had a few hundred million in the bank, and John, well he percolated that information for a while and, with a couple of nudges during our various conversations, he got there in the end. He started to see it as his route out, but it was too slow for me and more so for Sasha. I knew that she was using me, but she was intuitive enough to soon realise that I had an agenda too and that our objectives were, like our relationship, mutually beneficial for the time being.

It took me a few attempts, back then, to convince Williams that it would be worth the risk to siphon off the Portfolio funds for our own benefit. The turning point was really when he lost, and lost big at the tables, not owing anyone but having lost his life savings and no way to get it back once his stake money was gone. Once he had started it, I just kept a close eye on him as he inveigled that dodgy little Cheryl and her pals into the scam. Two of them were set against it, but Cheryl has a dark side to her and once they had been pressured and taken a few grand, they couldn't back out. I had been generous, too, letting them take the bulk of the stolen money and sending mine to an account which I had opened in Zoe's name, just in case.

It was a pity though that the Galloglas situation that Sasha and I had engineered too had got out of hand. A coincidence, as sometimes things are, was how it started. My sources heard that questions were being asked about the late George Galloglas, who his employers were and specifically who was responsible for his death. After Sasha and I spoke of this and she did some digging of her own, I met the investigators myself; false name of course, letting them know that the blame for his death lay solely with the Allantons. We extrapolated that their employer might well send someone to take revenge, giving me an opportunity to then leave the business unquestioned and for Sasha to fill the void. That was our concord.

We almost gave up on the likelihood that anything would come from this speculative mischief. The investigators had eventually sent a report, including our planted information back to Jim Galloglas in Thailand, but in the intervening period John Allanton had already decided to go legitimate. Sasha, who was meant to be monitoring that situation, claimed that she forgot all about it, but I suspect that she would not have been greatly perturbed if her rise to the peak of the UK Portfolio had been over the bodies of either her uncle or cousin, and perhaps even me.

Regardless, Galloglas' paid assassins had failed and, after my brief but effective trip to the Far East, there are no loose ends to tie Sasha or me to the whole debacle. She is more ambitious than I ever gave her credit for and I know full well that I served my purpose too, for her. Our agreement is now complete and all things having been settled. We are both satisfied by the outcome, both still in our early twenties and, her more than me for sure, as wealthy as we'll ever need to be. I have, it would appear, got away with a series of work-related serious crimes which are now unlikely to come to light as the bodies are no more, the witnesses dispersed or dead and all tangible evidence destroyed, no doubt overtaken by new problems for our valuable public order officials. To all intents, I am out of the whole thing, two years since I first fell into it. My primary reason for spending another week in the capital is to complete my sessions with Dr Schaffer, whom I feel is nearing the point where I can finally steer a hopeful path for my damaged psyche. Her general prognosis is that I've become too involved and too integrated into my business environment. She says I've lost sight of aspects of my morality which make up the building blocks of a functioning adult, and to be honest, it's as good an explanation as I could have expected. She is attempting to provide me with the toolkit to reset my moral compass, albeit I seem to be able to reset myself every time I get away from London and the Allantons bloody business. After my sessions are complete, I intend to take a sabbatical to test this theory. If the prognosis of Dr Schaffer is correct, and assuming that a breakthrough is possible, I figure that a period of time away will enable me to test my capacity to function again as a responsible adult or whatever I was before. This will, of course, depend on the circumstances and as such, I may choose to place myself under pressure to test her hypothesis, at a later point.

My parent's cottage in Mharisaig is still in its original decaying and neglected condition, so that is where I must begin my catharsis, if that is what it shall be. I was once, a criminal's lifetime ago, a trainee journalist who sought to make some kind of life as a grown-up, not at any point imagining I'd spend the next two years as an instrument of the heinous Allantons. Not that I disliked them, far from it. I must, out of loyalty if not gratitude, visit Sir Mathieson firstly, before my break, while he is still in Inverannan. If my call from John was correct, Sir Mathieson is now thinking about moving his repaired yacht to a more tax-effective arrangement in the

Caribbean or nearby as lately recommended by his new financial advisors. As I would be unlikely to travel so far for a passing visit, I may not see Sir Mathieson for some time and I feel that I should thank him, for in his way he recognised my hitherto well-hidden abilities and made me the developed if damaged, individual that I have become.

So, after leaving my new and modern apartment as free from individuality as my Portfolio office, I take my two hefty bags of clothes down to the basement garage and begin my drive north.

Driving has, since I learned and passed my test, become something of a chore for me, the roads of southern England being too busy to enjoy and certainly rather pressurised compared to the rural emptiness of Mharisaig. When the traffic clears just short of Carlisle it immediately becomes a more pleasurable experience. For once I don't have to think about my work; I'm not even heading anywhere to do anything unpleasant or businesslike. I am merely travelling to say thanks and goodbye to my employer, perhaps my mentor and certainly my sponsor in all things criminal. My car, a company vehicle which is both powerful and sleek, powers along the M74, past the Leadhills and up to the west of Scotland as the clouds lift and the sky turns blue, the fields beside the motorway verdant and I smile at the thought of my last visit, the land covered in deep, unforgiving snow as winter gave it's last blast before spring took over.

I slow as I pass Hamilton, then bypass Glasgow and up to Stirling and Perth, the traffic clear most of the way and in no time I'm on the road to Pitlochry. I stop for a coffee and lunch at Dunkeld, where my parents used to take me for a pit stop on the rare occasions when we were driving south to Edinburgh or Glasgow. While I'm there, I realise that I haven't spoken with them in a long time, just replying to their emails by repeating the same banal shit about hoping they are enjoying the sun and not working too hard. Perhaps I shall visit them, in the summer for a day or so. I can't even remember the name of the place they are staying, that's how little interest I have shown in their expatriate life. I'm over the childish feelings of abandonment now. Those idle emotions didn't take long to pop off after my tenure in the Allanton narcotics business took over my life. I head back to the car and start off again, towards Inverness and take a short diversion to the Dalwhinnie distillery to get a couple of examples of their finest. Then it's the final leg, north then west, the long drive to the Highlands and Inverannan. I'm not sure what I'll do about Gillian. Dr Schaffer has told me to stop pre-planning everything in my life, to sometimes be spontaneous and trust my inner emotions, which at the time sounded like a lot of shite, but now it seems to work quite well in the absence of any other apparent approach to my personal life. During our sessions, I have come to realise that I have been almost entirely shallow in regards to my personal relationships, which I'm still unsure if it's just down to my age and immaturity or because, in my doctor's opinion, I have a *borderline* psychological disorder. I don't agree with her about the borderline part, but in the interests of hiding my actual conduct at work, I had to make up a series of legitimate scenarios to describe my actions. This perhaps clouded her professional judgment in the process.

A smile plays onto my lips as I remember our conversations, Dr Schaffer asking me a series of obtuse and open-ended questions which were intended to probe my deepest psyche. I answered each as reasonably as I could, within limits and omitting the homicides. I'd also searched online for clues about myself, so generally knew what she was getting at after I had learned her professional leanings regarding psychoanalysis. The strange thing was that I had to pretend that I actually exhibited some of the other symptoms just to keep her interested in the important parts. For example, I told that I got angry at certain things, that I felt empty and that I had trouble sleeping, while in all honesty, I had none of these characteristics, not at that point anyway. I couldn't tell her the reality; that I felt like I was in a fucking B-movie, that I was living an unreal life and treating it as exactly that. Couldn't tell her that I felt absolutely nothing when I shot someone and disposed of their carcass because it was all illusory and had been since I accidentally shoved a little, deadly knife into my first victim and this crazy life began. I'd no doubt be in jail if I'd told her the truth, so I just had to use her prognosis and figure the rest of it out myself with some Internet-based amateur analysis.

I've lost track of time while I drive north, so I'm surprised that it's only 6 pm as I draw up outside Inverannan House. There's a guard at the front door who comes out to meet me, his hand kept inside his jacket on a pistol until he sees who it is. I nod to him and head inside to meet Sir Mathieson, who is in the library alone, and looking much better than the last time I saw him.

'Adam! Come in young man, it is wonderful to see you!' He shakes my hand warmly and we sit across from each other in front of the unlit fire.

'You're looking well sir.' I tell him.

'Thank you, Adam. I am feeling a damn sight better now that all that nonsense is over. John called this morning. He is certainly enjoying the lightness of his new life. The kids also love having him home so there can be no complaints on that front either. Would you like a drink?' I certainly would, so I'm rather pleased when the old man fetches me a large malt and a bottle of lager which I polish off quickly and settle into the whisky in a more relaxed manner.

'How is the London office looking?' he asks with his familiar clipped tones.

'It's running smoothly now, the new team are excellent and our projects are doing well, especially the commercial ones on the continent. We've got plenty of potential in the offing too, so we'll just let them run from one into another.' I smile at the thought of the easy profit and Sir Mathieson, well, he just smiles back.

I look through the window and see the guard patrolling. 'Is it all safe and secure here? Your man was on the ball when I drove in.'

'Yes, I've got two shifts working, eight men in total not including the estate workers milling around, so yes, Inverannan House is now much improved on that front. Took a while to repair all the bloody holes in the wall but we're there now.' Not a mention of the casualties, but hey, he's an officer and well used to the realities of combat. I finish my drink and get him another, I need to drive and he looks like he's ready for a chat. He starts on his army stories, some of which I've heard but not all, so we have an hour where he's back in the field, reminiscing over japes and larks. I'm trying to stay alert but wishing that, although I like the old guy, he would fuck off to his tax haven as soon as possible.

Eventually, Sir Mathieson falls asleep, three more whiskies and four, long, long, stories later. I put a cover over his legs and step out to the now-darkened hallway where a guard sits at the landing, not far from the place where Charlie's head was blown off such a short time ago. I grab my bags from the hallway and head up to find a bedroom. As Sir Mathieson told me, the decoration at Inverannan has indeed been fully repaired, no sign of the pandemonium and shot marks any more. My room, same as last time, is ready and clean. There's an envelope on the pillow and it's from Gillian, asking me to drop in if I have time. I shower, change as quickly as I can and then drive down to the village to see her. I'd phoned her a couple of times since we last parted, mainly to make sure she was still OK with me after the night of the armed idiots. Thankfully she and the others had nothing worse than a fright, a guilty feeling that they'd quite enjoyed themselves and a hangover to put up with.

At her parent's house, I get out of the car and ring the doorbell. Eventually, Hector comes to the door, an impressive figure of a man and momentarily, I think he's going to try and strangle me. Instead, he reaches out his arms to give me a bear hug, the like of which I have not personally experienced beforehand. He backs off and has a look of genuine concern on his face, while I no doubt have puzzlement on mine.

'I hear what happened at the big house son. It was a bloody terrible, terrible thing. Is Sir Mathieson all right now?'

'Aye, he's fine Hector. Got a fright at the time, but thankfully he got through it safe and sound. Is Gillian OK?'

'Yes, yes, she's made of stern stuff is my lassie. Just like her mother, but with a better nature.' He beckons me inside and his wife, thankfully unaware of his last comment, stands up and meets me with a hug too. I'm unused to being liked, so this is slightly unsettling to me.

'How are you, Adam? Is your leg all right?' I nod and tell her it wasn't that bad, all sorted now. This is more or less the truth, except I keep getting the odd sharp pain inside the wound when I don't expect it, and I think I am at some point going to need another x-ray to see if there's some metal floating around in there. This was unfortunately hinted at recently when I went through the airport checks and made the metal detector beep, momentarily panicking me in case I had something on me which I shouldn't have.

We sit together until Gillian joins us and I complete the trio of hugs with the one I really wanted and it all seems much, much better now. For some reason, Gillian seems to draw me towards her, to want to look at her. I think, at this moment, maybe I could still be the same person who arrived here two years ago. Maybe I'm projecting this onto her unfairly, or displacing Dr Schaffer's interpretation of my condition, but putting all that shite to one side, Gillian makes me happy, an old emotion which I'd like more of.

We have a drink together, another hefty portion of malt and I then remember that I brought some gifts from my stop en-route north, so give Hector and Katrina two bottles of 25-year-old Dalwhinnie, apparently labelled that

it was bottled well before that.   I hadn't actually realised
this when I bought the stuff, although I must admit it
tastes every bit as good as the price suggested it should.
Gillian, more to get some privacy than the need for
another drink, suggests that we visit the pub and it's off
we go again, the long day and the sudden influx of strong
whisky making me slightly unsteady as I go, particularly
when the cold highland air hits me. A short walk and one
passionate kiss later, we head into the convivial bar, a few
locals and a couple of walkers enjoying the booze, the
warm fire-heated room and some background music
which sounds like a band I know but can't place.

We say hi to the locals, one of whom asks in hushed
tones if I'm OK and I realise that the shambles at
Inverannan seems better known that I would like. I tell
him I'm fit as a butcher's dog and he laughs, I get a round
in for them and my local popularity continues unabated.

We sit as far away from the other customers as we can,
although the place isn't so large that this can be
considered a distance. I ask her how she really is and she
smiles.

'I'm fine, honestly. We all knew about the real business at
Inverannan, so we can't really say that we're surprised
when something like that happens. Well, we were at the
time, but it's over now, isn't it?' She looks at me with a
serious expression, so I have to respond, although I'm
not even sure if it is all over.

'Yeah, it's finished now. We're back where we should
have been before all that carry on. Better maybe, even.' I
tell her that John is pretty much retired and that Sir
Mathieson will probably be leaving soon too, so I'm as
much in charge as anyone, I suppose. I tell her that it's all

legitimate now and all that stuff is finished with. She is hard to read, for me anyway, so I don't know what she is thinking.

'Is it really though, for you?'

I nod.

'Everyone here knows what you did, all the Inverannan guys anyway. They liked Charlie and Jim, it's a shame what happened to them and to Magnus. He's still away at that hospital place.' I realise that I forgot to ask about him and then I remember that he shot those ducks and I was pissed off with him, but it doesn't matter now, not really.

'I hope he'll be OK.' I tell her, by way of appearing to care.

'Yes, he is a nice old man, just annoying when he was drunk all the time, that's all. My dad knew him when he was young. He told me that he was a real looker, all the lassies fancied him, but he went off to the army and never married, just came back and settled into the single life.'

The door goes a couple of times and a few more drinkers come in each time until the bar is busy and the music gets louder as the voices do too. Gillian does most of the talking and I love the sound of her voice, soft and strong and her laugh, well that gets me every time and I can't take my eyes off of her. We walk back to her house, her parents off to bed and she asks me to stay and I say OK.

I wake up beside her, the spring sunlight beaming through the lace curtains and onto her sleeping, stunning features, angular and with the curled black hair of her highland heritage. She wakens, perhaps sensing me looking at her, and I smile when she does, and we kiss, and stay in bed a while longer. It's maybe an hour later when we hear the door close and she looks out to see Hector and Katrina heading off in the car, perhaps to give us a chance to get up and about without the awkwardness of morning helloes. Good for them, I think. We head down and get breakfast and she walks me to my car, parked a decent distance along the road from last night. I don't know how long I'll be here, but while I am, I will be with her, absolutely. When I get to Inverannan House, there's some activity as the now-legitimate goods are being loaded onto estate vehicles, not so many as before but still trading and I remember that Gillian and the others had a plan for Inverannan. I had forgotten last night in the midst of all the whisky and her, her laughter and her beauty. I make a mental note to get that started before I go away, whenever that will be.

Sir Mathieson sees me arrive, knocking on the library window and waving as I walk past and into the hallway. Inside, we shake hands and he laughs as he tells me how he awakened at 2am in the library, confused as to his location but covered by a warm tartan rug I'd kindly placed over him. He seems smaller than he had been two years ago, a kindly old Scottish gentleman now, not a hint of his career to tarnish the image. We head down to the kitchen where some cold cuts have apparently been left for him and any visitors, so we tuck in and my hangover disperses with the food.

A bit of small talk later and I detect that Sir Mathieson is paused to ask me something. I feel some dread at the thought.

'Adam, now that we are done with all the unpleasantness of our former business, we must, ah, preserve our reputation going forward. Do you agree?' There it is, the

275

start of some fucking other thing, lets' see what the old bastard has in mind.

'I have a specific issue with some historical problems, which have recently come to light. An acquaintance of mine from many years ago has apparently been compiling his wartime memoirs, as it were, which may include some reference to my own part in both the narcotics trade and some other matters. This may, of course, come to nothing, but I would like you to take whatever action is required to ensure that this risk is mitigated. The last thing any of us need is a published document, naming me and my family as being connected with illegal activities, do you agree?'

Now, I absolutely do not agree that this is the case, but when I'm asked by Sir Mathieson Allanton to do something, I generally require a damn good reason not to.

'What needs done?' I almost lack the energy to discuss it but need to know what he is getting me into.

'There is a retired auditor, lives near here, as luck would have it, who was party to some of the projects we were involved in Iraq and perhaps elsewhere. He came to our attention courtesy of my contacts at your former employer, The Insider, which has been occasionally useful in allowing us to innocently examine potential news stories from an angle which we could not previously. In this instance, one James Forster has been in contact with them to ask for their assistance in the publishing of his memoirs, which I am reliably informed name certain names, including mine in connection with discrepancies and questionable activities.'

Here we go, I think, this is the nice old guy I interviewed two years back and here I am, about to pay him another visit.

Sir Mathieson went on. 'I should have told you, my chaps managed successfully to get through some very difficult snow to close down your own unpleasant indiscretion carried out while searching for young Balliol. We all have to help each other, Adam and now, now it is time for you pitch in with some more active duty, as I did.' The old bastard, he's got the devil in him that's for sure. He could send some of his trained monkeys that are guarding him, but he wants me instead, wants me to be less comfortable than I must have seemed. Fuck.

He tells me where Forster lives, but I remember it well enough, back then with my colleague Emma driving to the back of beyond and me trying to appear interested but now, it's just going to be me and there's no interview.

Sir Mathieson walks over to a writing bureau and opens the roll-top section, taking out a card and bringing it over to me. It's my old press ID.

'You might need this' he smiles, paternally.

John Allanton looked out of the floor-to-ceiling window of his home, the broad, well-tended garden outside and thence the stables, as yet unoccupied but in their plans. His children were at school and, after spending a couple of hours on some ongoing work to renovate the loft of their home, he took some time out to drink a coffee and give some thought to the past few weeks. He was, in all honesty, completely sick of the Portfolio and therefore acquiescent to Adam's approach to stabilise the business, replacing the disloyal and dead with a new and money-motivated anonymous team. Each member of staff was picked by Adam alone, fitting the bill as professional, emotionless and dull as could be found and operating within the strict spending approvals he set them. All future deals and transactions were to be approved and counter-approved by John and Adam, having joint control of the accounts and paying the staff well. Not city-level bonuses, but enough to make them stay for at least the medium term. John knew that Adam had compartmentalised the Portfolio, exactly like he had for their narcotics business, and with the same consummate efficiency. John liked that his own involvement now would only be to travel occasionally, to hear what their investment contacts had to offer, to agree to invest their immense capital into whatever schemes would let their money grow, as big money does.

The sun blinked, then stayed and the warm brightness illuminated the garden in front of him. Just under half an acre of fenced-off space, some for the children's trampoline but the rest for his wife to indulge her recently-found love of gardening. It was, to John, just wonderful. He was gradually discovering a new vigour after relinquishing his role as the CEO of the Portfolio, given freely to Paul Verratis and his daughter. John's wife was unaware that he had signed over many hundreds of millions of dollars of assets to them, although she would not probably care that much, as long as they still possessed considerable wealth, which they indeed did. John Allanton did not care that he'd discharged this fortune to them, for with the money came responsibility and indeed danger which he no longer wanted, could no longer bear. His hand felt inside the top of his shirt to the scars of his recent wounds. It had taken some time to persuade his wife not to leave him, or not to change the locks and leave him outside the family home, desolate without his children and all because of the Portfolio. Over the years she had turned a blind eye to his business, his absences tolerated and the rumours ignored, but when she realised the proximity of danger to her husband and potentially to her children, Sara Allanton could tolerate it no more.

So, John had to convince Sara that the business was changing, him too and that he guaranteed no more danger and no more extended absences after he relinquished the role of CEO. That was the simple and agreeable price of legitimacy and one which made Paul Verratis an extremely powerful man indeed, and perhaps his daughter too. John knew that Sasha was integral to their arm of the business despite her louche and detached persona. He had just received an expensive-looking invite in the post that morning, to the wedding of Sasha to her German fiancé whom John had met a couple of times. A titled aristocrat from an industrially wealthy family whose interests had benefitted greatly from slave labour during the Second World War, although this information had conveniently dissipated with the passage of time and the death of the offending grandfather in the late 1990s. The new generation, brought up with all the advantages of wealth and in control of some of the most significant and profitable companies in Europe were bona fide royalty and Sasha would soon be part of that too. The wedding was to be held in the family castle, or more accurately a series of events over a one-week period where relatives, friends and then a combination of both would be spectacularly entertained to celebrate their nuptials. John wondered if Adam knew, or if he had been invited. It had been somewhat awkward for John, knowing that Sasha spent occasional weekends with Adam while her fiancé was elsewhere, although, in their entitled and debauched milieu, such things were perhaps normal. In the end, Adam's relationship with Sasha was unlikely to have become anything greater, she being the driven and socially ambitious type and Adam, despite having his attributes, effectively nothing more than a diversion for her.

John spoke with his father every day, still and for the foreseeable future. He and Benny had, after some minor delays, recently taken up residence in a rather remote but highly desirable seafront property with private mooring nearby. Their neighbours were also from a decent position in the financial food chain, former actors, golfers and businessmen, so Sir Mathieson fitted in perfectly as an ex-military gentleman who mixed often and well with them. Benny continued his role, whatever that may be and they both were well looked after by the staff, including the new yacht crew who worked in the season, part-time, taking them around the Bahamian Islands when the weather and the notion took them. John hoped that he and his family would visit them, although the kids could not be taken out of school too long and they had to avoid the summer, so perhaps they would go over for Christmas and enjoy the sunshine.

In the meantime, John had no intention of going anywhere near the remaining Portfolio if he could avoid it. All their capital was, thanks to Adam, now tied into investments and until such time as he was needed, John would live on the generous dividends the business generated. He had his renovation work, he had a car restoration to begin on his father's solid but neglected Bristol Blenheim and he was sure, doubly sure, that time would not hang heavily upon his early retirement. Adam would pick up any slack from the business now, even though he was no longer needed as a full-time operative either. John Allanton wondered if Adam knew that he had let Zoe live, let her go abroad with a warning never to return. She had sounded so genuine, so desperately resolute that she was innocent of the insurgency, that enough doubt had been sown in his mind. He knew that some of the others had told him that she was involved, had been part of the artifice that some paid for with their lives and others with just their careers. John Allanton did not know who was pulling their strings back then, and it still might have been Zoe, but by then he'd had enough of it all and when Adam and he got the money back, thanks to Tim, well that was enough. John wanted to live now, without enemies, without rivals and without losing his life or his family. That was all it was about now.

The doorbell rang and he answered it, his kids back from school, off the bus and raring to get changed into old clothes and head out to play. He tried to offer them some food, but the thumping of feet and the slamming of the back door told him that their interests lay elsewhere.

281

He watched them as they sped into the garden and off through a gate to their neighbours' house and presumably to their friends. Smiling to himself, he followed their tracks outdoors and began to compile a list of the next days' tasks, the weight of life now light, very light indeed.

I decide to just get this over with. As I don't want to take my own car in case it gets used to track me, I borrow Magnus' old Land Rover, still waiting for its owner to return from his sojourn. I drive the long road to Forster's house, almost two hours of bone-shaking vehicular pain to reach the house, unchanged since my last visit. I have a pistol and a couple of other options with me, but I hope not to need any of them. I get out, walk up the steps to the front door and knock, but there's no-one in sight, so I walk around the back and see Forster through the window, alone at an antiquated PC, the monitor large and deep and a printer connected at its side. Although I know exactly what Sir Mathieson wants me to do, I'm trying to find alternatives, palatable solutions for the boss and for me and for Gillian whom I told that all this was finished. I watch him from my position, one hand inside my pocket touching the gun and one almost touching the door handle, for the longest time. There's no internet cable or connection visible, so it could be that the PC and any hard copies are all he has, if I am in luck. Sir Mathieson would have checked anything which went through The Insider, so I could in effect, close this down right here.

My sharp tap on the part-glazed door startles the old man, who then stands and comes over to let me in. I introduce myself and show my ID and he tells me that he remembers me, but wasn't expecting me. We sit in this sunlit writing room and I ask how he has been, my persona now that of the charming young journalist.

'My wife passed last year sadly. I thought that writing all this guff up would keep me busy, so that's when I contacted The Insider, just to see if I could get some representation and help with the publishing and all that. Been very helpful too, although I'm not quite finished the draft yet, as you know.'

'Do you not have any family?

'Yes, however they are making their way in the world, both based in London for now and doing very well. He lifts a picture frame and shows me his son and daughter, pictured with him and his wife on a long-ago day in the Highlands when they look just a little younger than me.

I nod and ask him how the book is coming along.

'Very well, the old memory hasn't gone as badly as the body, thankfully. I'm at 140,000 words and counting.' He pats a pile of unbound manuscript on the desk, neat and symmetrical.

'That's a fair sized book. It might need some editing!' I joke with an easy grin. 'Last time I was here, we were doing a piece on the Inverannan Estate if you remember. It didn't go ahead, but I wondered if you had anything in the new book about the man in charge back then?'

'George Galloglas? I did some checking on him, which might be of interest to you. He worked for a bloody scoundrel by the name of Allanton, who is the worst sort of criminal you could imagine. I met him, in Iraq, he had left the military around that time, but his minions were all over the place, Afghanistan too. He turned up, ostensibly as an advisor to someone or another, but he was a major part of the criminal fraternity then, of that, I have no doubt. What I do have is copies of the building contracts he was awarded and never built – money our government and the Americans poured into the area and buggers like him stole. Do you know that they actually pretended to have some buildings erected then blew them up, part-built? Just to steal money and spend nothing, the swine. People like him held the whole thing back, disrupting the real work and I'll tell you, they were involved in the opium business too, although I don't have any evidence of that, unfortunately.'

'What evidence do you have of the contracts? It's OK to know something, but do you have the paperwork, actual hard copies?' He nods and heads off to another room, coming back moments later with a box file.

'These are the only copies left. I would assume Allanton's lackeys and crooked contacts would have destroyed everything in the offices over there before they left.' He extracts a file with about half an inch of yellowing originals, signed copies of contracts and starts to tell me the legal significance of them, which I pretty don't much care about, but these are exactly what I need.

'So, there are no copies at a solicitor or, centrally in some government office in London?' He shakes his head impatiently.

'No, no, that's what they did. Budgets were paid into accounts, and then the specifics lost in the manufactured chaos of the local situation. The civil service has nothing, I can assure you. I, however, am more diligent and retained these in my personal records of the audit.' He spoke proudly, a man who kept records assiduously and all credit to him, there's not enough of them in the world.

Its five minutes later and I'm walking down the steps to my car holding the manuscript and the contracts and trying not to let any of them blow away. Going back inside, I get the computer then return for the printer and monitor, which are all every bit as heavy as they look. I know I don't need either, but I'd prefer for it not to look like there was ever a computer there. As I get into the Land Rover, Forster stares down at me from the front window; warned, threatened, scared, impotently angry and still alive, my gift to him.

It takes me another arduous couple of hours to get back, via stops at two anonymous lochs into which the computer and then the peripherals are separately launched, and on my return to Inverannan I have a short debate with Sir Mathieson to justify my actions in leaving Forster alive. He really is a bloodthirsty old bastard, underneath his cardigan and toffee grandfatherly veneer, and I currently hope that he fucks off to somewhere sunny and I never see him again. Here's me striving to be all legitimate and responsible, and he's trying to get me to murder some poor old sod whose only crime was to uncover the sordid past of the Allanton millions. Fuck him, is my primary reaction, but I need to stay calm as ever; explaining my assessment of the risks, not having to overplay the situation as I'd left Forster with no evidence, no book and a fairly graphic indication of the consequences of trying to start it up again. Sir Mathieson, I realise now, can be very magnanimous when the infringement does not involve him directly, but can be most sadistic when it does. I takes me a while, but I stick with the defence of my judgement and eventually, he calms down enough to move on, although I wonder if he'll just send one of his other guys to finish the job properly after I've left. That is his decision, entirely.

Exhausted from my day-long venture into the central wilderness of the highlands and with some resultant back pain from the Land Rover, I crash out in bed until there's a knock at the door and one of the guards tells me that there's dinner in the kitchen. Sir Mathieson is already at the rough kitchen table and I join him, our meal a basic one, perhaps made by the guard himself as it strongly suggests army-quality cooking. He's back in his usual positive and benign patriarchal mode, so we have a good chat over dinner and retire to the library for a drink afterwards. I'm wondering when to tell him that I'll be heading off for a while, but the subject comes up from him first.

'So, I expect you'll need a break now Adam? This has been an unexpectedly busy few weeks for us all, perhaps mostly for you.' He could easily have helped this situation by not asking me to terminate Forster, but I decide to put that firmly in the past and agree with him instead. I just hope he doesn't have any other requests, as I'm feeling all murdered out after the past two years and I don't want to regress after all that expensive therapy.

'It is rather unexpected how all this has turned out, although I am not unhappy that the Portfolio has been taken into new markets. Perhaps now we can put everything behind us and simply enjoy the fruits of all our hard work?' I nod in agreement and sip the whisky, another of my Dalwhinnie gifts, not quite as expensive as the one I got for Gillian's parents, but still, one to savour. We sit and chat for a while, he tells me that the yacht repair has been approved; however, he will perhaps sell this one and settle for something less obtrusive.

'So where will you go? Not back to the Med?'

He looks at me with a slightly morose expression. 'No, that particular location is no longer the same for me. I have one or two properties in mind farther afield, not ideal at all times of the year but I will primarily base myself over there.' I guess he wants as few people as possible to know the specifics, and I fundamentally couldn't give a fuck where he's going, so I smile pleasantly in tacit approval of his choice.

There's something been nagging at me since I got here and I suddenly realise that someone is missing.

'Is Benny OK? I haven't seen him since I got back.' I ask with some faux concern.

'Yes, he's taken some time off, you know Benny. He likes to do his own thing every now and again, just a few days to get the sun on his back.'

'Nice. Where's he off to?'

'Portugal, I think.' He whispers, his eyes fixed on the amber whisky glowing in his crystal glass.

31   TIM RETIRES

The buzzing alarm awakened him at 8.15am and, after dressing for the sun, Tim stepped out into the morning light and into the waiting car. This was the most uneasy part of the journey for Tim, the one where he knew that if they were just screwing with him, he wouldn't end up at the airport. The feeling of relief as he was dropped at the car park of Heathrow wasn't just tangible, it was sublime. It was like being given another life, the nightmare ended and its memories already diminishing. Tim bought a newspaper, contrary to his normal routine, but handy to hide behind as he sat in the café for breakfast and waited for the departure gate to be announced.

Five hours later, Tim emerged from Faro airport into just about the warmest heat he'd ever felt, the spring heatwave burning the clouds from the sky and leaving those below to seek shade. Pulling his case behind him, he got into the first taxi at the rank and told him his destination. The driver said something that Tim did not understand, but nodded in reply from his seat in the back. His tone was pleasant at least, so Tim settled down for the long drive to the distant village where his semi-retirement could begin. It was a solid, long hire for the taxi driver, who, after realising that Tim was not acquainted enough with the language to hold a conversation, settled into the trip and mentally calculated that this hire would mean that he wouldn't have to work the following day. His passenger was an odd chap, even for an Englishman. He had a whopping set of scars on his face, the left side looked like it had been cut really badly at some point, maybe plastic surgery or something but it was still messed up. Maybe this guy had been in a car crash or something, as he had a pronounced limp as well, so maybe he was just nervous about being in a car.

Tim's journey continued for just over two hours until they reached the rural village where he had secured a rental property. He paid the driver, including a few euros tip, which Tim knew that he didn't have to do but hey, it was a start of a new life and he might be more open-handed in this one. He felt the exhilaration of being somewhere hidden then, somewhere anonymous. The lady at the real estate office was very helpful, even giving him a lift in her car to the apartment after he'd paid her and smiling as she left him there. Tim looked up at the three-storey building, its rough plasterwork radiating the accumulated heat of the day. Hefting his bags inside and upstairs, he ignored the faecal feline odours, the dust on every surface and instead ploughed upwards, the pain in his knee aggravated somewhat by the uneven steps and the weight he bore. The lock proved to be another physical challenge. No Yale locks here, just a proper, prison door sized key and a lock which clearly hadn't been oiled for some years. Almost bending the key, Tim strained until finally the bloody thing gave in and opened with an almighty clank. He shoved the door and, soaked with sweat, pulled his bags inside and closed the door over, taking mental note not to lock it again until he could apply some lubricant to its workings.

He stood woozily, wiping the nipping, salty sweat from his eyes and cleaning his glasses with his handkerchief. It was apparent that the realtor had been somewhat whimsical with her description of the flat, which, while it did have a traditional Portuguese rustic charm, was also the source of the fetid cat odour and host for a few cockroaches, which Tim did not like one bit. Shoulders slumping, he knew that he had work ahead, starting with the scuttling pests which were heading for the base of the rusting cooker. He searched the kitchen cupboards, finding more bugs along the way in the low, curtained recesses of this 19th century hovel and finally emerging with a box of what appeared to be insect poison, the skull and crossbones logo encouraging him to translate the label as best he could, although his Portuguese vocabulary was, at best, limited for this type of chore.

Guessing at how best to administer the poison, he settled on surrounding the base of the cooker with it until he could seek help the next day. Checking that underneath the bed was free from these unwanted visitors, he did the same thing with the powder there. It did cross his mind that the poison might not be ideal for him if inhaled; however, he kept spreading it around as the roaches were his immediate concern. He took off the musty bedclothes and gave them a shake, then spent ten minutes trying to clean the critical part of the flat with a wet cloth and bucket before the pain in his knee and exhaustion caught up with him and, Tim, his meagre frame saturated with sweat, collapsed on the bed and slept the sleep of the innocent. Despite wakening at first light, Tim pulled the covers around him again and went back to sleep, right through to almost lunchtime when hunger and dehydration called him back to consciousness. He sat up, his hair sticking up at an angle, and looked around. The floor showed no sign of insect visitors and barring a fly or two zipping around, he appeared to be blissfully alone. He lay back and planned his day.

A short time later, Tim emerged into the sunlight and, leaning more than he had needed to before on his stick, set off for the village centre, to find a shop and perhaps some assistance. He found a small general store, which lifted his spirits, and tried to converse at a basic level with the shop assistant, whose local dialect Tim found virtually impenetrable. After many, many efforts, he managed to make her understand that he needed cleaning materials and, giving up on any further requests until he could speak to the realtor, limped onwards in search of sustenance. A bakery was his saviour, the aroma drawing him to the concealed shop and giving him his first opportunity to stock up on water and provisions. He hadn't drunk anything since early the previous day and Tim felt ill, even worse after he'd rapidly polished off his first small bottle of mineral water. He spent the rest of the afternoon cleaning the apartment, poisoning bugs and eating pastries and bread, the room being cooler now after Tim belatedly realised that it had a ceiling fan and that the windows could open.

That night, Tim washed, dressed in his best linen trousers and casual shirt and set off to find the hostelry which he remembered from the apartment advert. It was indeed as wonderful as he had anticipated, a café painted white like every other building in the main part of the village, but with an air conditioning unit projecting from the wall which suggested a welcome respite from the relentless heat. The waiter even spoke broken English and, after careful consideration of the menu, Tim ate and drank his way through a range of reasonably-priced tapas and four large beers. He was not used to alcohol at all, so almost fell on his last trip to the toilet. At that point, he decided to pay the bill and take a leisurely walk back to the apartment, which turned out to harder to find than he thought. Tim limped around the surprisingly confusing small village for forty-five minutes until he spied a building he recognised and from there, located his flat.

This idyllic existence became Tim's routine for the next couple of days. There was another café in the village, only open during the day, but ideal for breakfast and lunch. With the help of the realtor, he secured the employment of a cleaner, working twice weekly to keep the place tidy and do his laundry for a relatively paltry wage. He found a safe place in his apartment for his passport and the money, hidden in an alcove in the bedroom behind a cabinet. There was adequate Wi-Fi in the café and after the fifth day, Tim went online at lunchtime to start to build his future as a rurally-based investor, accessing his bank accounts first to ensure that someone, Adam Darnow specifically, hadn't got someone to go in and steal his funds. It was also at this time that he started to feel uneasy, for no particular reason. He'd survived the Allanton family business, been medically repaired by them even, helped them fix their current and future finances and they'd let him escape to Portugal, but still, Tim couldn't escape this renewed sensation of angst. He sat in the café, seeing nothing but locals, old women and men going about their business, and trying to calm his fears.

So, after more or less suppressing his anxiety, Tim completed his stock analysis, checked a few indicators and moved some money to test his theories and make some early profit. That complete, he packed up his laptop and finished his water, heading home for an afternoon nap. As was becoming his habit he woke around 3.30 pm and took a beer from the noisy fridge, sitting on his balcony to watch the little children returning home from school, before some light reading and a visit to his tapas café. By nine pm, Tim was again pleasantly drunk and slowly winding his now familiar way back to his apartment.

As he limped along the otherwise empty street to his flat, an old man was strolling, almost as slowly as him, towards Tim. Cheered by the food and beer, Tim raised his head and smiled at the old gentleman as he reached him, however, the thump in his stomach and then his chest, then his back, left Tim on a quickly reddening pavement, his semi-retirement in Portugal abruptly ended. The man ambled away, round the corner to a waiting car, which would take him speedily but surreptitiously to a private airport after disposing of his weapon at a river bridge and cleaning himself thoroughly with a forensic kit he'd brought for that very purpose. New clothes donned and the old ones to be taken away and burned, the car dropped him at the aerodrome. His plane was waiting as he didn't want to leave Sir Mathieson for long, not with all the packing to do before they went abroad again.

I stayed that night in Inverannan House, just calling
Gillian from the office landline to ask if I could see her
the next day, Saturday. My concept of days has been
rather vague recently, as the various requirements of the
Portfolio have taken precedence over any personal or
weekend time to myself. My sleep is unusually sound and
it's a surprise when my watch tells me that I've just passed
the 9.40 am mark before stirring. Showering in the
Victorian over-bath contraption, I dress in jeans and a t-
shirt and prepare to head down and meet Sir Mathieson
before I leave. He's in the library, coffee and biscuits on
the go and I join him, wolfing down as many as I can
while he's burbling away about his plans to visit John and
the family before the various flights to the tax-friendly
sand pile where he plans to spend his second-phase
retirement in blissful isolation, albeit probably with Benny
and as many nubile assistants as he can procure. It's with
great pleasure that I shake his hand for the last time
before I take his leave.

'I wish you well for the future Adam. I shall, of course,
be in touch to see how you're getting on.' His handshake,
in place longer than is usual, feels like it could still crush
my hand if he was minded to.

'Thanks for all you've done for me.' I tell him, and I mean
it.

He takes just a moment longer, still gazing at me. 'No, it
is I who must thank you, Adam. You have earned all that
comes to you.'

With that, I turn and take my bags to the car, we wave to
each other before I pull away and I'm left wondering if

that last statement was a kind farewell or a barely disguised warning. Maybe my head is indeed fucked up after the past two years, I'm reading way too much into things, although it's not paranoia if everyone is indeed out to get you. I force this one out of my thoughts and skim quickly along the road to Inverannan, down the side road and along to meet Gillian. She's in the back garden of the house, with Hector and Katrina as they clear the winter debris from their land and into black plastic bags. I say hi and despite their remonstrations and my underlying laziness, pitch in to help them. Since the four of us are working pretty full-on in, it only takes about an hour, although this is mainly due to the fact that Hector is blootering every overgrown shrub and tree with his chainsaw. I think to myself about the last time I used one of those, and it certainly wasn't on an unruly conifer.

I head inside to wash up and help Gillian make some sandwiches. The sun has come out and it's as warm as it gets up here, at this or any time of year. We sit in the bucolic aroma of cut trees, looking over the loch to the coastal hills, drinking strong tea and eating cold meat sandwiches. Gillian laughs when she realises that Hector has a twig in his thick, wiry hair, this sets off Katrina and then Hector and I can't resist their snorting guffaws and we're all laughing like loons while Hector paws at the thorny stick which has entrenched itself in his thatch. We sit for the rest of the lunch break there, Hector and Katrina telling us about their young life, doing up the house while the kids were tiny and I wonder how the fuck I'm going to tell Gillian that I'm leaving but I need her and I don't want to leave her, not now or ever.

After we clear up the plates and take the bags to where Hector can load them up in his four-wheel drive later, I finally get a chance to sit alone with her. Even a few scrapes from the clearing of the naturally defensive highland weeds makes Gillian even more attractive, and above all, she is now perfect for me. I tell her a heavily redacted version of the past day or so at Inverannan and ask her to work with Eilidh to get their proposal ready for Inverannan, the guys in London will have a look at it and, if it's OK, we'll get back to them as soon as we can. All a bit formal, but that was the last work-related thing I have to do before leaving. The rest is purely personal but I'm not sure how it will go, my never-good judgment with women having possibly worsened since the onset of what I am now coming to think of as my Two Year Psychotic Episode, which I hope has now passed and will continue its absence as long as I stay away from the Allantons and the narcotic trade in general. As per Dr Schaffer, to ensure my own compliance with the unregulated norms of acceptable behaviour, I have to carefully consider the consequences of my interpersonal actions in future. This is especially important to me as I no longer have a supportive infrastructure of paid thugs who can clean up after me, incinerate and threaten until all is well. In short, time for me to chuck the criminality malarkey for good, along with the whole associated murder thing and focus on my new reality.

Gillian is, right now, my priority. I ask her to go for a walk with me and we head along to the loch, the path ending but a track still taking us around the waterside until a headland blocks our way. We sit in its lee, the sun-warmed rocks behind us and the glistening loch in front.

'So, where are you heading now, back to London?' She's bright and breezy about it, but I really, really hope that she just wants me to be closer, for a while.

'No, it's on auto-pilot down there, for a while. John is a sleeping partner now, so we've got the main team doing all the delegated work. I'll keep in touch with them, but I'm not needed as much down south from now on.' She looks down but smiles involuntarily, and I hope that's because of me, so I keep going.

'I'm going back to Mharisaig for a while, my mum and dads house will be a wreck unless I get it fixed up soon. They will probably want to come back when their hips and knees need replacing, so I'd better do the right thing and keep it habitable for them.' She laughs, a sparkling sound to me.

'So, that'll keep me going for a few weeks, there are some guys in the village who can do the work, albeit they do need a bit of supervision.' I think for a moment about my friends, who I've hardly seen in such a long time and momentarily wonder what they will think of me when I get back. After two years of working out, training and boxing in the evenings at my gym in London, I seem to be somewhat heftier than I was when I last was with them. I tell Gillian that I've not seen them since I left and she laughs.

'Well I think you're a bitty taller than when we first met, and the rest of you has filled out a shade too. Mum and I were watching when you helped dad with that tree and we reckoned that you're even taller than him and a bit more muscle too. Need to watch mum, I think she fancied a trade-in.'

She sniggers at the thought of this, and my lack of self-awareness is reconfirmed by the fact that I thought Hector was both taller and broader than me. I file this away as yet another thing I don't fully comprehend. This has, however, taken the pressure off me for a moment. Then I remind myself what I have to ask.

'Is it OK if I come back up, you know, to see you? Maybe you could come down to Mharisaig too, once the cottage is in better shape.' I'm babbling slightly, which is unlike my recent persona.

Gillian turns and kisses me, long and slow, our faces warmed by the sunlight and the highland breeze. She breaks off and gazes straight at me.

'Maybe, if you stop being such a complete fucking idiot.'

I'm lying, laughing on the sand, she is too and I wish I knew how to, I really do.

Printed in Great Britain
by Amazon